"LET'S SHOW NANNY ROWAN her room, shall we?" says Sha. But then—instead of leaving Flossy's room—she crosses to a door on the far wall and opens it. "Bring your suitcase!" she cries.

We enter a tiny room. "This *was* the nursery," Sha explains. "But now Flossy's such a big girl, it's a perfect nanny's room, don't you think?"

No, it's bloody well not! I rage, but silently. It's a box, a cell, with a skinny little window and a very narrow bed and a telly the size of a brick. "So there's no . . . actual . . . *way out.* Other than through Flossy's room, I mean."

"No. But that'll be OK, won't it?" Sha says. "You can be quiet."

There's a long silence. I'm feeling kind of sick.

Also by Kate Cann

Spanish Holiday

Grecian Holiday

Love Trilogy
1: Ready? 2: Sex 3: Go!

California Holiday

Or, How the World's Worst Summer Job Gave Me a Great New Life

KATE CANN

AVON BOOKS

An Imprint of HarperCollinsPublishers

First published in the UK by Scholastic Ltd., 2003.

Library of Congress Catalog Card Number: 2004095707
ISBN 0-06-056161-0

First Avon edition, 2005

AVON TRADEMARK REG. U.S. PAT. OFF. AND IN OTHER COUNTRIES,
MARCA REGISTRADA, HECHO EN U.S.A.
❖
Visit us on the World Wide Web!
www.harperteen.com

To Megan and Chris,
with love.
And to Sylvia,
with many thanks.

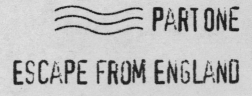

PART ONE

ESCAPE FROM ENGLAND

TUESDAY AFTERNOON, FIVE O'CLOCK, and death is looking like a positive option. I'm completely knackered and strung out, sinking under the weight of fear and despair and half-digested A level revision. I've got a big sociology exam two days away, and to get even the basics covered I'll have to time-travel back three weeks.

And as I don't have a time machine, death it is. If I spend five more minutes crouched over my useless moron notes at my fetid desk in my stinking bedroom I'll die anyway, so . . . From downstairs, I hear Mum come through the front door, call out her automatic "Hi!" A tiny spark of hope activates me. I creak to my feet and slump down to the kitchen, longing for sympathy.

"Hello, Mum," I groan, "you're back from work early . . ."

"That's 'cos I got in early!" she says unsympathetically, and starts briskly unpacking the supermarket bags she's dumped on the kitchen counter. "That's the good thing about flexitime! I get an early start as often as I can, so I don't end up trying to catch up with myself the whole day."

"I know," I mourn. "I've been trying to catch up—"

"Oh, *Rowan*!" she erupts. "You wouldn't know an early start if it jumped up and bit you on the leg! When I phoned at eleven to see how your revision was going *I woke you up*!"

"I was only having a little nap," I lie. "I'm just so *exhausted* . . ."

"You shouldn't let exhaustion stop you. Heaven knows *I* don't. I *can't*. What would happen if I did?" She dives into the cutlery drawer, comes out with a potato peeler and shakes it in my face. "These are *your* exams, Rowan, *your* future. I warned you— months ago—to get down to some proper work. No one else can do them for you—it's up to *you*!"

Mum has missed her calling in life. She runs some kind of administration department at the local council, but what she should really do is run a battalion of soldiers. She never gives in to depression, confusion, fatigue or self-doubt. Or to me. "If you *fail*," she goes on, injecting about twenty litres of venom into the word, "it'll be your fault, no one else's!"

I feel so battered by her unfeeling criticisms I sink on to one of the kitchen chairs and start snivelling. Mum starts violently peeling potatoes. I snivel louder; she carries on, hurling them one by one into a saucepan, *bing, bong, bang*. She gets to five, then she slams down the peeler, stomps across the kitchen floor and puts her arm round my shoulders. She squeezes them as if what she'd actually like to be doing is breaking my neck, and barks, "Look, love—you need a break. Get some fresh air. Get some *exercise*."

Exercise is Mum's answer to everything, from boredom to a broken heart. "Go on," she says, squeezing my shoulders again, this time till the bones crunch. "Get out for a *fast* walk in the *fresh* air."

And just then little brother Jack swaggers into the kitchen, stripped to the waist and holding a large dumbbell in either hand. He seems to be completely unaware of what a prat he looks because he's got his usual arrogant grin plastered across his irritatingly handsome face. "Walking ain't exercise," he sneers. He braces his legs and starts to pump the dumbbells up and down. "If you're feeling—*uuugh!*—a bit stressed out, sis—*uuuugh!*—you should come to the gym with me. *Uuuuugh*."

"Now *there's* an offer!" exclaims Mum, smiling at him fondly and spotting the chance to offload me and my moaning on to someone else. "That's *thoughtful* of you, Jack."

"It's not *thoughtful*!" I snarl. "Well—only thoughtful in the way a sadist puts thought into planning his next torture session."

"Don't be silly, dear."

"He just wants to *humiliate* me! Get me on one of those running belts and turn the speed up till I catapult into a brick wall!"

Jack scoffs with laughter, doubtless enjoying the image.

"Don't be *silly*, dear," Mum repeats wearily. "You know, you really do need to get out."

"Certainly does," agrees Jack. "Look at 'er. Like something the cat sicked up." He swaggers out of the room, calling back smugly, "Offer still stands, sis."

I glare at his sweaty naked retreating back. I glance at Mum, who's shaking her head despairingly over her last potato. And I hear myself saying, "OK, smart-arse. Let's go."

Ten minutes later I'm in a grubby pair of trackies trailing behind Jack along the towpath to the gym, regretting it like anything. Probably he's really regretting it, too. Probably he only asked me to suck up to Mum so she'd slip him another tenner at the weekend.

Mum thinks Jack's wonderful. She wishes I had more go, more drive like him—I know she does. Dad does, too. I went along to one of Jack's rugby matches once, and I ended up watching Dad instead of the game. He was shouting Jack on and I don't think I'd ever seen him so enthused, so full of excitement and pride. It made me feel kind of weird, hurt.

If I'm honest, both my parents think Jack's rung on the ladder of life-achievement is way, *way* above mine. Not that that's hard, because I've never really achieved anything. I gave up swimming, I gave up piano, I gave up horseriding, I gave up dance. I hated all that grading and certificate-earning that went along with it, all the pressure.

Jack, though—he's thrived on pressure ever since he started to walk. Ten months younger than I did. And now some big-shot rugby club has just "spotted" him and put him on an "Elite Development Course", so he can play for them when he's older. This course includes unlimited use of the rugby club gym and a workout plan geared to beefing up his muscles. After three weeks the only obvious enlargement has been to his head, but it's still one hell of an achievement.

We round a bend in the towpath. "Come on, fat-arse," Jack calls back. "Move it, can't you? I usually jog there."

I don't jog. I don't even reply. I look down into the river as we walk along and imagine myself sliding into it, letting the weight of the water cover me, sink me down away from Jack, from exams, from everything . . . it's then that I hear the frantic quacking. It's then that I see the tragic duck and her three tragic little ducklings. I stop dead in my tracks. "Jack—come back—*look*!"

He glances over the towpath rails. "Yeah. Ducks. So?"

"But she's trapped in the barge! Look at her— she's frantic!"

At this bend of the river, stranded on the river bed, there's a rusty old metal barge, riddled with holes. When it's high tide, the barge floods and disappears under water. But now the water level's low, just a few shallow centimetres inside the barge, much, much lower than its sheer, steep, unclimbable sides. And the poor mother duck's swimming round and round on this water, followed by her anxious offspring, desperately looking for a way out.

"Stupid thing," grumps Jack. "It must've gone in when the water was high, and got trapped when the tide went out."

"Oh, so it's the duck's fault, is it?"

He shrugs. "Obviously. Come on, I want to get to the gym."

"God," I erupt, "you are so *unfeeling*!"

"It can get out if it wants to! Ducks *fly*!"

"What, you think she'd leave her babies behind? Not everyone's as callous as you, Jack!"

"Oh, for God's sake, come on."

"We can't just leave her—look how panicky she is! It'll be ages till the tide comes in again, and floats them out. And I bet they've been in there for hours already. I bet they're all *starving*." Then a thought strikes me. "Hey—did you bring your usual enormous sandwich with you?"

"Forget it—you're not having that."

I grab the end of his sports bag, tug on it. "Don't be so *selfish*! Who needs it more—that poor exhausted duck or you?"

"Me!" His voice rings with self-righteous indignation. "Coach says we gotta eat after we work out! Got to replenish spent energy, build ourselves up." He tightens his grip on the bag.

"Look, Jack—*God* I hate you!—look—let me have it. I'll buy you a better one."

"Yeah, you say that now but you won't. Sod the stupid duck. *Fuck* it. *Ha ha ha*—geddit? Fuck the duck—" He breaks off as I violently yank on the sports bag and rip it out of his grasp. I spin away from him, pull the bag open, see an enormous peanut butter sandwich wrapped in clingfilm. Jack's lunging at me, roaring, so I simultaneously grab the sandwich and drop the sports bag on his foot, distracting him long enough for me to tear the wrapping off the sandwich and spit—*pah, pah, pah!*—all over it.

Jack stops dead, in shock. "You *cow*," he hisses, mouth all screwed up in loathing and disgust. "You evil fucking *cow*."

"Shut up. Still want it?" I wave the spitty sarnie at him, then I tear it into nice little duckling-bill-sized bits and shower them down into the rusty barge. The duck and her brood fall on the bread, gobbling it down frantically. "There!" I retort. "See how famished they were?" I stand and watch them and I feel this warm glow spread inside me as they feed slower, and slower, and then stop, with still a few bits left.

Jack too has watched the ducks gorge. Maybe he even allowed a little bit of altruistic pleasure to infiltrate his self-obsessed skull. At any rate, he's not thumping me or trying to chuck me into the river for gobbing on his sandwich. "We've got to get help for them," I say.

Any altruism Jack was feeling vanishes. "Oh, for Christ's sake—we *got* help! You gave them my whole *sandwich*, for God's sake."

"They can't stay there swimming until the tide comes in again. They'll die of exhaustion."

Jack turns to me. "*Ducks*," he says, annunciating clearly as though explaining to an imbecile, "*float*."

"Not all night. They sleep on land. I know! If we get them a raft—"

"*Jesus—H.—Christ*. What the *hell* did I do to deserve such a wacked-out lunatic for a sister? *Great*. So you're gonna make a duck raft now, are you? What—twigs lashed together with string and a teeny little *sail*?"

I give him a withering look, which unfortunately fails to wither him, turn from the towpath railings, and start scanning along the wall on the opposite side of the road where various bits of rubbish have been dumped. "I didn't say *make*," I growl. "I said *get*. I'll find them a piece of wood, something that'll float . . ."

I spot a likely-looking plank, head over the road and pick it up. "This might do. It's a bit thin, but . . ."

"What about that big bit next to it?" demands Jack, drawn in despite himself. He points to a huge piece of wood covered in asphalt.

"That's *far* too big," I snap. "It looks like a whole shed roof. You'd cause a tidal wave, dropping that in."

"Not if you help me drop it in carefully."

"*No*. I'm trying this." I march back across the road with my plank, and gaze into the sunken barge again. The ducks look happier now they've fed, but they're still circling round and round hopelessly. There's absolutely nothing for them to roost on. "Go up the other end, mother duckie," I call. "Go on—then I'll drop you this nice raft up here and you can have a lovely rest on it with your babies and—" I break off.

Something huge has risen up behind me. It's the shed roof, Jack's got it, and before I can scream out or stop him he's lifting it shoulder high and *letting go of it*—oh, Jesus, it's sailing over my head, it's crashing down into the barge, it hits the water with a nuclear boom.

A great, drowning wave surges up from the impact, the mother duck squawks in terror, surfs the wave half flying, then she turns, frantically searching for her babies. . . . One duckling's caught in the wave, it's smashing against the wall of the barge, the other two have disappeared completely, I feel sick, I'm peering in desperation at the surging water, and as it settles, sloshing against the metal sides of the barge, I see the other two ducklings bob up all dazed and terrified.

There's a weird calm, like the calm after a terrible accident. Then the mother duck, quacking in rage and fear, gathers her three traumatized babies to her on the still-heaving water.

I turn round to Jack, still clutching the plank. My stomach's knotted up, my throat's clenched like a fist. I realize I've got two tears running down my face.

"Muscle power, see?" he says, cockily. "Lifting that bloody great thing over the railings all on my own—pretty good, eh?"

And that's when my arms quite of their own accord raise the plank like a baseball bat and swing it—*crunch!*—into the side of his head.

I DON'T USE ANYTHING LIKE all my strength in the blow. If I'd used all my strength, the way I'm feeling, I reckon I'd've take his head off. But even so, Jack's knees buckle and he goes down at once, really satisfying, like a ninepin. "*Groooogh*," he groans.

I stand there completely stunned by what I've done. Then I kind of block it out, and fix my eyes on the barge. The water is almost calm now, the babies have stopped frantically cheeping and are staying as close to their mother as they can get. She's looking up at me with hate in her duck eyes. "It wasn't me!" I plead.

"*Yes it was!*" howls Jack.

The duck turns her back, swims as far away from the shed roof as she can. It's taking up over a third of the barge, floating beautifully, like an island.

"*Aaaargh!*" wails Jack. "*Aaaaargh*—I've gone blind!"

The baby ducks look all right, they're swimming fine, but who knows what the shock will do to them, or maybe they've got internal injuries, or . . .

"*Grrrooooogh. Oh my Go-oo-oood . . .*"

A trickle of reality seeps through into my consciousness. There'll be one hell of a fuss at home if I've wounded the little sod. Irreparably, I mean. Or even reparably. I suppose I ought to see to him.

He's holding both hands clasped in front of his face. Worryingly, a fast trickle—a torrent, even—of blood is coursing through his fingers. "I'm blind!" he groans. "I'm bleeding!"

I hold my breath, preparing for the worst, and prise his fingers away from his face. *Shit!* My first thought is I've split him like a melon. Running from just above his right ear all the way down to his jaw is a cut, streaming blood. I feel faint just looking at it. I fumble in my pocket, draw out a wad of tissues, press them to the wound.

"What're you doing?" he wails. "You're making it worse!"

"No, I'm not, I'm stopping the blood."

"Why should I trust you? You just tried to kill me—you *blinded* me—"

"Jack, get a grip. You're not blind, you've got your eyes shut. Open them, go on."

"I can't! I *can't*! You knocked my eyeballs out!"

"Jack—*shut up*—you're getting hysterical!" I think about slapping him but veto it as too cruel, even for me. "You got blood in your eyes and screwed them shut, that's all."

Whimpering a little, he starts to open his eyes. And now I've mopped up a lot of the blood, I can see that the cut isn't too deep. *Relief*. It's gaping, though, a bit like the stomach of a gutted fish. It needs to get seen to. "Jack—can you stand up?" I take hold of his arm, hoping he's not concussed as well.

"Stop it!" he wails. "Leave me alone!" He's blinking piteously, but he's starting to focus.

I V-sign in front of his face. "How many fingers?"

"Two. *Bitch*."

"Are you dizzy?"

"*Yes!* You just slammed me in the face with a plank of wood—*course* I'm dizzy!"

I start pulling on his arm. "Come on, Jack. You're OK. Look—I'm sorry. I dunno what happened to me—I didn't mean to hurt you." That's a solid lie, but I've got to get him moving somehow. "Come on—we need to get you to the gym—

they'll stitch you up there. It's not as bad as it feels, honest. It looks OK now the blood's stopping. They'll stitch you up and you'll mend in no time and have this sexy scar, just like a duelling scar . . ." At last I get him to his feet and we move off along the towpath. He's leaning on me a bit and I keep clucking and chuntering away, just to keep him moving, comforting him like I used to do when we were little kids and I'd look after him if he hurt himself in the playground or something.

God. That feels like centuries ago.

We're in luck once we get to the gym. The first-aid guy who's usually on hand at rugby matches is there in his fully equipped medical room, and he takes Jack's wound totally in his stride. "Hmm," he says, swabbing at it with an antiseptic wipe, "it's shallow. See far worse than this on the pitch every week. I'll butterfly it—no need to stitch. How d'you do it?"

"She—" groans Jack.

"He tripped," I interrupt at speed. "He tripped and fell against a lamppost."

The first-aid guy peers at the wound, pulls a pair of tweezers out of a drawer. "There's a splinter in here."

"It was—it was a *wooden* lamppost."

"Hmm," he says, suspiciously, giving me a searching look. "Well—the cut'll heal fine."

I watch as he dresses the wound fast and expertly. Then he gives me another suspicious glance and says, "Better check for concussion." He runs through various vision tests, rotates Jack's head on his neck, then slaps him on the shoulder. "You'll do. Get off home now. Give your workout a miss today, right?"

"Oh, *what*?" huffs Jack. "If I don't work out today, my schedule'll be all out—"

"Don't be a prat," says the first-aid man amiably. "Now—d'you need a cab?"

"No," I say. "I'll see him home. You could do with some fresh air, couldn't you, Jack?"

And I bundle him out of the door before he can argue. I want the time on the way home to try and persuade him not to land me in the shit with Mum. But he's not having any. He won't let me take his arm like he did on the way to the gym, he'll hardly talk to me—as he starts to feel better, he walks faster and grows angrier. "I should've *told* him," he rants. "I should've *told* Mike you did it!"

"What, and admit your sister beat you up? Come on, Jack. Let's forget it, eh?"

"Forget the fact you tried to kill me? No way," he snarls. "*No* way." Then he comes to an explosive halt by the railings overlooking the sunken barge. "Look!" he yells, pointing, his hand shaking with anger. "Fucking *look* at that!"

I dart guiltily to the railings. The ducks—I'd forgotten about them!

I look down into the barge. The mother duck is roosting peacefully on Jack's floating shed roof, a picture of maternal calm. As I stare, a little fluffy head peeps out from under her wing and then nestles back in again. I scan the water. No ducklings; all three must be under her wings. And I know that when the tide comes in the shed roof will float gently up to the rim of the barge, and the four of them can swim happily away.

I realize that Jack's face is about two centimetres away from mine, contorted with fury. "Look *ALL RIGHT*, don't they?" he bellows. "Look like I did them a real *FAVOUR*!"

And he rages off home.

CHAPTER 3

THE FUSS ONCE WE GET back is out of all sane proportion. The first thing Jack does—of *course*—is relate my misdeed in glowing technicolour to Mum and Dad. Who are entirely predictable in their responses. Mum is all shut-eyed, disgusted disbelief—"What came over you, Rowan? I just do not understand *what came over you*! I mean—yes, you were angry over the ducks, but to hit Jack so hard he needed *medical attention* . . ."

Dad is stony-faced and trying, painfully, to be a bit more understanding. "This isn't just about the ducks, is it, Rowan? I know you're tense about your exams, but you have serious issues here, too, about your little brother. They're not just going to go away—we need to talk about them."

Both look at me with concern and horror in

their eyes. Both insist I *explain*. I can't, though—not in a way that would satisfy them. I just mumble on about his arrogance and how he could've killed the ducks and how I just snapped. I mumble on about how I didn't hit him that hard anyway and how he gets worse knocks than that on the rugby pitch. I start to say I'm sorry, but I gag on it. I suddenly feel really pissed off, *bored*, with all the fuss, and I'm hungry, too. I ask when dinner's going to be ready.

Big mistake. They exchange an ominous glance at that, appalled at how cold and callous I'm being. I could be an axe-murderer phoning for pizza midslaughter, the way they're looking at me. There's a frosty silence, then Dad says, all reproving, "I don't suppose *Jack* feels like eating."

"Yeah I do!" interjects Jack, who up to now has been sitting smug and silent at the table. "What I mean is—" correcting himself hastily—"I'm gonna *try* to. I think I *ought* to eat something. Even though my jaw hurts."

"Oh, shut *up*, you self-pitying little git!" I explode. "I wish I'd *broken* your stupid jaw!"

"*ROWAN!*" Mum chides, horrified. She moves to stand behind Jack, a comforting hand on his shoulder. He smirks. His white head-bandage glows like a badge of martyrdom.

"I really don't know what's come over you, Rowan," mourns Dad.

And something kind of splits inside my head.

"*Nothing!*" I rasp out. "Nothing's come over me! I just acted on what I always feel for that superior little shit, that's all! It wasn't just the ducks, you're right, although the way he treated them was the way he is with everyone—*I'm me, I'm great, I'm riding over you, deal with it*. Maybe he has to be that way playing rugby but in normal life it absolutely *sucks*. I'm sick of it and I hate it and I *let that out*, for once! And you know what? It feels bloody brilliant! You're waiting for me to come to my senses, say I'm sorry, aren't you? *Well, I'm not going to*! I don't regret it, not a bit of it!"

There's a stunned silence. I sweep out of the room, grab my purse and key from the hall table, and slam out of the house. At the end of our road I turn to check no one has burst through the front door to come after me, and barely register any hurt when I see that they haven't. I head down the main street, and go into The Pasta Place on the corner. I've eaten here before with friends, and normally I'd feel embarrassed about going in on my own. Not tonight, though. I march over to an empty table, and plonk myself down. When the waiter arrives, I order a huge bowl of spaghetti carbonara, a round of garlic bread and a mixed salad. And when it arrives, I really tuck in.

I'm *starving*.

CHAPTER 4

I'D HATE TO GIVE ANYONE the idea that whacking your little brother round the head with a plank of wood is a good thing to do. I don't want to suggest it will help your self-development in any way— free you, even. But something fundamental shifted in me when my arms lifted up that plank and followed through. It was like something blocked got unblocked, the real me got flowing again. Like I'd plugged into an energy source I didn't even know I had inside me.

And from that moment on, somehow everything was different.

My feelings about the big sociology exam, for a start. It was only two short days away, but that night, after my pasta blow-out, I sleep like a log. The next day, I get up and in my pyjamas read through what I thought were hopeless, muddled revision notes. And I find out they're not that crap after all. In fact, everything starts slotting together in my brain—I discover I know a lot of this stuff! I get dressed, read the crib book I bought. Not only can I follow it—it slips beautifully into my knowledge, adding to it, shaping it. Like everything's falling into place.

I drop the crib book. My brain feels like it's electrified. I pace my room, stop in front of the mirror. My face looks different, it looks as though I know what I'm doing, as though I'm in charge for once. I'm going to do OK in this exam, I tell myself. It is not a world-shattering big deal and I'm not going to get shot if I don't do OK. But I will. Do OK.

Mum has a half-day off work. She's treating me nervously, like I'm a cross between a rabid dog and a headcase. She's probably worried I'm cracking up completely and I'm going to miss the exam and start the downward slide to full-on heroin addiction or something. She'd love to know if I'm actually working up here in my room, or just lying on my back on the bed, drooling. I don't enlighten her, though; I pretty much ignore her apart from saying *yes, please* when she asks me if I want a sandwich at lunchtime.

At three, I need a break, so I walk back down to the river. The tide's been up and gone down again; the shed roof is at the other end of the barge, and the duck family is long gone. I gaze about, scanning the water for them, but they're not around. I lean my elbows on the railings and imagine them all swimming away over the rim of the barge. Somehow I know they're safe. I can still see them gobbling up the bread, roosting peacefully on the raft.

The plank of wood I hit Jack with is there on the towpath, near my feet. I pick it up, remembering what it felt like to take a swing at him, and laugh. Then I drop it over the railings into the river like some kind of offering to the Fates.

Back to work. By eight o'clock that night I'm so far ahead of the game I'm actually making short revision notes on cards. I haven't covered all the topics, no way, but if I'm lucky—and somehow I know I will be—I'll be able to answer a question in each section. I eat a huge dinner, avoiding all dinner-table conversation. I go to bed early, and fall asleep wishing I'd belted Jack round the head at the start of the exams so I could have done all my revision in this new, clear state of mind. God knows what a psychiatrist would make of it. Drama brings shift in attitude? Energy comes from releasing anger? Whatever, I'm all for it.

The next day I'm a little lower on dynamism

but I still work hard, and sleep well that night. And the exam the day after that is *fine*. I have to seriously waffle in one answer, but in my new assertive state of mind I reckon I make even waffle sound convincing.

I'm so pleased I give myself a whole day off, afterwards. Not *take* the day off in a dreary, knackered, inevitable way—I *give* it to myself. Like a present.

It's during this day off that I notice the second thing that has fundamentally changed—my family's attitude to me. Jack's is the most uncomplicated. He's clearly decided to pretend that from now on, I don't exist. He walks by me in the hall, skirts round me in the kitchen, ignores me in the living room. Fine by me. He's only ever insulted me before so it's a nice change.

Mum and Dad's attitude is a bit more complex. They're still basically appalled at me, and worried and concerned on top of that. Early that evening I overhear them discussing me in muted voices: *Sibling rivalry, exam tension, not herself, so sweet to him when they were little.* They watch me, anxiously. There's one comic moment when I'm standing with my back to the kitchen door, buttering toast with the breadknife, and someone walks in. I swing round, see it's Jack, and Mum (who's following him) shrieks, *"Rowan-NO!"*

"No what?"

"Put that knife down!"

"What? I'm doing some toast!"

"Yes, but . . ." She dithers, back-pedalling frantically. "Surely there's no need for such a large knife!"

"There is if you've just cut the bread with it and can't be arsed to get another one out the drawer." I start to laugh. "You thought I was gonna stab Jack with it, didn't you?"

"Don't be silly, dear . . ."

"Slit his throat like a sack of flour. Slice his stomach, watch his guts spill out on the floor . . ."

"Rowan—*stop it! Please!*"

"You're sick," snarls Jack. "You need to be put away."

"Yeah?" I say. "What, for murder?" And I advance on him, still with the knife.

"Rowan!" shrieks Mum, at the top of her voice, *"PUT THAT KNIFE DOWN!"*

She's so loud she makes my ears ring. She's *really* upset with me. The sight of Jack backing fearfully out of the kitchen and banging painfully into the heavy oak table in the hall makes it all worth it, though.

* * *

After a tense and silent family dinner, I neglect to offer to do the washing up and head for the phone. Fifteen minutes later, I've rounded a few people up for a drink at The Link, just about the only pub in our town that hasn't been a) colonized by pensioners or b) turned into a trendy over-21s bar that won't let us in. And I leave the house, not telling anyone where I'm going.

My best mate Mel's already there at the bar when I arrive; she hugs me and gets me a drink. "We're outside," she says. "We grabbed a big table. It's actually warm enough for once."

"Lovely. Why does the one bit of summer we're probably gonna *get* this year have to be full up of exams?"

Mel shakes her head mournfully, and we go outside. The pub garden's got honeysuckle climbing its walls and it smells really good. Five of my friends—people we've been in a group with since school—are drooped round the table. Most of us ended up at the same sixth-form college, but you don't make friends there like your school mates. There's just time to have—in my case—two doomed, pathetic relationships. One that lasted three weeks and Billy who I had the Full Thing with for nearly five months. *God*, he was dull. Even the sex was dull. Especially the sex, come to think of it, once I'd got over the novelty.

We swap news and go through the usual thing of groaning about the exams and promising each other we're not going to get rat-arsed, we've got to work tomorrow. And then I say, "I'm thinking I might do a gap year after all."

I don't know where that came from, 'cos I hadn't been thinking about it all, but now it's out there I know I'm going to *start* thinking about it.

"You want to get off the treadmill for a bit, don't you," nods James. "Sensible." James is just about my best male friend. At college he gets loads of girls after him (lucky sod) and I can see what they see him, but I don't fancy him myself. I've known him too long—since he was a geeky little kid, just starting at big school—it puts you off. Anyway, it'd be like incest.

Mel's looking at me. "But Ro," she says, "you were absolutely fixed on getting straight to uni."

"I know I was."

"Won't your parents mind? I thought . . ." She trails off, then she says, "So—d'you want to come to Costa Rica with me and Annie and save the turtles? I bet there'd still be a place."

I smile at her. Mel, Annie and I love anything furry, feathery or scaly; when we were in junior school we'd hold garage sales for the World Wildlife Fund and fight over who got the "Thank you for your £13.74 donation" certificate. She's got her sights set on working in a turtle nesting-site protection area in Costa Rica for part of her gap year, and I've toyed with the idea of going with her, but . . . "What puts me off about that, Mel," I say, "is they make *you* pay to do it."

"I know. But it'll be worth it. I'm gonna get a job at Tesco or something for six months or so first, I'm gonna *make* myself save . . ."

"That's it, though. I want something that'll get me out *now*. Like—as soon as the exams are over."

There's a sort of pause round the table. Then James says, "Is something up, Ro?"

I empty my glass. I wonder about telling them about the Duck Event. I wonder about telling them what's happened at home over the last few days. In the past, James and Mel have been great, listening to me moan about Jack, propping me up when I feel inadequate in front of the expectations of my family. But then I realize something. I realize I don't need to tell them. "No, I'm fine," I say. "Anyone want another drink?"

I go home and go straight up to my room, thinking about how everything's changed here. Ever since I crossed the line, burnt my bridges, went beyond the pale (what pale? and what's so bad about going beyond it?), I've felt this weird, drifting sense of . . . *freedom*.

I've only been in ten minutes when Dad comes up and knocks on my bedroom door with a cup of tea, all solicitous. I take the tea, tell him I'm fine, and more or less shut the door in his face.

And I am fine, too. I sit on the bed slurping my tea and realize the biggest change of all is in *me*. I don't *care* any more! Not the way I would've done once—scurrying round, trying to put things right, make up with everyone. The whole family's treating me like I might blow my top again at any minute and, far from wanting to reassure them, I'm *enjoying* it. It's the nearest thing to respect I've ever had.

CHAPTER 5

THREE MORE EXAMS TO GO until the end. Part of me wants to just say sod it and coast through them, not even turn up maybe, but I keep at it with my bold new revising technique and they go pretty well.

And then I'm *really* free. Free every-which-way, free in a way I've never been before. It's the weirdest sensation, like someone suddenly taking the top of your head off and everything inside just blowing about.

And after it's all blown about it starts to slot into place, *click, click, click*. I start to see things clearly. It's all about pressure, isn't it? Endless *pressure*. Not just from my parents, though they're Grand Masters at it, but from everyone and everywhere. Pressure to achieve in every aspect of your life, like some kind of self-improvement quiz in a magazine. *Are you taking charge?* Tick the box. *Are you energized?* Tick. *Are you popular?* Tick. *Are you pretty? Are you a success? Are you worth your space on earth?* Tick, tick, tick.

Add up the score. *Ooops, sorry—our lowest score yet! But don't sink into self-defeat. Turn that failure around today. Revolutionize your diet, do our popularity workout, attend our life-management course, categorize your aims, organize your time, set goals, look great, achieve, achieve, achieve . . .*

Jesus, who needs it? I want to live my life like a *life,* not some stupid attainment quiz. I want to relax into it, look around and enjoy the view. I want to feel what I'm feeling, not wonder how I'm coming across the whole time. I want to find out what I want, what I *am.*

The gap year idea grows. I come to the conclusion I'm yet again playing safe in planning to go to uni right away—a couple of weeks' package holiday somewhere hot maybe and then that's it, back on the treadmill again. Doing something that looks OK from the outside, where I just have to follow rules and timetables again, something with parental approval.

I start to think about taking a risk, getting off that treadmill. Going somewhere where I can take chances, see what turns up. Not caring about what

I look like on the outside any more—caring about what's going on in the inside. As in inside me. My thinking scares me but mostly, I'm thrilled by it.

I start believing I could act on it.

Three days after my last exam, there's a heatwave. I meet James early evening down at one of the crowded riverside pubs. He's got a job assembling cardboard boxes in a nearby factory, and he's got loads of cash. He buys me a beer and tells me he can get me a job there too, if I want.

"I can't afford the energy," I say.

"What you on about?"

"I'm putting all my energy into *planning*. I got to work out what I'm doing. 'Cos I'm going. Soon as I can sort something out, I'm off."

"Wow. Tell me."

"Well, there's not exactly a lot to tell, yet. Just the decision that that's what I'm gonna do is scary enough." I stare down into the river, then I blurt out, "All my life I've done what I thought I *ought* to do. I've never just gone with what I want, with what I *am*. And I reckon if I can just *get out*, go somewhere where no one knows me, *judges* me, I can . . . go with the flow, see who I am. Sorry to sound like a hippy. But there you are."

There's a bit of a stunned pause, then James says, "Good for you, Ro! Where you gonna go?"

"That's just it. I have absolutely no idea."

"Ah. Well, you could just go. Step outside, see where the road takes you."

"Now who's sounding like a hippy?"

"Head off to Thailand or somewhere, look for work when you get there . . ."

"What, and find it in the sex industry? No thanks. James, this is *me* we're talking about. I'm too much of a coward to just take off like that. That's the trouble. I want to get out, but I'm scared to just *jump*, you know? I need to have somewhere to go *to*. I'm hopeless, aren't I?"

"No. You're sensible."

"That's as bad as hopeless."

"No, it's not. What you need is—a job with accommodation!"

"Yeah. But those kind of jobs—they're for people with skills, aren't they. And I've *got* no skills! I've no experience, I've never worked, not properly. I had to give up that Saturday job at Top Shop after three weeks 'cos Mum insisted it was detrimental to my homework . . ."

"Babysitting."

"What?"

"My mum reckons you are the best babysitter

she's ever had. Even if *I'm* free to stay in and watch the brats, she phones you. Bloody rude I call it. Rejecting her own son."

"Babysitting . . ."

"And Jane's mum—she really reckons you. *And* Tom's. Come on—you make a pile out of it, don't you, Ro? All those parents recommending you to other parents. And kids love you. You even seem to quite like kids."

"Good with kids, bad with blokes, that's me. James—babysitting isn't a *job*!"

"It is if you call it nannying. And you get a place to live. It's a great way to get away. Loads of time off when the brat's asleep to go trawling for men—Jesus, Ro, this is a brainwave. Seriously, I want commission on this."

"But nannies have to be *trained*. They have to do courses, get qualifications . . ."

"Do they? You sure about that? Seems to me that references from people like my mum—who's just been promoted to deputy head, by the way—"

"Has she? That's brilliant!"

"—and Jane's uncle, who's a *doctor*—you've babysat for them too, haven't you?"

"Loads of times!"

"Seems to me references from people like that'd carry a lot of clout. I mean, au pairs—they don't do courses, do they, and people trust them with their kids? You could get old Markham's reference too. About how reliable you are."

Mr. Markham is our college principal. He probably doesn't know who I am, but even so . . . "James, you're a genius! This could actually *work*."

"What you need to do is phone round some nannying-type agencies, find out what they want. And think where you want to go. If you don't want to improve your French—"

"What French?"

"Then Australia, America—"

"America."

"Yeah?"

"It just—it feels like the best place to get lost in. Not to have to fit *in* in. If I went to Australia I'd have to get all hearty and surf and stuff."

James laughs, clinks my empty glass, takes it from me and heads back into the pub to get another round. I sit and watch three kids throwing bread at some over-stuffed ducks waddling about on the slipway, and feel like something's really begun.

After that, everything moves with amazing speed. I shut myself away in the spare room with the computer and surf the Net for all the international nanny agencies I can find. I make a list of any that are not completely hopeless and the next day, bright and early, I ring round. Most are frostily dismissive of the fact that I'm "just a babysitter." They want qualifications—experience at least. A couple tell me I could work as an au pair but the pay "takes into consideration that you'd be attending college for some of the time." In other words, the pay's crap.

Then I get a glimmer of hope. I phone an agency that I skipped past the first time, mainly on account of its vomity name: "Nursery Sprites." And the woman on the other end of the phone doesn't immediately tell me to forget it. "We pride ourselves," she confides smarmily, "on providing a flexible service, both for employees and clients. All our girls are subject to thorough checks and assessments and come fully recommended and guaranteed by us. But we have placed several girls who are not accorded full nanny status. They have less responsibility and more support from the family they're with." In other words, the pay's crap. But so what. By the end of the conversation, I've arranged to go and see her. *Tomorrow!* Bring it on!

CHAPTER 6

"MEL, I'M DOING IT! I'M *going*. In five days' time. Well, subject to references, but they'll be fine. *Jesus*, I can't *believe* it!"

I'm on my mobile to Mel outside Tottenham Court Road tube station, trying to earth my frantic excitement. I've just come out of the tiny offices of the Nursery Sprites agency. And not only have I landed a nannying job in Seattle, but a job that starts *next week*. Just as soon as Nursery Sprites have done the necessary checks to make sure I haven't got a police record for armed robbery or selling infants' body parts.

Mel screams questions back at me down the phone. She can't believe it either. I'd let her into my plans as soon as I'd made the appointment with the agency, and we'd talked it through, but— "*God*, I never thought it would be this quick!" she squawks. "I mean—you sure it's OK? It's kosher?"

"Well, unless the woman I saw is a serious confidence trickster, yeah! They've checked out this couple thoroughly—they'd already placed a nanny with them but she got a better deal at the last minute and let them down. There's only one kid, a girl, four years old. They both work in marketing and they don't pay amazingly, but they really wanted an English girl and it's OK, it's a start, isn't it? And I get my own room, and all my food, and my plane fare paid for. And they sort out my work permit and give me an open ticket to return if it doesn't work out—" I babble on, giving Mel all the details, and she agrees it sounds fantastic, so fantastic she'll even put up with how much she's going to miss me.

And then she utters the lead-heavy words: "You told your parents yet?"

"A nanny."

"Yes, a nanny! What's wrong with being a nanny?"

"Nothing. It's just—"

"Just *what*? You see—*this* is why I didn't discuss it with you—I knew you'd sneer and be disappointed, put the dampeners on it."

"Rowan, we're not *sneering*—we're trying to keep up with you! What about university, what about—"

"*Don't* pretend this is about university! I can still go—I can defer entry for a year."

"Well, that's fine. But if you want to take a year off, there are all *kinds* of challenging, exciting things you could do—"

"I don't want challenging and exciting. I want *un*challenging."

"*Un*challenging," repeats Mum, disgustedly. The alien word has to force its way through her gritted teeth.

"Yes, *un*challenging. I want peace, I want space."

"Oh, for *God's* sake, Rowan—"

"You SEE?" I scream. I'm half hurt, half triumphant. "Nannying's just not thrusting and cutting edge enough for you, is it? If I'd sorted myself out a gap year stopping the rain forest being hacked down or working as junior reporter on the *El Salvador Weekly*, you'd be thrilled, but *nannying*— that's too safe, isn't it? Not *challenging* enough. Well, I don't care. It's away from here and I'm doing it."

Mum glares like I've slapped a custard pie in her face. Dad raises his hands like a supplicant to heaven. "Rowan," he wails, "why are you so *angry* with us?"

"*I'm not angry!*" I roar, and stomp off to my room.

* * *

Things normalize. Once they've accepted I'm going, you could almost say my parents are supportive. Mum helps me sort out deferring uni entry for a year. Dad checks over my nanny's contract and tells me to open a bank account in Seattle as soon as I can, so he can transfer money if I ever get short. Mum takes me shopping for "practical clothes to wear around a child" and doesn't argue when I insist on some pretty impractical stuff too. They both keep telling me they'll write, and I'm to reverse the charges any time I want a chat. Even Jack says the odd almost-pleasant word to me.

It would be sweet if it wasn't for the growing feeling in the house, a feeling of relief, palpable as a sigh when a heavy weight's been lifted. Relief that the difficult kid, the cuckoo in the nest, is clearing off at last.

I spend my last few days in England preparing and packing (one large case, and my old college backpack as hand luggage), saying goodbye to friends, and trying not to think too much. As strongly encouraged by Nursery Sprites, I phone my new employer, Mrs. Bielicka, two days before the flight, and have a brief, slightly hysterical chat about how great it's all going to be and how much we're both looking forward to it and how she'll be sure to be at the airport to meet me.

And then I'm on the ten-hour flight to Seattle. For a while I sleep fitfully with my neck cricked, and I dream in scary snatches, something about being left, terrified, on a great open road . . . When I wake this wonderful feeling of calm descends on me. There's no going back now, so there's no point in any more agonizing and worrying. As I stare out at the clouds a memory comes in of a game I played when I was a kid, that I was a changeling, a princess swapped by evil elves, who had to find her way back to her real parents. I laugh, think back to Mum and Dad waving me off at the airport. One day, after several courses of expensive therapy, maybe I'll forgive them. Maybe—*maybe*—the fact that I don't fit in so well at home is not entirely their fault.

The plane lands, and I follow the crowd along a long, grey airport corridor. My heart's thumping with the fear of all the things that can go wrong. My case'll be lost, I'll be stopped at passport control, my papers will be wrong, I'll be arrested . . . with a mouth as dry as sandpaper I finally stagger through into the arrivals lounge, sure there'll be no one to meet me. And there's my name right in front of me. *Rowan Jones*. In black letters on yellow card. Held by a thin, stylish-looking dark-haired woman with a broad smile on her face.

I belong!

Weak with relief, I totter forward to introduce myself.

PART TWO

ESCAPE FROM SEATTLE

CHAPTER 7

"HI ROWAN!" SQUEALS THE WOMAN, seizing my damp paw in her bony, red-nailed hand. "I'm Sha Bielicka! *Wel*come!"

"Oh, Mrs. Bielicka, hello!"

"Sha! Call me Sha! We don't wanna be all formal now, do we?"

"Er—"

"I was gonna bring Flossy along to meet you. She was *pestering* me to bring her! But I thought you and I should take an hour or so just to chat and get to know each other. Without Flossy interrupting the whole time! OK?"

I'm warming to Sha, warming to her fast. She seems a little hyper, a little wound up, but then so am I. It's a big thing, this meeting for the first time.

"Why don't we put your bags in my trunk and then go get ourselves a coffee and maybe a tiny bite to eat. I'm sure you couldn't eat that garbage

48

they serve on the flight!"

"Er, no," I lie. I'd eaten all of it. "Yeah, that would be great."

"Well, let's get to the car, shall we?" she says, and high-heels off ahead of me.

I struggle after her with my weighted-down trolley. She's unnervingly *chic*. She's so thin, and her shoes exactly match the clutch bag she's toting. Still, she'd have to be chic, working in marketing, wouldn't she? She'd have to have the image.

The first thing she does once we reach the car is hand me her cellphone so I can phone home and tell Mum I've been collected. It's kind of her, but I feel dead awkward, talking to Mum with her right next to me. As we drive out of the airport she tells me about Flossy. "Her name's short for Florence. We wanted a cute old-fashioned English name— we just *love* England! And the name suits her, 'cause she's the *sweetest* kid you could imagine, seriously. A little high strung—things upset her. Sometimes. But she's so sweet and sensitive. I'm *sure* she's gonna like you."

I'm gazing out of the window, trying to make the right noises in response. I'm *gobbling* up the view. It's the same as home—streets, houses, roads, but different, right down to its bones. Bigger, broader, newer, wider, more *space* . . . *I'm in America,*

I think. *America, land of the free—free is what I'm gonna be!* We draw up outside a trendy-looking snack bar, go inside, and get ushered to a table. Sha pushes the menu towards me, says, "Have anything you want!" She doesn't look at a menu herself. When the waiter comes, she orders just a black coffee, and I mentally switch my order from steak to a small salad to avoid looking like a pig.

"You want me to quickly run through what I'll want you to do?" she says, smiling at me brightly.

"Er—sure."

And suddenly she's in top gear, firing words at me like bullets. "I wake Flossy up at seven thirty a.m. I leave for work at seven forty-five a.m. So I will need you to *take over* as soon as we've had our morning hug, as soon as she's on her way to the bathroom. That's so important. I can't have her hanging on to me, getting wound up."

"Er—right."

"You get her washed, dressed, give her breakfast, leave for school at eight thirty to be there well before nine."

"School?"

"Nursery school," she hisses, and the slightest chill seems to settle around my shoulders. "Mornings only, nine to twelve. We're not entirely happy with it, though. We're looking for another. We may be pulling her out."

"Oh, that's a shame—"

"They just don't *understand* her, that's the problem. They haven't taken the time to find out the kind of little girl she really is. I've had *endless* discussions with them."

Sha's face has gone all frigid and bitter-looking, and my shoulder chill has intensified. If I was a real nanny, a nanny who'd read books on parent psychology, right now my brain might be warningly flicking to the problem chapters at the end.

But I'm not a real nanny, so all I say is, "So this nursery's open all summer, is it?"

Sha's eyes snap shut, as though in disbelief at the question. "Of course. People have to have somewhere for their kids when they *work*, don't they?"

"Of course," I echo, ingratiatingly. I think it's pretty vile to send your kid to school in the summer, but I do really want to get on with Sha, so I smile attentively and ask, "What kind of things does she do there?"

"Oh, all kinds. The curriculum is really varied. It's the *personal* side that's kind of a let-down. Still! It's OK for now. One of the reasons I chose it was that it's near enough to walk to. I think it's so important that a child doesn't only see the inside of a car, don't you?"

"Oh, absolutely."

"And walking's so good for a child."

"Oh yes. Great exercise."

"And such a useful space of time, too. I'd like you to *use* that space to learn times tables, or sing songs, or do homework, or discuss how the seasons are changing . . . you can collect pretty leaves in the fall. Flossy keeps a Seasonal Nature Diary. I'd like for you to work with her to make sure it's up to date."

The attentive smile I've got stapled to my face cracks. *Space of time? Homework? Seasonal Nature Diary?* I'm hoping she's going to burst out laughing, say, "*Kidding* you!" But she doesn't.

"From nine thirty to eleven thirty you can do Flossy's laundry, tidy her room and so on, and I may leave you the odd chore you need to get done. But basically, that's *your* time!" She beams at me, signalling that I should now display gratitude and pleasure. Like a coward, I beam back. "You pick up Flossy from school at twelve," she goes on, "and then take her back for lunch, or have a picnic if it's nice outside, or if she has a play date that involves lunch, you take her there. Then it's on to the afternoon. She has music Monday, swimming Tuesday, free time Wednesday, dance Thursday, free time Friday. When I say free time, I mean a play date or something organized with you. Oh, and do *not* let her nap in the afternoon. She'll be up all night if you do."

Christ. I'm exhausted just listening to this litany, and the poor kid can't have twenty winks? Panic rises up inside me. I've stopped battling to feel positive about Sha, started battling to keep sitting here and not run back to the airport.

"Dinner at five, bed at seven. I'm usually home in time to take care of that. Is there anything you want to ask?"

"Er . . ." I really feel I ought to ask something. To show I care. But I'm so blasted by the itinerary, I can't think . . . "What kind of things does Flossy like to do?" I bleat. "In her free time?"

There's a pause. Sha's frowning, as though she either doesn't actually know what her kid likes doing, or doesn't think it's relevant. "Well—a museum maybe. Or sometimes there's a Kiddie Event going on, like a puppet show. The arty kind, you know, not something gross and commercial. I'd be glad if you'd draw and paint with her, too. She's very gifted at art, and I couldn't get her into art class this term . . . they had waiting lists *way* long . . ." She

53

trails off, demands, "Any questions about her actual schedule?"

"No," I gulp. "You've been very clear. I just hope I can remember it. . . ."

"Oh, I've written it *down* for you!" she cries, as though it would be unthinkable *not* to write it down. "I know it must seem like an awful long list, but I just think things are simpler if they're organized, don't you? And children *need* routine. Don't they? I mean—we're not *rigid* about it or anything."

I have the strongest sense that "not rigid" for Sha means very, very occasionally deviating from her timetable. Like if Flossy breaks a leg, say. Or on Christmas Day.

"How's the salad?" Sha enquires.

"Um—delicious," I mutter, choking down another few strands of shredded carrot.

"Weekends, of course, you're off duty. We have family time then."

I heave a shaky sigh of relief. I'd forgotten about weekends. Maybe it'll all be all right. She's tense, worried whether I'm going to work out OK, she wants to get telling me about my duties out of the way first, and now we can relax and have a chat, like she said we would—

Sha checks her watch. "We should go," she

raps out. "Taylor—my husband—he wants to meet you, and he has to go out this evening."

I put my knife and fork down and stand up—to my horror, I find I'm fighting back tears. She hasn't asked me anything about myself, not even how the flight was . . . *Stop it, Ro, you creep*, I tell myself. *You're just tired. You wanted people to stop interfering in your life, you wanted space. Now enjoy it.*

CHAPTER 8

WE GET BACK IN THE car and drive pretty much in silence to Sha's apartment. I risk a couple of glances at her profile; she's rigid as a sheet of steel. "I'm sure Flossy's gonna like you!" she suddenly squawks. Followed three minutes later by, "Flossy can take some time to get used to people!" Basically, she's nervous as hell that her kid's going to start screaming as soon as she sees me. And I'm suddenly struck by how weird it is, how unnatural, for this little girl to be about to spend most of her waking hours with someone she's never even met yet . . .

Sha swings into a driveway leading into an underground car park; the gates roll back ahead of her. She parks in a bay with number 34 above it, and we get out. She gives me no help wrestling my case and college backpack from the boot of her car, just collects two expensive-looking carriers from the back seat and taps ahead of me to the lifts.

"I *hate* this parking garage," she says. "I know there's security, but somehow it's so sinister—I won't come down here by myself at night, not even to go to the gym."

My ears prick up. "Gym?"

"Yeah—it's part of the apartment complex, there's an outdoor pool too. Taylor uses it. That's the entrance over there—"

"Could I use it?"

Silence. Maybe she disapproves of me planning for my time apart from Flossy. "I guess so," she says, at last. "I'll see if I can get a pass for you."

"That'd be great," I enthuse. "One of my aims for this trip is to get fit, you know—do more exercise."

Another silence. It crosses my mind that she could ask me what my other aims are. But she doesn't of course. The lift arrives, we shoot up two floors, and then she's letting herself into flat 34. I take in a deep breath. This is it.

"Mo-oommeeee!"

A tiny girl in a bright red tracksuit with black hair in pigtails spurting out just above her ears hurls herself theatrically at Sha. Who sinks elegantly to her knees and grasps her daughter's arms in a hold which is more about keeping sticky hands

57

away from her smart suit than motherly affection.

"Floss-*eeee*!" she coos. "Now—are we gonna say *welcome* to Nanny Rowan and give her a nice big hello hug?"

Oh—my—God. "Nanny Rowan," for Chrissake. And "hello hug." I may throw up.

"*Noooooo!*" wails Flossy, burying her face in her mother's side. "No, I *wo-oon't*!"

"Now Flossy—we discussed this, didn't we—we said Flossy had to be a Big Girl and be nice to Nanny Rowan—"

"I *hate* her!"

"Now, Flossy, how do you think that makes Nanny Rowan feel, sweetheart? It'll break her heart to hear you say that! And you know what? It can't be true, can it? And why not? Because you don't know Nanny Rowan, do you? So how can you say you hate her if you don't know her? You've got to be a good girl and—"

"*Oh, for Pete's sake, Sha, stop harping!*" A disembodied male roar has broken through Sha's monologue. Then the owner of the roar—a stocky alpha-male type with cropped grey-blond hair—strides into view.

"*Taylor*," hisses Sha malevolently, "will you *please* not interfere when—"

"You fuss with that kid too much. No wonder

she's such a little prima donna."

"*Taylor!*"

"She's four, for God's sake!" He scoops Flossy up and sits her on his arm. "And you treat her like she's at a philosophy seminar!"

"I'm just *trying* to get her to think through her reactions, Taylor!"

"*Think through her*—oh my *God*. She's a *kid*. Just let her be and go on like normal. She'll be fine!"

Sha turns a shattered face towards me, bright smile in place. "*Excuse us*, Rowan!" she squeals. "I guess we're both a little tense—this is such a big thing for us! This is my—er—husband, Taylor. Taylor, this is—"

"*Nanny Rowan*," says Taylor, all sarcastic. "Yeah, I guessed. Hi, Rowan. I have about ten minutes to get to know you before I have to go out. I *wanted* to come to the airport to meet you, with Flossy, but my *wife* decreed otherwise."

"Why don't we go inside and get a drink?" strangulates Sha. Taylor grunts, dumps Flossy back on the floor again, and everyone heads off down the hall. Flossy seems unperturbed by her parents' behaviour, which probably means this is how they often behave, which means I've arrived in a dysfunctional, psychotic *hell* . . . Heart thumping, brain spinning, I follow them down the hall.

We go into a big kitchen-diner, huge and glossy like a style magazine centerfold. Gleaming granite counters, white walls, soft lighting . . . I edge closer to Flossy and smile at her but she tosses her head and huffs away from me. *Fine*. Taylor might be a pig to show Sha up like he just did, but I kind of agree with what he said, about just letting Flossy *be*. I'll try to talk to her when she's had time to check me out.

Sha's pouring out drinks from a bottle she's pulled from an enormous fridge. Judging from the picture of herbs on the label and the fact that she's pouring some out into a little plastic beaker, too, it's going to be depressingly non-alcoholic. *God*, I could use a beer.

Taylor turns to me; his eyes pass over me like I'm a car that doesn't excite him much. He raises his glass, says, "Well, welcome, Rowan. I guess my wife's gone through the *schedule* she has mapped out for you. All *I* want is for you to keep my kid safe and not get too damn spoiled. Shouldn't be difficult, should it?"

"Hope not," I gulp.

For some reason this answer seems to please him. He grins at me. "You look like you have common sense."

"Well—I think so."

"That's what we need around here. Simple common sense. Isn't that right, Floss?"

Floss glares first at him, then at me. Then she goes over to Sha and buries her face in her skirt.

"Great start, Sha," snarls Taylor. "*Great* start." Sha's face works like a vat of acid about to boil over, but you can tell she wants to avoid another scene. Taylor checks his watch. "I gotta go."

"Oh, Taylor—not already!"

"Yup, I'm afraid so. Oh, come *on*. You know you want me outta the way." Then he ruffles Flossy's hair, so hard she squeaks, "*Ow*, Daddy!" and marches out of the room.

Sha turns to me again, still with a big smile on her face. It's so out of place now it's grotesque, like a clown's grin in a horror film. "Why don't we go into your room?" she shrills. "So you can unpack?"

Dazed, I pick up my case and backpack, and follow her and Flossy (now attached to her mother's leg) down a corridor. The decor is a bit like a smart office, kind of impressive, impersonal. She pushes open a door. "This is *Flossy's* room, isn't it, sugarpie?"

"My room!" squawks Flossy. She bowls over to the bed and jumps on it.

I leave my case at the door, and walk into the large room. It's kitted out entirely as you'd expect.

Tasteful, coordinated and very costly—especially as the kid's going to grow out of it in a couple of years. There's a tiny bed in the shape of a boat with a star-spangled duvet on it; a tiny wooden desk and chair by the window. On the curtains, the rug, and stencilled on to the walls, are legions of yellow ducks. ("Flossy loves quacky-ducks, don't you, baby?") Shelves display old-style wooden toys and teddies that look like they've never been played with. As I gawp, Sha stoops, picks up a dodgy-looking Barbie (naked apart from a chain round her neck—masochist Barbie?) and slings it into a huge wooden chest by the door. "We like to keep Flossy's room tidy, don't we, sweetie?" she murmurs. In other words, no naff toys on show.

I'm expected to say something. "It's *beautiful*!" I enthuse. "What an absolutely gorgeous room, Flossy!" I risk a look at her. She's looking at me, but as soon as our eyes meet she flings her head to the side.

"Let's show Nanny Rowan her room, shall we?" says Sha. But then—instead of leaving—she crosses to a door on the far wall and opens it. "Bring your suitcase!" she cries.

Jesus, what is this? Am I sleeping in a cupboard?

We enter a tiny room. "This *was* the nursery,"

Sha explains. "And we slept in that big room, right next to it. But now that Flossy's such a big girl, it's a perfect nanny's room, don't you think?"

No, it's bloody well not! I rage, but silently. It's a box, a cell, with a skinny little window and a very narrow bed and a telly the size of a brick—

"Look at this!" squeals Sha, and pulls open the only other door in the room. A very nasty doubt is taking shape in my mind, confirmed as soon as I see the huge cupboard, all fitted up with rails and drawers. "You have the *best* closet in the *house!*" she gushes. "I hang a few of our coats in here, but—"

"Did this used to be a dressing room?" I ask.

"I guess so. In the old days."

"So there's no . . . actual . . . *way out.* Other than through Flossy's room, I mean."

"No. But that'll be OK, won't it? You can be quiet."

There's a long silence. I'm feeling kind of sick. I can be a coward, I think, and just grin and bear it, or I can . . . "The thing is, Mrs. Bielicka," I blurt out. "I sort of thought I'd have a bit more privacy than this."

"*Privacy?*" she squawks, indignantly. "But goodness, Rowan—you can shut the connecting door! And you have to be near Flossy. If she wakes up at night, you won't hear her!"

I feel *really* sick now. "At *night*?" I croak.

"Yes, at night! Rowan—I was *very clear* with the agency people. During weekday nights, if Flossy wakes up, you take care of her. I have a very demanding job. I *can't* have sleepless nights."

Feverishly, I think back. I can remember the smarmy Nursery Sprites woman saying something about me "taking care of the child during the night sometimes." I'd assumed she'd meant babysitting if the Bielickas went out. I remember thinking at the time I might even get paid extra. But *this*—

"Is there a problem, Rowan?" hisses Sha. "If so, we really shouldn't be discussing this in front of Flossy. . . ."

"It's fine," I groan. "Really."

"Good!" She's got her wide, fake smile on again. "Now, how about we go to the kitchen and make Flossy's supper and you try and get to know each other a little, *hmm*?" There's definite reproach in her voice. She's obviously disappointed I'm not best buddies with her kid yet.

As we head back along the corridor, I'm holding a panicky little conference with myself. This is going from bad to bloody awful. The killer daily itinerary and realizing the Bielickas are the couple from hell—that's bad enough, but not having my privacy, my *nights*—that's too big a shitty thing to overlook. I want to ask—*So what happens at weekends? Where's* your *bedroom? Are you even in earshot?* But I daren't.

We go through into the kitchen. Sha takes Flossy to one side and whispers urgently to her, then Flossy trots sulkily out of the room again and comes back with a large, professional-looking folder. "Would you like to see my artwork?" she peeps.

Oh, God. *Artwork.* For a four-year-old. But hey—she's *talking* to me! "I'd *love* to!" I enthuse.

We sit side by side at the table, and I take refuge in the daubings and stickings and sketches that Flossy pulls out of her folder. They all look a bit too careful, a bit too controlled, but they're good, good enough for me to praise quite genuinely. "I love this cow, Flossy!"

"It's a goat."

"Yeah? So it is! And this little girl, she's so sweet—is she you?"

"Yes! At my *dance* class. Mommy—when can Rowan see me at my dance class?"

"On Thursday, sweetie," beams Sha, from behind the plate of teeny-tiny bits of food she's preparing. "She's going to be *taking* you—won't that be nice?"

Flossy clambers down from the table and starts

pirouetting somewhat sickeningly about the floor. I force myself to coo and clap. Sha's smile is now threatening to split her face. At least I've made up some lost ground in her dwindling opinion of me. "Sweetheart, come and eat supper now!" she yodels, bringing the plate over to the table. Flossy clambers back into her chair, and Sha and I, seated either side of her, watch her eat. She seems completely unperturbed by this, as though it's normal to have two adults entirely focused on what she's pushing into her mouth. I eye the tiny sandwiches, apple quarters and raisins with hungry envy. God, I could do with some energy food. That salad I felt obliged to order at the café was nowhere near enough.

Then out of the blue Sha asks, "I bet you're feeling a little jet-lagged, aren't you?"

This is the first real question she's actually asked about *me*, and I'm almost touched. "Er—it certainly feels like way past my bedtime."

"Well—good. I thought—this being the first night and everything—it would be nice if you went to bed the same time as Flossy. So she knows you're *there*, next door."

Oh, *great*. *Charmed*. "Sure," I mumble. "Why not."

"I have tomorrow off. I thought we'd have like

a—*training* day, if that's not too awful a word! Then it's over to you, Rowan. And I know things are going to be just *fine*." She does her horror-clown smile at me and I make myself smile back. Then we troop off to get Flossy in the bath.

MAYBE IT'LL BE ALL RIGHT, I tell myself desperately, as I stand at the end of the big bathtub holding a huge pink fluffy towel and trying not to cry, while Flossy cavorts in the bubbles and Sha clucks adoringly, looking up at me to check I'm adoring her daughter too. *Maybe Flossy hardly ever wakes up at night. Maybe Sha's coming over as Queen of Neurosis 'cos she's as nervous as I am. Maybe once I've settled in— once I'm used to this mammoth change in my life . . .* Sha keeps up a kind of running commentary about how perfect Flossy is, but I don't contribute much. Tiredness has hit me like a baseball bat to the back of the head—I'm having to use all my concentration to avoid dropping comatose to the floor. I watch weepily as Flossy is swung out of the tub, dried and dressed in her lacy nighty, and tucked into her little boat-bed.

"Now, Nanny Rowan is going to get *her* nighty

on, sweetheart," gushes Sha, "and she's going to go sleepy time right next door! And if you wake up, you just call for her! Won't that be good?"

I don't like the sound of that one bit. Neither does Flossy. "Want *Mo-oommy!*" she wails.

"Well, now, if you wake up and want Mommy, then Rowan will come and get Mommy, OK?" And she gives me a look that tells me I'm to do no such thing.

When Flossy's settled, if not asleep, I collect my night stuff and totter off to the shower room at the end of the corridor that Sha has pointed out with the implication that I'm not to use the family bathroom.

It's kind of surreal as I walk in. Like I'm surrounded by myself. There are mirrors on all walls, angled so I can see both my profiles and the back of my head, and my face reflected on and on to infinity . . . it shocks me awake, and I exhaustedly register that this will be great when I'm dressing to go out. Then a great wash of loneliness comes over me. Go out where, with *who*? When am I going to get the chance to meet anyone here? Dazedly, I clean up and hobble back to Flossy's room.

Her quiet breathing tells me she's asleep, thank God, and a tooth-strippingly twee bedside lamp (rabbits cartwheeling inside a glowing toadstool) lights my progress across to my door.

I'm in bed within ten seconds, deeply asleep within ten seconds more.

I'm coming up to the surface from way, deep down underwater—someone's shouting and I'm swimming, swimming up, there's this huge weight of water on me, it's so hard to swim up—and then I'm at the surface, almost awake . . . I feel sick with the shock of it, being woken when I was so deep down, so fast asleep. Oh my God, it's *Flossy*! I'm not asleep at home, I'm in America to take care of Flossy and she's *screaming* . . . In panic I topple out of bed, blunder towards a dim column of light, collide with the window, fight my way back out of the curtains, wake up a bit more, fumble to the door, stagger into her room...

"*Mooo-ooommy! MOOO-OOMMY!*"

"*Shh, shhhh*, Floss, hey, it's me, it's Rowan . . ."

"*GO 'WAY! I WANT MOOO-OOOMMEEE!*"

"*Quiet*, baby, quiet, come on, what's wrong?"

"There's a bad *dog*! He's got big, big teeth, and he's chasing me, he's gonna *bite* me! Want *Moo-oo-mmee*!" She bursts into frenzied sobs. I swoop down on to the bed, wrap my arms round her, hug her little shaking body to mine. "It's OK, Floss," I croon, "it's just a dream, all gone now, just a dream . . ."

"Want *Mo-ooommy*!"

Oh, God—how can I stall her? I mustn't fail at my first attempt at protecting Sha from her daughter, must I?

"*MOO-OOMMY!*"

"OK, *OK*, I'll fetch her . . ."

Two tiny hands suddenly grip my arms. "*Stay! Stay!*"

"OK, I'll stay, I'm here, you're safe . . ."

"Want *Mo-oommy. . .!*"

"Floss, I can't get Mommy unless I *leave* you, can I? You *want* me to leave you all on your own?" I stop short of adding, "So the bad dog can come and get you?" but even so I'm risking permanent psychological damage here . . .

It works though. Flossy stops screaming for her mom and subsides, sobbing, down into bed, still gripping my arm. I stroke her hair and burble on about being "all safe now." My nerves are jangling, but I feel pleased I've done my job. I try to sit upright but Flossy won't let go of my arm—she's still trembling with terror. *Poor little sod*, I think, and I stretch out beside her, curving my legs inside the little boat and my body round hers. "I'll stay, Floss," I whisper. "I'll stay till you're asleep."

I've no idea who falls asleep first.

When I wake for the second time that night, I

wake naturally. I stretch my cramped legs to the end of the boat and disengage my arm from under Flossy's head. There's no chance whatsoever of going back to sleep again—not in this bed, anyway. And my throat's dry as dust. Carefully, I lever myself out from beside Flossy's warm, sleeping shape. The window's black; the only light in the room is from the toadstool lamp. I check my watch—three forty-five a.m.—try to work out what that is in *my* time, decide it must be around midday, which explains my wakefulness, and creep out to the corridor.

I had meant to get a drink of water in the shower room, and go back to my own bed. But I'm *wide* awake now, and not only so thirsty I could die, but starving too. What I want is a nice cup of tea, and toast, and cheese, and jam . . . I make my way to the kitchen. Shit—I deserve it, don't I? After I got Flossy back to sleep so well?

In the kitchen, greed and instinct lead me to all the right places. First I sink about a pint of water from the tap, then I put the kettle on. I find some reassuringly English-looking teabags, and crackers in a jar. In the huge fridge, I discover cheese and ham. I *need* this. I feel faint just looking at it. And if I'm breaking house rules, too bad.

I top half a dozen crackers with cheese, grab a couple of slices of ham, make a mug of tea, and sit up at the granite counter to gorge. And just as I've crammed my mouth to splitting point, I hear the front door creak open.

I STAY AT THE BAR, frozen. Who the hell is this, in the middle of the night? Someone breaking in, that's who. My heart's going like a piston. The door to the kitchen swings wide—

"*JESUS!*" explodes Flossy's dad, as we both jump about half a metre in the air at the sight of each other.

"Oh, Mr. Bielicka, I'm so sorry!" I wail, through my mouthful of food. "I'm all jet-lagged, I was starving—"

He's starting to smile. Thank *God*. "*Shit*, you scared me," he slurs. "Thought you were a ghost or something, sittin' there."

"Sorry," I bleat again.

"No problem. I scared you too, right? Coming in at—" he checks his watch and whistles. "Business thing. Ran late. Hey—any coffee?"

"Er . . ."

He reaches across the counter, smiles right at me—he's got a good smile—and helps himself to one of my crackers. He smells pretty strongly of alcohol. "If there's no coffee, guess I'll just have to have another beer. Is there any in the fridge?"

I have two options here. I snap, "I'm your kid's nanny, not your bloody servant!" or I go and get him a beer. Cravenly, I decide on the second option. As I hand the bottle to him, his eyes pass over me again, but this time like I'm a car he might consider driving. I put this down to all the drink he's had.

"So—Floss fall asleep OK?" he asks.

"Yes. She had a nightmare, but I got her back to sleep . . ."

"Great, good job. God, that kid has bad dreams. Sha's been going crazy with it—" He breaks off, grins at me. "Ooops. Shouldn't say too much. Hey—don't look at me like that. It's the mother you should look out for, not the kid. *Ooops*. Said too much again, didn't I?" He laughs, swills some beer back. I climb numbly back on to my stool "Rowan, it's all gonna be *fine*, trust me," he goes on. "And I'm really glad you're here."

He stumbles towards the counter, leans up against it, and helps himself to another cracker. "What's it all for, huh?" he demands. "Life, the universe, the whole damn thing. Don'cha ever ask yourself?"

I go "Ha!" weakly, gulp down some tea, and bite into the last cracker, planning to scarper as soon as I've finished it. There's something too overpowering about Taylor. Especially when he's drunk.

"You're not going, are you?" he slurs, as I slide off my stool and self-consciously take my plate and mug over to the sink. I can feel his eyes on my backside as I move. Jesus, I wish I had a nice thick towelling bum-concealing dressing gown to put on.

"Yeah, I'd better," I say. "I'm gonna try and get back to sleep. I've got to adjust to US time some-time."

"Don't see why," he guffaws. "I never have."

I giggle weakly, say goodnight, and speed from the kitchen. Flossy's still asleep as I creep past her. This time, I'm glad she's there.

I lie in bed in the growing light for the next two hours, wide awake, brain going like a speeded-up tumble-dryer as I turn over everything that's happened to me since I landed here. I keep telling myself not to panic, not to judge too hastily, but it's hard. I'm even feeling homesick, for God's sake, so things must be bad. Around six a.m., full of nervous energy, I get up and unpack my suitcase. The enormous walk-in closet swallows up my few clothes like it hasn't eaten for a month. On the table beside the brick-sized telly, I arrange the few things I've bought with me—my jewellery case and make-up kit, a notebook, address book, airmail writing kit. I have to fight back a wash of loneliness, just thinking about writing to Mel. Then I head off to the shower to get ready for Training Day.

Training Day. It sounds like a particularly bad military movie. Which is not a bad description for the day that follows. Especially as I feel like I'm in a film, looking on at myself the whole time. Mostly in disbelief.

At seven thirty on the dot, I hear Sha march into Flossy's room. "Floss-*ee*! Wake-*ee*!" I appear in the adjoining doorway to show Sha that I'm fully dressed and ready. She ignores me. "Come on, baby, wake up!" she cries, shaking Flossy's shoulder.

Flossy groans, pulls away, mutters, "Go '*way*."

"She's tired, she had a bad night," I say. I'm concerned for the poor kid, and I'm also eager to let Sha know how fabulous I was coping with her. "She had a terrible nightmare—"

"*Flossy!*" squawks Sha. "It's *up* time!"

Not until Flossy, bleary-eyed and miserable, has been hauled from bed on to her mother's lap, squeezed, told how much Mommy loves her, and then shunted off towards the bathroom, does Sha turn to look at me. But not to talk about the nightmare. "At this point, Rowan, it's *over to you*!" she hisses, like it's a matter of life or death. "OK? At this point, I *have to leave the house*!"

"Er—right," I gulp.

"Good. Come on."

Sha is determined it's going to be an exact dress rehearsal of an average, high-attainment, full-on-pressure day. I watch as Flossy's washed and dressed, listen with sinking heart to the running commentary and advice. "We use this *timer* for toothbrushing, or Flossy can be lazy about brushing for long enough." And "Her *school* underwear is in this drawer. Picture panties are for weekends only." And "We do hair *after* breakfast. Or Flossy plays with it when she's eating."

Breakfast is another catalogue of anxieties. "Flossy can choose whole-wheat toast, or bran muffins, or whole-wheat cereal. Juice or two percent milk. And try to get her to have a piece of fruit."

I get offered breakfast too, but only as an afterthought, like it's inefficient to need to eat. Sha has black coffee, nothing else. As we sit at the counter, she switches into "quality time" mode and starts asking Flossy questions about her Nature Diary. Flossy, still grumpy and sleepy, refuses to reply. "Breakfast," Sha whispers to me, "is a really good time for Conversation. A lot of times, Flossy is too tired later. So try to chat *now*." Flossy yawns, won't finish her whole-wheat cereal.

As we head out of the front door, Sha consults her little gold watch for about the nine millionth time. "Strictly speaking," she says, "we're five minutes late. I like to be outside the *main* door by eight thirty."

We judder down in the lift, and I watch Sha from the corner of my eye. She's *radiating* tension. I imagine her undernourished bones splintering and shattering inside her skin with the sheer pressure of it all.

After a march down broad, tree-lined streets, we reach the nursery school. At the gates, a beaming Spanish girl seizes Flossy's hand and swings her off inside. Mother and daughter seem equally relieved to be parted. "So hard to say goodbye," murmurs Sha, then she storm-troops off with me in her wake.

Back at the Bielickas' flat, I'm handed—as

promised—a comprehensive list of my duties. We go through this line by line; ditto Flossy's scary Organizer hung prominently in the kitchen. I'm shown her Seasonal Nature Diary and also her Daily Diary, in which Sha says I should jot down events and achievements. ("It's for me, Rowan, in case you and I don't get time to chat at night—but it's also to keep *you* focused on your aims for Flossy's day.")

Jesus Christ, she'll be wanting flow charts next. Beam me up, someone. Anyone.

I'm given a crash course in how all the household appliances work and where everything is kept, although Sha keeps insisting I won't have that much to do domestically because a cleaner comes twice weekly and most of the food is delivered. By ten thirty I'm desperate for coffee (none is offered) and I've given up the last shrivelled bit of hope I ever had that Sha and I might get along.

We won't, ever. Not in this life or the next. She's a nightmare. She never lets up. She gives a whole new dimension to the words *control freakery*. It's like spending time with a huge, focused wasp.

She shows me round the flat, but implies that general rooms other than the kitchen are out of bounds. When we've finished the tour, she stops by a door she hasn't opened yet, checks her watch, then demands, "Do you like plants?"

"Er . . ."

"We've got a roof terrace. It's ridiculous, it's up a flight of stairs, *all wrong* for dining, and it's not like it's *visually* accessed from any of the rooms, but—" She pulls open the door, starts clipping up the steps. "I never use it," she calls back over her shoulder, "but Taylor likes to hide up here sometimes with a drink. . . ."

I bet he does, I think—and then I stop.

We've entered the most beautiful space, full of green and light. Huge plants are everywhere, climbing the walls, snaking across the tiled floor, crushing their leaves against the glass roof. There's a large cane table and chairs in the center, and even this is partly overgrown by tendrils creeping out from the two vines either side of it.

"It's so *scruffy*," says Sha, sourly. "Totally out of control. It was great when we first moved in, but Taylor won't do enough to it."

"Everything looks so healthy, though," I say, walking further into the delicious green space. The air's moist, warm, relaxing. I take in a great breath of it.

"Well, it's watered automatically. That's one good thing. And the plants get so much light—" She indicates the arching glass roof.

"It's lovely," I murmur.

"Come up here any time you like," she announces, beaming at me to make sure I've registered her generosity. "You can bring the baby monitor if Flossy's in bed."

"I'd love to," I say, "it's—" I break off. There's a scratching, rasping sound, over behind a bunch of palm leaves.

"Oh, *God*," snaps Sha, "that's the lizard."

CHAPTER 11

WITHOUT MEANING TO, I TAKE a couple of fast steps back, away from the scratching noise.

"Oh, don't worry," says Sha, dismissively. "It's in a cage. Come see."

The cage is tall and thin, made out of wire mesh. Hanging from the top there's a cone-shaped metal light-shade, the bulb beneath glowing. Below that are two thick wooden branches, suspended at right angles to the wire sides. And straddling the top branch, staring straight at us, is a large green lizard. "Hideous, isn't it?" says Sha.

Something catches in my throat when I look at him. He seems so utterly alien, like a cartoon, something out of a space-movie, with his head-spikes and skin-scales, but his eyes are beautiful, luminous, weirdly knowing. "I hate lizards," says Sha, "don't you?"

His tail—twice the length of his body—curves

sinuously down to the branch beneath. His back legs hang either side of the branch like a frog's. His scary dragon's claws rasp against the wire mesh. He's . . . *wonderful*. And before I can stop myself I blurt out, "He hasn't got enough *room*!"

"Ridiculous!" erupts Sha. "Lizards only grow to the size their cage allows."

"*What?* That sounds like footbinding. Poor thing!"

"Rowan—we *are* talking about a *lizard* here." She glares at me, non-comprehending, as though I'm concerned about the welfare of a pile of cat shit. "And anyway, that cage is absolutely state of the art. Heat control, automatic feeder—even that little pool is drip-fed." At the bottom of the cage is a filthy-looking basin, with a pipe running into it. "Taylor's supposed to clean it," she sighs, "but he doesn't, of course . . ."

"Is it Taylor's lizard, then?"

Sha shrugs. "It came with the apartment. The guy who owned it moved overseas—we had to promise him we'd take care of that creature before he'd sell to us! He used to give it the run of this conservatory, can you imagine? Taylor lets it out now and then but I absolutely *can't stand* it—it comes up to you for food! Flossy's terrified of it."

The lizard's blunt, patient head nods away

from us, and I'm filled with pity for it. But Sha's checking her watch again. "Time to get Flossy from nursery school!" she carols.

Once we've collected Floss I offer to prepare the lunch of wholemeal pasta and fresh tomato sauce, thereby gaining Credit Points and ensuring I at last get enough to eat. Over lunch mother talks at daughter with a few fake, failed attempts to include me. Then, as it's Tuesday, we go swimming. I pack my cozzy but once we get there I learn that Floss has a swimming lesson and my job is to sit with Sha in the poolside café. So I sit and watch Flossy splashing up and down and listen to Sha obsessing yet again about her schedule and needs, and I'm full of this weird, panicky feeling that I've been kidnapped, that my life's been taken out of my control and it's now being run for me by a lunatic.

I switch off, try to sort my head out. I'm longing for tomorrow, when Sha's at work. Any nervousness I feel at being in charge is more than outweighed by my desperation to get away from my new boss. I start to put some shape on how I'm going to be able to run things without her around. I reckon if I'm efficient with all the little morning tasks and do them first thing, I should be able to get some real freedom while Flossy is at nursery. Plus I can swim while she's having her swimming lesson, read while she's at dance class . . . eating with her most of the time will be fine, too. I'll not only have an obsessively healthy diet, it'll be cost-free. Leaving me with more cash to have a wild time at the weekends.

The weekends. They're like this great, echoing, empty space. Terrifying. I'll think about them later.

Pretty soon after suppertime, jet lag catches up with me again. I read to Floss but *Burglar Bill* is interspersed with jaw-cracking yawns. Floss finds this funny, and keeps trying to stick her fingers in my mouth. She's OK when she's not in the full beam of her mother's attention—when I pretend to bite her hand, she shrieks with laughter and her whole face comes alive. She's starting to warm to me, but I'm not pushing it, not till Sha is out of the way.

I go to bed at the same time as Floss again. I've survived Training Day.

I'm woken once more in the early hours by Flossy screaming. This time it's a witch after her, a witch with a long nose and dirty fingernails who hides in trees and hangs upside down and *snatches* you . . .

It's quite spooky, listening to her terrified little voice describe the horrors she's been through. This time I get straight into bed with her, and hold her while she cries. We're both asleep really quickly.

I wake up in time to get back to my own bed before Sha bursts in, in a power suit and very high heels, and hauls Flossy out of bed, protesting how much she loves her. She embraces Flossy like she might never see her again, turns her over to me, and flies from the room.

And I'm on my own.

CHAPTER 12

FLOSS AND I ARE GETTING on fine. It not quite nine a.m. and already we've broken at least half a dozen of Mommy's rules. Floss insists on wearing picture panties; she refuses to clean her teeth for more than ten seconds; she has butter as well as jam on her muffins, and absolutely no fruit; we don't leave the apartment till eight thirty-five a.m. and I brush and clip up her hair going down in the lift. Then we dawdle so much I end up putting her on my back for the last hundred metres and jogging her up to the nursery gates, which she loves. I get back to the apartment quite elated.

To find a note I hadn't noticed before, magneted to the huge fridge.

Dear Rowan—Just a few chores to do after the usual cleanup. (fyi—the bathroom is GROSS!)

1. *Dry cleaning: tickets and money on side, please pick up from Fresh Start Cleaners, address is . . . etc etc*

2. *Please pick up from store: whole wheat bread, bananas, light cream cheese . . . etc etc*

3. *Please phone Val Williams at 206-674-2485 to confirm play date for . . . etc etc*

4. *Please do Flossy's ironing, basket in . . . etc etc*

Bitch, bitch, bitch! I rage to myself, as I stomp off to the bathroom. I work flat out clearing up that, the kitchen and Floss's bedroom, then I rush out to the dry-cleaners, get lost on the way to the store, hurtle back to the apartment and phone Val Williams, who's clearly half-barking with boredom being what she calls "just a stay-at-home mommy" and who keeps me talking for *months*. It's eleven forty-five by the time I race out to pick Floss up, and I haven't even touched the sodding ironing. I arrive at the nursery eight minutes late. Flossy is not impressed. "Mrs. Marks was going to call *Mommy*," she accuses.

"*What*? Why?"

"To say you hadn't come to get me."

Oh, great. I go over to Mrs. Marks, grovel to her, explain I'm still getting the hang of everything.

She's so sweet and understanding, tears come into my eyes.

I need chocolate.

"*Mommy* never lets me have chocolate," says Floss, mouth smeared with sticky brown.

"Well, I couldn't buy it for me and not share it with you, could I, Floss?"

"No. That would be *mean*."

"Two squares won't spoil your lunch."

"No." She munches happily for a while, then demands, "Do I have a play date today?"

Shit, shit, *shit*! I forgot to check her stupid Organizer before I came out! With my luck, it'll be some big-deal lunch that's been arranged, and we're supposed to be there in two seconds' time . . . "It's a surprise, Floss," I bluff. "You wait till you get home. Now—play horsies again?"

I jog her back to the apartment in record time, dump her on the floor and fly over to the dreaded Organizer. *Relief.* She's supposed to play with Kelly Oswald at Mansion House, Grover St., Apt. 3B but not till two p.m. I check the map Sha left me, calculate it will take maybe twenty minutes to walk there, and jam my head in the fridge.

"What about omelette for lunch, Floss?"

"Don't like it. What is it?"

Luckily, Floss doesn't like my omelette all that much, so I have something to eat in snatched mouthfuls while I'm doing the ironing. We're late leaving again. Floss says she doesn't want to go, she hates Kelly and she's tired. I tell her she's got to go, the Organizer says so. She pulls a face. I consider phoning for a cab but bottle out, especially as I'd probably have to pay for it myself. We leave on foot and I end up being her horscy again. Once again I get rather lost and I'm nearly dropping from exhaustion when I arrive at Mansion House, ten minutes late.

A sour-faced Hispanic woman answers. "Kelly in playroom," she barks. "Come in."

This apartment is very like the Bielickas'. Expensive, stylish, soulless. In a square room bursting with toys, a little blonde girl sulks and won't say hello to us.

"You watch them, OK?" raps out the woman.

"Er—OK. Are you Kelly's nanny?"

"No. Maid. The nanny, she go out."

Oh, *I* get it. Organize a play date for your charge so you get another kid's nanny to mind her while you scarper. What a cheek. Maybe I should try it sometime.

Hostilities are breaking out already. Every time Floss picks up a toy, Kelly takes it off her. Flossy's lower lip starts to tremble. "Oh, come on, Kelly, can't she play with anything?" I ask, indignantly. Kelly's lower lip starts to tremble. "Hey," I trill, desperately, "let's play a board game, shall we?" Silence. "What about this *ladybird* game, huh?"

The game is a rip-off of snakes and ladders with mega-twee plastic ladybirds you have to shunt around the board. Floss can't resist them; she sits down and plays with me. Kelly watches like a sniper from the side of the room. As soon as we've finished one game, she marches over and wordlessly packs the board away. After a brief fight over her ladybird, Floss gives it up and bursts into tears.

"OK, Flossy babe," I murmur, "come with me." I take her by the hand and we go in search of the maid. She's in the kitchen, polishing a huge silver cup with a picture of a golfer on it. "I'm afraid it's not working out," I say.

"No?" she shrugs.

"No. They seem to hate each other."

She shrugs again.

"If I take Floss home, you'll look after Kelly, won't you?"

"Sure. You know way out?"

* * *

Flossy is dragging by the time we're halfway back to the apartment. "I'm *ti-i-ired*," she moans.

"I know, sweetheart," I say. "Me too. *Exhausted*." I squeeze her hand. It's starting to feel natural, holding it in mine. "You want another piggy-back?"

"No," she says bravely. "It's OK."

"You know what, Floss?"

"What?"

"When we get home, you and I are going to have a nice little *nap*."

Which will be Rule Number Eleven—or is it Twelve?—broken.

And which will be too sodding bad.

WHEN SHA LETS HERSELF IN the apartment at six forty-five that evening, she's met by a beaming, happy daughter all refreshed from her hour-long sleep. When Flossy woke I wiped her face and said, "I hope Mommy won't be mad that you had a nap, Flossy."

To which she replied, "Let's not tell her, Rowan!"

Oh, Jesus. A guilt-pact with a four-year-old. Well, fine—I'm up for it if she is. The apartment is tidy and the dry-cleaning and groceries are sitting there next to the pile of ironing and Flossy is fed and happy. Sha need never know I've been anything but perfect.

"How was the day, Rowan?" she asks, as she peels her daughter's arms from her waist.

"Fine, thank you!" I reply, brightly. And I give her a rundown—edited, of course. In my version, chocolate doesn't feature, Kelly and Floss play for the allotted time, and no one so much as yawns, let alone sleeps. I wind up, expecting some kind of praise.

But all Sha does is grimace like she's swallowing bile, and say, "Rowan—could you please not call her Floss? It's—well, it's so *dental*. Uuugh . . . I have *such* a headache. Could you bathe her tonight? I've got to go and lie down."

And without waiting for me to answer, she embraces Floss and totters out of the kitchen, shutting the door firmly behind her.

Choking, I tow Floss into the bathroom, promising her that Mommy will come along later, when her bad pain's gone. Floss, who'd started to cry when Sha exited, cheers up a bit when I pour twice the bubble bath I should into the running water and the bubbles foam right up and creep over the edge of the bath. While she splashes about I sing stupid songs like *One Man Went to Mow*, which Sha would no doubt hate and Floss loves. I dawdle over drying her; I dawdle over getting her into her nighty. Seven thirty-five and still no sign of Sha. *Bitch, bitch, bitch!*

"Let's tuck you up, Floss," I murmur. "And I'll go and tell Mommy you're ready for her to read to you, shall I?"

Outside Sha's bedroom door, I hold my breath and listen, ear next to the wood. Nothing. I tap softly, then louder. "Hello?" I waver. "Sha?"

"What is it?" she wails.

"Flossy's in bed—"

"Isn't she *asleep* yet?" Her voice—a vitriolic whine—makes my skin creep.

"Well—nearly—but she wants you to read to her—"

"For *Chrissake*, Rowan, what am I *paying* you for? *You* deal with it!"

I feel like she's slapped me. Or—more to the point—slapped Flossy. Without answering, I turn on my heel and go back to Floss's room. "Want *Mommeeee!*" Floss cries.

"Mommy sends you a big kiss," I lie, "and says she needs to stay in bed a bit longer till the pain's gone away. *I'll* read to you till she comes." I put my arm round her and she cuddles up to me, sniffing, and suddenly I feel this huge wash of pity for her. I pull back her long dark hair from her face and say, "Hey, Floss."

"Hey," she says back, all tearful. Her face is a little white doll's in the dark. It's like I'm seeing her for the first time, and I see that she's not just my means of earning money, not just my reason for being in America, and she's not just a series of problems, either—problems like keeping her quiet in the night, getting her to nursery on time. She's a little kid with her life ahead of her and nothing— no kindness from me now, no wonderful friends and lovers later—will change the fact that she has a screwed-up control freak for a mother.

"What book d'you want, Flossy?" I ask, gently.

"*The Biggest Apple*," she whispers.

I hold her close as I read to her and put in lots of expression, which is all I can think of to do to make things better. I'm silently cursing myself for letting her sleep so long earlier, because now I'll just have to read and read and read, till I bore her to sleep. But before I've even got to the end of that first book, something unexpectedly good happens: Flossy falls asleep against my arm. I cradle her down in her bed, and tiptoe out.

I go into the great empty kitchen, make a cup of tea, and try not to brood. After all, I can't change anything, can I? All I can do is take care of her and distract her from the crap. And now—what do I do with the rest of the evening? The tempting options on offer are: watch miniature TV very quietly in my room, stay in the kitchen and flick through those three old magazines over there (one of which advertises an article called *Angel in the Office, Bitch at Home?* which could be highly relevant), or write to Mel.

I go for the first option. Flossy's still fast asleep as I creep past, and I feel quite good as I switch on and settle down to watch. But after an hour or so of inane channel-hopping I'm going stir-crazy. And cabin-crazy too, stuck in my cupboard of a bedroom.

It's then that I remember the roof terrace. Oh, *yes*. Perfect. All that space, up away from everyone among the stars shining through the glass roof, and the plants breathing out oxygen (or is it nitrogen?) at night and . . . and . . .

And the lizard. Stuck in its too-small cage, trapped in the corner.

Suddenly I'm not so keen on the roof terrace.

Don't be an idiot, I tell myself. *It's probably got more room in that cage than you have in this cell. And anyway—the poor thing's stuck there whether you're looking at it or not*. I make up my mind not to be squeamish, and tiptoe past sleeping Flossy again, remembering to collect the listening part of the baby monitor on the way through. Then I climb the stairs to the roof terrace.

* * *

I push the door open, feeling weirdly excited. Dozens of little spotlights are scattered among the plants, lighting up a group of leaves here, a thick twisted stem there. It's spectacular. The glass sides and roof reflect the lights back and I feel like I'm in a space ship travelling through the night, a space ark maybe, with its own little jungle . . .

I can hear the lizard stirring, scraping its claws against the cage. *Get it over with*. Face it, then it won't seem so bad and sad . . .

It's looking straight at me, through the wire mesh. It's in exactly the same spot as it was yesterday when I first saw it. Jesus, it may as well be nailed down for all the space it's got. I guess it can climb down to that other perch, and then maybe to the floor—the water basin's still mucky and unfilled. "Bastards," I mutter to myself. It peels back its lizard lids, gazes at me blankly.

And then I sense someone behind me.

"Hey—wanna let him out?"

CHAPTER 14

"MR. BIELICKA!" I SQUAWK.

"Taylor, *please*."

"God, you scared me—I didn't hear you come up!"

"That's because I didn't come up," he slurs. He smiles at me; raises his beer bottle in salute. "I've been up here a while. Sittin' over there." He jerks his head to a reclining chair, half-hidden by a huge shaggy fern. "The one night I get home in time to *eat* with the wife, like she's always nagging me to, and she's in bed with a *migraine*."

I'm silent, thinking he must have been back for ages, and yet it didn't occur to him to call in on Flossy, say goodnight to her. Pointedly, I bring the baby monitor attachment up to my ear, and listen. I can just hear Flossy breathing, deep and calm.

"Still asleep?" he asks.

"Soundly."

"Atta girl. It go OK with her today?"

"Fine. Well—we're still getting to know each other, but—"

"She's lucky to have you," he says. Then he reaches round me, and unclips the cage. "Let's let poor old Iggy out. He likes running around."

"Is he—is he—?"

"Housetrained? Doesn't matter, with lizard shit. Good for the plants."

"I meant dangcrous."

"Only if you get in his way." Then he laughs, scoops up the lizard two-handedly, and lifts it out of the cage. Its tail rasps against my bare arm as it passes me, mid-air. It feels warm, very alive.

"What type of lizard is it?" I gasp.

"A green iguana. They *told* us one of the smaller ones." Taylor puts it on the ground and it waddles purposefully off towards the leafy planters along the side. It's like a squat little dragon—it's like having a dragon for a pet. He's clearly loving moving after being cooped up so long. I can't take my eyes off him.

"He's beautiful," I say.

"You think? Sha can't stand him. A while ago I couldn't find him, so I left him out. Left the cage door open so he could get back in to bask under the light. *Boy*, did I get shit for that. It *had* to be the one time *Madame* came up here. She saw the open cage door and went crazy."

We watch until Iggy disappears into the leaves. "I got takeout," Taylor says, pointing at an inviting selection of Chinese takeaway cartons on the cane table. "Want some?"

I hesitate. Taylor makes me nervous. I'm not sure about being up here alone with him. It's not like I think he'd actually *try* anything, he just makes me nervous. "Should still be hot," he goes on. "Here—have a beer too. You over twenty-one?"

"Almost," I lie.

"Strict laws about underage drinking here. You *Europeans* let little kids drink alcohol, right?"

"Er—the French do sometimes."

"C'mon. Eat."

I succumb, sit down, and pick up a carton. After all, I don't have to stay long, do I? Taylor hands me cellophane-wrapped chopsticks, and I unwrap them and tuck in. I feel a bit self-conscious but I'm OK with chopsticks, especially if it's noodles. It tastes *great* after the diet of health-conscious kid-food I've been existing on. The beer tastes great too.

"So," says Taylor, tipping himself back in his chair, "think you're going to be able to stand us?"

"Sure," I mumble, glad the food's making talking hard.

"Big change, new country and all. You'll take a while to get your bearings here, I guess. And you know—meet people around your age." He shrugs, palms turned out, and looks at me hopelessly, but I feel quite touched. At least he's aware I have needs too—unlike Sha who so far has treated me like a baby-care robot. "If there's any help you need, Rowan, you just ask, OK?"

"Actually, I was wondering," I say, swallowing down a mouthful of beansprouts, "if I could use the gym here, you know the one in the basement car park?"

He grins. "Fitness freak, eh? *Sure* you can, no problem. I'll get you a pass. Maybe we can work out together sometime. Or—you know—swim."

I smile queasily, dreading him adding, *Or—you know—take a sauna*, when some leaves high up to my left rustle loudly. I look up and laugh out loud with shock. Iggy's vivid, grinning face is about a metre away from mine, peering through the foliage.

"He *likes* you!" Taylor exclaims. "Look at him checking you out!"

Iggy's sprawling along a branch in one of the shrubby trees, tail and back legs dangling. He seems so incredibly pleased with himself I laugh again.

"Better get him back in his cage," says Taylor, and he stands up and unceremoniously plucks him off the branch.

"Can't you leave him free a bit longer?" I wail.

"He's had enough. If he disappears, it takes forever to find him. Unless you've got some salad with you. He'll come for that."

I stand up, follow them over to the cage, and bravely demand, "Isn't he awfully cramped in there?"

"Nah, not really. Iguanas—they like to preserve their energy. They stay in one spot for hours, just soaking up the heat."

"But he looked like he liked moving too!"

"Look—if you're feeling so sorry for him, grab that water bowl at the bottom and go give it a scrub. There's a sink on the wall over there. Fill it up too. Then he can have a dip." I do as I'm told, and when I get back Taylor's cleaning out the bottom of the cage. "There you go, Iggy—all this because the lady feels sorry for you. Enjoy." Iggy seems to sense the clean water. He slithers down the sides of the cage, and lands in the bowl with a satisfied splash, filling it like a turkey in a roasting tin.

Suddenly there's a piercing, banshee wail from

the baby monitor. We both jump. "*Jesus*," Taylor blurts out. He sounds appalled, disgusted even. I give him five seconds to offer to go to his daughter, then I speed towards the door.

"No hurry," he calls after me. "Sha can't hear her in our room. That's why we moved over there."

THURSDAY DAWNS. SHA IS UP bright and early and makes no mention of—let alone apology for—her absence last night. Pointedly, I ask her how her migraine is and she says sourly, "Better. Thank you." As she leaves, she spits at me, "Rowan, have you remembered to work on the Seasonal Nature Diary? And can you start keeping Flossy's Daily Diary from today on? We did talk about it. Remember?"

Bitch bitch bitch, I chant, under my breath. I seem to have taken to chanting this, like a monk chants his mantra. God knows what it's doing to my karma.

Floss is miserable and uncooperative from the moment she's woken. She throws a real wobbler when Sha leaves and I'm forced to practically sit on her to prevent her from racing after Mommy. She won't wash, she won't eat breakfast. Through a mix of bribes and bullying I manage to get her to nursery on time, and once I'm back I get through the long list of chores magneted to the fridge, take delivery of a consignment of groceries, and field two inane phone calls. Then I collect Floss, and feed her lunch. She's still miserable and I'm having about as much fun as a hamster on a wheel. A pre-booked taxi conveys us to her Thursday dance class, which I sit through with gritted teeth. Lots of vain, spoilt brats being extolled to act even more vain and spoilt by vomit-inducing chat from the pastel-clad matron in charge. ("Pointy toes, Lara— not lazy toes! Now *spin* like falling leaves!")

I'm aware other nannies are sitting long-sufferingly on the line of chairs at the back of the room and now would be an excellent time to make contact—say hi, swap phone numbers even. But I'm in such a foul and dejected mood I even avoid eye contact, and the negative energy I'm giving off surely repels anyone thinking of approaching me.

Back at the flat, Flossy says she's going to fetch a toy, so I put the kettle on, get down the Daily Diary and vent some of my anger by writing a fake and sickly report of Flossy's day. *Flossy skipped on the way to school and spotted a jay bird! She helped prepare the salad for lunch and counted out the carrot sticks! She got praised for being the best little snowflake at dance class!* Etc. etc. *ad nauseam.*

Halfway through my mug of tea, I realize Floss has not reappeared. I make my way to her room pretty sure what I'm going to see. And sure enough there she is, curled like a puppy on the end of the bed, no toy in sight. The poor kid made her way here wanting sleep like a junkie needs a fix.

Quietly, I settle down on the floor facing her, back against the radiator, and finish sipping my tea. The peace is delicious. *You sleep, Flossy*, I say to her, silently. *We both need it.*

The next day—thank *God*—is Friday. As I force myself out of bed (jet lag having been replaced by what feels like terminal exhaustion) I keep telling myself *Tomorrow I'm free, I have time off*. I'm not worried about weekend loneliness any more. I just want to *stop*.

"Flossy's free time this afternoon!" Sha barks at me, in lieu of saying good morning. "What do you have planned?"

Planned? I want to scream at her. *What d'you mean PLANNED? I've been here less than a week, my head's still reeling with trying to fit into your hideously dysfunctional life, and you expect me to PLAN things??!!*

But what I do is clear my throat and say, "I thought a Nature Walk. In the woods we pass on the way to nursery? And then we can do some work on her Nature Diary."

She smiles at me sourly, not wanting to do anything so positive as actually approve. "OK, Rowan, but don't let her play dates get behind, will you? Maybe you should make some calls this afternoon—people get booked up really far in advance. And play dates are so important. She needs the social interaction."

Then—before I can punch her in the face—she swivels round and stilettos off.

The day is hot and dry, so before I pick Floss up from school I make a packet of sandwiches. If we drop into those woods on the way home we can claim we've had a stupid Nature Walk—and a picnic—and save at least an hour.

In the woods, Floss sits glumly beside me on a bench and munches her sandwiches. She refuses to get excited about the squirrel we see, or the crow. So I pick up a few plants to press and take her home.

We sit down at the kitchen table, both dreaded diaries in front of us. I open Flossy's Nature Diary. It's a testament to her rebellion against being made to keep such a thing. She's drawn lots of pictures, but the trees are purple and growing at crazy angles, frogs have wings, birds balance one on top of the other, and the rain is spouting up into the sky from clouds creeping along the pavement. It's like the kid's been on an acid trip. "Has Mommy seen this?" I ask, nervously.

"I'm not showing her till it's finished. At the end of the seasons."

That's a relief. I plan to be well gone by then. "Well, I love it, Flossy," I announce. "It's very imaginative."

"What's . . . *imaginive*?"

"Things that people make up. Like—fairies."

"They're not made up," she says, scornfully. "They're in books."

"Just 'cos they're in books doesn't mean they're not made up. They're made up, and written down!" She looks unconvinced; I launch into a story about unicorns and witches, mermaids and fairies, all mixed up with something nasty called a Grobbert thrown in for spice. Just as the Grobbert's about to chop all the mermaid's hair off and use it to stuff a cushion, I stop.

"Now you carry on," I say.

"I *can't*!" she says, eyes like saucers.

"Yes you can. You use your *imagination*. You decide if the Grobbert gets stopped, or if the mermaid loses her hair. *You* decide."

Squealing with laughter, she's off. It's probably the first time in her over-organized life that the poor kid's been in control of anything. The Grobbert gets mashed to a pulp by the unicorn. The mermaid says she'll be the witch's friend and goes home with her and they make cakes and ask the fairies to a party. It's *great*. It's just about the happiest I've ever seen her.

We fetch juice and biscuits, and she sets about drawing the squirrel and crow we saw (the squirrel's pink, and riding the crow like a horse) and I proudly write *Interactive creative storytelling* in her Daily Diary.

CHAPTER 16

THE WEEKEND. WHAT MADE ME think it would be good? It's worse than the week. Saturday, everyone sleeps in; Flossy wakes me around nine thirty by singing loudly in her room and lobbing toys about, quite a few of which hit my door. She tags after me to the kitchen so I end up making breakfast for the two of us. Sha appears half an hour later in a wannabe Hollywood nightgown and looks put out that I'm there. I slink off to shower; then I slink out.

I set off down the streets and walk. And walk. After an hour or so, it stops feeling so alien and special, and starts feeling tiring. I reach the shops; I window-shop. In a streetcorner café, I make a cup of coffee last an hour. Then I walk again. I'm like a bag lady without the bags.

By two thirty in the afternoon I'm starving, but reluctant to eat on my own like a saddo, or to spend my money on food—so I go back to the apartment. Happily, it's empty. I fill a plate from the fridge like a thief at top speed, and I'm exiting the kitchen to go and hide in my room just as the front door opens.

The family outing has not been a success. Sha's spitting at Taylor, Taylor's fuming, Flossy's pouting. Sha spots my piled-up plate, does a double-take of sheer disbelief, and demands, "Have you got someone here?"

"No," I mutter.

"Then what on *earth* is all that food for?"

"I—I dunno, I'm starving—"

"Obviously," she sneers.

"Leave her alone, Sha, will ya?" snaps Taylor. "Let the kid *eat*, for Chrissake. Not everyone wants to look like a praying mantis."

Hastily, I scuttle off to my room, dropping a bit of cheese that I don't pause to pick up.

I stay shut in my cell for the next four hours. I eat; I watch TV; I write a bitterly complaining letter to Mel; I nap for a bit. *I'm getting acclimatized*, I think gloomily. *I'm adapting to life as a prisoner*. Then, around seven p.m., there's a tap at my door.

"Rowan?" It's Sha, sounding saccharine-sweet. "Rowan—can I come in?"

"Of course."

She half-opens the door and slithers round it. "Are you going out tonight?" she asks.

I shut my eyes—I feel like I might start blubbing. How can *anyone* be this stupid? I want to scream at her, *I'm alone, I just got here, I know no one, I've no idea what to do, where to go* . . . But what I do is sniff and croak, "No."

"Well, in that case, would you keep an ear open for Flossy? Taylor and I thought we might duck out to eat."

I stare at her stonily, and she rattles on, "We need some *us* time—by ourselves. We haven't eaten out for *weeks*—Taylor said he'd like takeout but I put my foot down, I told him he was taking me somewhere nice and expensive!" She smirks at me, expecting me to mirror her women-against-mean-men face. I continue to stare stonily.

"Flossy won't be any trouble," she simpers. "She's in the bath right now, Taylor's watching her, she's had such a *full* day, she'll go right to sleep the minute her head touches the pillow . . ."

"Until she wakes up screaming," I blurt out.

Sha looks like I've slapped her, which is fine because it's what I'm longing to do. "Is that a problem for you?" she hisses.

In for a penny. "No, not when I'm on duty. This

is meant to be my night off."

"But I thought—if you're going to be here *anyway* . . ."

She's a monster. A vile, exploitative monster. May as well play her at her own game. I lift my head, stretch a fake smile across my mouth. "It's *fine*," I coo. "What are your babysitting rates?"

All the way through the closed bathroom door, I can hear the Bielickas warring over my demands for payment. Sha's going on about how ungrateful I am, how sordidly money-obsessed I am, how if I really cared about Flossy I wouldn't ask to be paid. It doesn't seem to occur to her that slagging me off in front of Flossy might not be the wisest child-care move.

Then Taylor says, "Look—it's fair that she should get paid for extra work!" and this uncorks a new stream of bile from Sha, during which Taylor groans in repressed rage, like he's trying to stop himself ramming his wife's head down the toilet.

Trapped in my room, I listen to Taylor putting Flossy to bed. He's bluff and efficient; she's sulky and shrill. Neither—clearly—are enjoying the other's company. I start to really *really* need to pee, but I tell myself I'll resort to peeing in my suitcase before I leave my room. I cross my legs, strain my ears. It goes quiet, then there's another tap on the door. "Come in!" I squeak.

It's Taylor. He's smiling apologetically and holding out a twenty-dollar bill. "Still OK to watch Floss?" he asks.

"Sure. Look—I feel bad about asking to be paid, but honestly—"

"Don't say any more about it, Rowan," he goes, all warm and avuncular. "You're right to expect to be paid." Then—worryingly—he sits beside me on the bed. I cross my legs tighter. "Look—Sha's a demanding woman," he says confidingly, as though telling me something I don't already know. "Thing is—she cares so damn much for that little girl I guess she thinks there's something—you know—not quite *right* about wanting to be paid to take care of her. Like you should just do it out of—*love*, or something."

This is so insane I can't think of a reply. Especially as Taylor has picked up my hand from the bed and is pressing the folded twenty-dollar bill into it. "Now—you take this, OK?" he says, still gripping my hand in his. "We won't be gone more'n a coupla hours. We're just—"

"*Tay-LOR!*" Sha's shriek cuts through his voice like a chainsaw. "I'm all ready—what the hell are you *doing* in there?"

Taylor jumps guiltily to his feet, and leaves my room without a backward glance. I hear the Bielickas snarling at each other as they head towards the front door. I hear the door shut. I count to five, leap to my feet and hobble at top speed to the shower room. There, I pee fountainously, sighing in pleasure and relief. Then I check on Flossy, who's out for the count, collect the baby monitor attachment, head for the fridge and pick up two beers and some lettuce.

Then I climb up to the roof terrace.

CHAPTER 17

HE'S STILL THERE, STRADDLING THE top branch, with the warm light coating his green skin like honey. "Hiya mate," I mutter. "Want to stretch your legs?" Then I reach out and unhook the cage clasp.

On the way up here I'd decided if I was going to let him out, I'd better do it quickly. Before I got cold feet.

His weird lizard eyes watch me as I swing the door open, and he shifts on his branch. What now? Do I lift him like Taylor did? I'm just gently raising my arms when he shunts forward and suddenly *drops*, like a stone, right off the branch. I gasp, jump backwards. He's bypassed the lower branch and landed half in, half out of the water basin.

Then he's still again, looking up at me.

"D'you want out?" I quaver, trying to summon up the courage to pick him up. I reach out slowly and he makes a rush forward. "*Shit!*" I squeak, sidestepping. He swarms across the cage bottom, over the edge, and drops again, on to the floor. Then he's away among the stems and foliage.

I take in a deep breath, watch him disappear. Then I head for a reclining chair and open one of the beers.

I relax for at least three quarters of an hour, staring up at the spaceship glass ceiling twinkling away with all its reflections. If "relax" is the right word—it's more like I'm poleaxed. I lie unmoving, catching a glimpse of Iggy's tail here, nose there as he forages about, and I try to come to terms with my weird new existence. In an attempt to pull myself together, I start to make a mental list of things to do to make friends—try to talk to other nannies at the school gates, at the dance class, at the pool . . . it's not exactly cheering. I feel like I'm using all my energy just holding at bay a great dark cloud of depression that will engulf me as soon as I let it.

A rustling to the left distracts me. Iggy appears, a twig in his mouth like a huge Cuban cigar. I laugh, get off the lounger, and hold out a piece of the lettuce I'd bought up. He senses it, starts plodding towards me. He looks like a dinosaur as he moves. I feel a thrill of fear, but I keep the lettuce held out. And then he's taking it in his wide mouth, and very carefully I lever both hands under him, really squeamish and scared to touch him, but I do, I lift him gently off the ground. He's heavy, solid—his skin is warm and alive. I carry him back to the cage. He's chewing happily as we go. Then I deposit him on the floor of the cage, and fasten the door, high on the success of it. "Bye, mate," I breathe. "Till next time."

The Bielickas slam back an hour or so later, while I'm still awake reading in bed; I hear them rowing in the kitchen. Neither of them comes to check on Flossy. She wakes with her usual nightmare at about three a.m. and I fall asleep beside her in the tiny boat-bed.

Sunday is spent once more avoiding everyone. I make myself eat lunch out—just a fast-food joint with lots of other losers and loners, but I still feel humiliatingly conspicuous. Apart from that I lurk in my room, battling cabin fever, making occasional sorties into the kitchen to steal food, make tea. I daren't even visit Iggy 'cos I suspect Taylor's hiding out up there. All in all the weekend is about twenty times worse than the week when my life might be total shit but at least it has a purpose, at least then there's a *reason* for my miserable existence on earth.

The Bielickas clearly share my weekend loathing. On Sunday night there's an almost palpable feeling of relief in the apartment—relief that the new week's about to start and everyone can get away from each other again. Sha drags me into the kitchen and subjects me to a floral-tasting "tisane" and what she nauseatingly calls a "mini planning session" about play dates and a swimming test and a trip to the dentist in the week ahead. And then Taylor wanders in, sees me, strikes his forehead with his fist and goes, "Shit—I forgot! Gotta pass for you, Rowan! For the gym, and the pool!"

Great. What wouldn't I have given to have been able to go there this weekend?

Stupid, amnesiac *bastard*.

CHAPTER 18

TIME PASSES. CARING FOR FLOSS settles into a routine. She and I seem to have silently agreed that Sha's rules are psychotic and we can break as many as we like as long as she doesn't find out. My worry about Floss's welfare is growing, though. It's no good just to cuddle her, give her as much fun as I can, let her take naps. The kid needs help. She needs—face it—different parents. But what can I do about it?

I've served three long weeks of my sentence here. I have no rights, no needs recognized, no life outside this dysfunctional home—I exist just for the kid. I feel like a twenty-first century Jane Eyre. The only difference is *my* madwoman isn't tucked away up in the attic, she's down here in the kitchen ordering me about.

After only three weeks six things are abundantly clear:

1. Sha is a fake, cold, insane, controlling, ungrateful bitch who lives in the outward appearance of things and has no sense of anything real. No wonder Floss gets nightmares.

2. Floss needs therapy for her nightmares. If only so I can get some sleep.

3. Floss is an OK kid with me and a prima donna monster with her mommy.

4. Taylor is a sleazebag who's going to make a move on me sooner or later because he's desperate (see 1).

5. I'm overworked and miserable and so lonely I could die. I've met no one. I see no one. Jane Eyre was a party animal compared to me.

6. I NEED TO LEAVE.

I haven't talked to anyone about leaving, of course. It's a thought—not yet a plan—that I've only just admitted to myself. How can I leave after only three weeks? Where can I go? I can't admit failure and go home. During the bi-weekly phone calls to Mum (which I *look forward to*, so things must be bad) I'm chatty and cheerful, glossing over the ghastliness. I can't let them know it's gone so stupendously wrong.

Four things are just about keeping me sane:

1. THE GYM AND POOL. I go nearly every evening. Floss's hi-tech baby monitor works in there and the staff are really good about keeping it on the desk and giving me a shout if she wakes up screaming. This has meant I've done a wet towel/sweaty shorts and T-shirt dash up in the lift a couple of times but by and large it works, as her nightmares usually only kick in around dawn. Going early also means I manage to avoid Taylor. ("Hey—wanna do laps together?" "Hey—coming in the spa pool?") I'm feeling pretty thin and fit. My skin—with the health diet—is clear, the best it's ever been. The multiple mirrors in the shower room confirm how good I'm looking. But there's no one to see me.

2. THE ROOF TERRACE. It's an oasis, an escape from the concrete jungle, an Eden complete with its own snake in the form of...

3. IGGY. Who has become my friend. I read somewhere that prisoners in the Bastille made friends out of rats—well, Iggy's a whole lot cooler than a rat, isn't he? As soon

as he sees me now he does his nosedive off
the branch, and waits on the cage floor for
the door to be opened. Then he roams
about, occasionally trotting over to see me
as I lie on the recliner. I feed him fruit and
salad and I talk to him. I have this whole
fantasy going that he's a lizard (as opposed
to frog) prince and if I kiss him he'll turn into
a complete stud.

Yes, I am going mad. Clearly.

4. THE MONEY I'M SAVING. They're not paying
me well but I'm hardly spending a dime. I
get most of my food here and I never go
out. What's there to spend it on? So my bank
balance is beginning to look very healthy
indeed.

Which is good because I've started to think
of it as my escape fund.

At the Thursday dance class in interminable week
four, I get talking to a couple of nannies, Sara and
Melanie. They were born in Seattle and seem a
tiny bit dull, but I think, *Beggars can't be choosers*,
and throw myself into the conversation with flattering gusto. When they hear I'm recently from
England and don't know anyone here, they ask me

out with them on Friday night.

I'm thrilled to actually have a social event to go to.

First hurdle is negotiating Friday night off. Sha thinks only Saturday night is the weekend, meaning I'm on duty six nights out of seven. She doesn't actually *say* this, as that would expose her as a slave-driver, but it's clear from all the obstacles she puts in my way that she thinks it.

Luckily, Taylor steps in. "Shit, Sha—let the kid have some *fun*! It's great she's met some girls her age."

"Taylor, could you please keep out of this?" hisses Sha. "You're interfering when you don't know the full story—"

"*What* full story? It's not a *story*, for God's sake—Rowan just wants a Friday night off!"

"I'm not arguing with that. I'm merely reminding her that Flossy's bathtimes are important—they're wind-down times. If she's rushing through it so she can get ready to go out—"

"Oh, for *Christ's* sake, Sha—"

"And, anyway, this Friday I can't guarantee to be home before nine! I've got an important client meeting—and I'll need to have drinks with them afterwards—I suppose you think it's *OK* to leave Flossy unattended here if my meeting runs late?"

"*NO*, I didn't say that—look, I'll guarantee it—OK? I'll be home by eight thirty. *OK?*"

In the end he's not home till nine ten but as I've managed to put my make-up on perched on the end of Flossy's bath, I'm still ready to go out at nine fifteen. I meet Sara and Melanie at a bar, as arranged, and we go on to a club, and I know by eleven thirty it's going to be a complete washout. Sara and Melanie's idea of a fast time is to huddle in a corner and *watch* people. That's as hot as it gets. They giggle hysterically when I try to get them on to the floor to dance—they won't budge. In frustration, I take off on my own—and fall prey to the deranged attentions of a guy with two scars and eight ear-piercings, who's high on something seriously brain-altering. I flee back to Sara and Melanie, who—horrified at the sheer sight of him—decide it's time to share a cab home.

It's not even one in the morning when I'm letting myself in the front door. Taylor's propped at the kitchen counter, five empty beer bottles beside his elbow.

"Hey, kid!" he slurs. "Have a good time?"

"Not really."

"Me neither. *Me* neither. Sha got home, said she's exhausted. *Big* fight over whether I should go out or not, meet my buddies for a few beers. She said I gotta stay in in case the kid wakes up. Seeing as I told you you could go out."

"Mr. Bielicka—I'm *supposed* to have Friday nights off—"

He raises both hands like he's surrendering. "Hey, hey—don't look at me! I'm on your side! Anyway—I stayed in. Sometimes—sometimes it just isn't worth it."

"And did she wake up?"

He looks at me vacantly, and for a moment I think he's going to ask, "Who?" But then he shrugs, points at the baby monitor attachment, and says, "Quiet last time I checked."

I pick it up and listen to Flossy snuffling and wheezing. My stomach contracts with tension, like it always does when I hear her breathing on this thing. She's like a time bomb waiting to go off.

"Have a beer?" Taylor asks.

Something in my head tells me to say good-night and leave, but he's putting a decapped cold beer in my hand, and I know it's going to be me on duty when Flossy wakes up screaming, so I take the beer and say, "Thanks."

"Some crummy Friday night, eh?" he says, chummily. "Here—sit down."

Gingerly, I sit on the stool next to his. And he starts telling me what a great job I'm doing, how he knows Sha's difficult, and Floss is demanding, but I'm doing great. "We're gonna get this weekend thing worked out, trust me," he says. "You deserve your nights off for the good work you're doing."

I'm just starting to think I've misjudged him when the clammy weight of his hand lands on my thigh. I push it off, fast.

"Hey, OK," he slurs. "I was just thinking—if you wanna little fun, there's no need to go out to get it."

"Are you—are you *saying*—?"

"Yeah, baby, I am. I think you're really cute." He turns to face me. "Come on, don't act so scandalized. We could go up to the roof terrace, spend a little time together."

I shoot to my feet; my stool scrapes loudly back on the floor. "I don't fucking *believe* this!" I spit.

"Hey—watch your language!"

"Oh, that's *great*! You're trying to *jump* me and you're worried about me swearing?"

"I don't like to hear someone who's in charge of my daughter *ever* using bad language."

"You—*hypocrite*!"

"Keep your voice down!"

"You had your hand on my *leg*, and then you lecture me on—"

He stands up too, towers over me. "Look, you little British *madam*, what happens between us has nothing to do with Floss. Your language does."

"Well, personally, if I was Floss I'd be far more upset about my daddy trying to *fuck* my nanny than my nanny saying it!"

His head jerks back. "You disgust me. Keep my daughter out of this."

"Keep her *out* of it—I'm here because of your daughter! You employed me because of your daughter! And—and—*I'm somebody's daughter too*!" Then I burst into tears, and run out of the kitchen.

I speed past Flossy, shut myself in my room, wildly consider shifting the bed against the door. Seconds later there's a soft tapping. "Hey, Rowan," Taylor whispers. "Hey—I'm *sorry*."

"Go away!" I hiss back.

"Look—I'm drunk, OK? And lonely. I like you but I'd never hurt you, I'd—"

"*Go away*."

There's a silence, then a tiny scraping at my feet. I look down. A fifty-dollar bill is being posted under the door. I pick it up, screw it between my fingers. *He thinks he can keep me quiet with a pay-off, the creep.* In my head I'm flinging open the door, chucking the money straight in his face.

But only in my head. In reality, I'm smoothing it out, opening my purse and tucking it inside. That's fifty dollars for the escape fund, fifty dollars nearer to freedom.

CHAPTER 19

FROM NOW ON, TAYLOR GIVES me a wide berth. He even seems a little scared of me. And when he and Sha go out for another vitriolic dinner *à deux* next Saturday night, he pays me double to babysit.

In an odd way I miss his friendliness, which shows how desperate I've become.

Then, the Tuesday after that, everything comes to a head.

It's the evening and I'm feeling slightly more cheerful than usual because I'd phoned home earlier to discover little brother Jack had broken his arm in a rugby match. "He's an *awful* patient," moans my mother. "You'd think the world had come to an end. When I think how good you were when you had glandular fever . . ." On the way back from swimming I let Floss choose a get-well card—a bunny wabbit with a tartan waistcoat and a leg in plaster, off the Richter scale for tweeness. I write a condoling message inside that I know will irritate him enormously, only feeling slightly sick at how small my pleasures have become.

Things stay good, because Sha's back early and insists she'll put Floss to bed single-handed. But then she seeks me out in the kitchen where I'm peacefully glugging my second mug of tea, and she's looking distraught. "Flossy says her *eye* hurts," she wails.

I sigh. "Have you had a look at it?"

"No. She won't let me. She's too *upset*."

Here we go again, I think. M&M for Flossy doesn't mean sweets, it means Mommy Manipulation. "I *thought* her eye was looking swollen earlier," I say, and head into her room.

As soon as she spots that her audience has increased, Flossy's wails take on a hysterical edge. "*Hurts!*" she screams. "*HURTS!!*"

"Aw, Floss, does it? Let me see."

"*No-o-oo! N-OOO-OO!!*"

I sit on the side of the boat-bed while Sha hovers behind me, wringing her hands. "Come on, darling," I say. "If I can't see, how can I make it better?"

"*NO-OO-OO!!*" She starts banging her head against the pillow. I grab hold of her shoulders, and while I make like I'm hugging her, I pin her down, hard. She's immobilized long enough for me to see the tiny, angry-looking pustule on the edge of her eyelid.

"Thought so!" I announce, triumphantly. "It's a sty."

"A *what*?"

"It's where an eyelash root gets infected. It's agony, but easily fixed. My brother used to get sties a lot. You just pull out the eyelash, and the relief is immediate, it's—"

"*Pull out the eyelash*?" You'd think I'd suggested drilling a hole in her daughter's skull.

Catching the panic in her mom's voice, Flossy increases the volume yet more, and I shout, "*Yes!* I'll go and get my tweezers."

When I get back to Flossy's room, Sha is stretched out beside Flossy, just about howling with her. "I can't take this!" she sobs. "I'm calling the doctor!"

"You can't call a doctor out just for a sty! They'd sue you or something! Look—you hold her, and I'll—"

"Hold her? You want me to *pin her down*? You can't just attack her with tweezers, Rowan! Her eye hurts so much it—"

Half of me just wants to give up, walk away from Flossy's dreadful screaming saying, "OK, have it your way, call a doctor." But the other half can't bear the monumental fuss that's being made, and that half wins. I get hold of Sha very firmly by the arm, pull her to her feet. "This will be over in a *minute*," I say. "Now go and get me a little bowl of boiled water and some cotton wool." I propel her towards the door. "Go *on*!"

With a strangled sort of cry, Sha exits. And I turn to Floss. I know I've only got a few minutes. I put on my scary voice and say "Flossy, *shut up*! *NOW!*"

Shocked, she shuts up.

"Now *listen*. You have a nasty, *naughty* eyelash. It's hurting you, isn't it?"

"*Ye-ees!*"

"So if you let Rowan pull it out—all the hurt will go, OK?" I start to put my weight on her, lie half on top of her. "Look at me, Flossy. *Oh*, it's horrid. *Oh*, what a nasty, mean, *horrid* eyelash." She stares at me, mesmerized. "OK, Floss. Let's get it." I take hold of her chin to steady her face, bring the tweezers round. Flossy scrunches her eye up, hard. "Come on, baby, open it up. Let's get rid of that horrid—"

She opens her eye and I go in, fast and steady. The sty eyelash is at an angle, so I can clamp it right away. Then I *pull*.

Flossy's anguished scream brings Sha bursting back into the room, water sloshing from the bowl she's carrying. "Oh, *God*," she yowls, "what have you *done*?!"

"I've got it out, that's what I've done," I announce triumphantly, silently thanking the ghoulish, not to say sadistic, interest I always took when Mum used to nix Jack's sties. "Now give me a bit of that cotton wool, will you?"

I have to take the bowl off her. I squeeze out the cotton wool, wipe the tweezers on it, and say, "Want to see that nasty eyelash, Floss?"

Flossy stops crying immediately and sits up in bed. I hand her the swab. The root of the eyelash is gratifyingly gunky, all blood and pus. "*Uuuurgh!*" she squeals, revolted and delighted in equal measure.

"Does your eye feel a bit better?"

"Yes. *Yes!*" Absolutely compliant, she lifts her face to me and, with a fresh swab, I wipe her eye clean. Then she settles back in bed.

"Sleepy time," I say.

"Don't frow it away," she murmurs.

"What, the eyelash? I'll leave it here, on your bedside table. You can see it again in the morning."

I stand up. Flossy's already asleep. I walk from the room, Sha following, and turn out the light.

OK, bitch, thank me! I'm thinking. And then I

see her face. "That's your idea of taking care of Flossy, is it?" she seethes.

"What?"

"Pinning her *down*, attacking her *eye* with a metal instrument—you could've blinded her. If she'd moved at the wrong time you could've *blinded* her!"

"But you *knew* I had tweezers," I say, as calmly as I can. "I remember you saying—*you can't just attack her with tweezers*—"

"Yes, I did say that, and you chose to ignore me, didn't you?" she shrieks. "I'd like to remind you, Rowan—*I'm* her mother. Not you. *I* make the decisions about her health and well-being. And I don't appreciate being *shoved* out of my own daughter's bedroom by some *girl* who thinks she can override *MY DECISIONS*—"

"SHHHH!!"

"WHAT?! Don't you *dare*—"

"D'you want to wake her up again?" Sha glares at me, then shoulder to shoulder we march into the kitchen. And I get my blow in first. I take in a big breath, turn on her and say, "Flossy is *asleep*. The pain has *stopped*. *Some* people might be grateful for that—some people might even *thank* me for what I did!"

"I'm not denying you got the pain to stop," Sha

hisses malevolently. "Although I will take her to a doctor tomorrow to get her eye checked out, and if there's *any* sign of damage, *any* at all—"

"There won't be. It was just a *sty*!"

"Don't interrupt me! I'm giving you notice—*now*—that if you *ever* try to override me again like that in front of her, your employment here will stop immediately! Do you understand? *Do you understand?*"

She's insane. There's no point trying to talk to her, none at all. So I just look at her, and make the mistake of letting exactly how sick and foul I think she is show on my face. Her hand shoots out, fingers clawed, but—partly because I flinch back, partly because she pulls back—she makes no contact with my face. Then she bursts into tears and runs from the room.

Heart thumping, I flee straight to the sanctuary of the roof terrace and let Iggy out of his prison. "All right, mate?" I croak, and he grins at me and perambulates off among the plants. I follow him about, feeding off the sight of him, telling him all about what happened, telling him that's it, the last straw, and I've got to get out. His total indifference is quite soothing. Then I sit on the lounger and wrap my arms round my knees. I can't bear to remember Sha's face when she flipped out, but it keeps coming into my head. I try to drive it out by replaying that intensely satisfying moment when I pulled out the infected eyelash. Which I think is a bit dodgy of me until I work out that it all goes back to the apes. We're programmed to like that kind of stuff, so we can look after each other, aren't we? Pull out ticks and eat fleas, scrape off scabs. Me the groomer. Me the *healer*.

I can't heal the rest of Flossy though, not in the way she needs healing.

No one can.

THE NEXT MORNING SHA DOESN'T appear as usual to get Flossy out of bed, and I hear screaming and shouting coming from the master bedroom at the other end of the apartment. Taylor's bellowing, *"This can't go on!"* and Sha's screeching, *"If your mother comes here I'm leaving!"* I tell Flossy Mommy has another of her headaches, and I see from her sad little face that she knows it's a lie, but she goes along with it because the truth is too terrifying to face up to. We both pretend we can't hear when Sha's voice accelerates into full-on hysteria, and over breakfast I turn the radio on and am very, very jolly.

On the way back from nursery, I brood. My need to escape has just gone into the urgent red zone. But Flossy—how can I abandon Flossy? I'm just about the only stable thing in her life right now. I decide to talk to Taylor as soon as I can. I'll confront him, make him face up to how things are.

But when I let myself into the flat, he's waiting to talk to me.

"Hi," he says sheepishly. "Guess you heard the fight?" I nod. "She's just tired. She's been working really hard, and with Sha, things just come to a head . . ."

"She nearly hit me last night," I say, bluntly.

He shudders, then carries on with what he was saying, like only his body heard what I said. ". . . but she gets through it, she comes around in the end. Rowan—I'm asking you to hang on in there, 'cause things are gonna change. I'm getting my mother down for a coupla weeks. Flossy's *Babcia Stasia*."

"Babcia—?"

"*Babcia* means Grandma. She's a real Polish granny. She's practical. She'll inject some good ol' common sense into the situation."

There's a silence. Then I say, "Mr. Bielicka—"

"Taylor."

"I couldn't help hearing that . . . well. Sha's not too keen on your mother coming."

"Oh, she says that *before* the visit, but she loves having her here once things calm down. And I've got a plan to cheer her up. Sha's been getting on me for months now to get outside caterers in to throw a big classy dinner party. All her friends are doing it. Well—we can't afford that. But Ma's an ace cook. Sha can throw a big dinner party, and Ma'll do all the food."

I stare at him. I can't think of a single word to say to this plan, so inadequate, so clearly doomed from the outset.

Taylor's got his wallet out. He peels off a twenty, and lays it down on the counter. It's queasily reminiscent of the time he tried to get off with me. "I know you had a tough night last night," he says. "Just hang in there a little longer, OK?" Then he turns on his heel and leaves the kitchen.

I creep along to my room. I'm dreading hearing Sha wailing and muttering like mad Mrs. Rochester up in the attic, but there's only silence. I shut my bedroom door, stow away the twenty dollars. Then I get my bank book out and stare at the total line of my escape fund.

How far will 729 dollars get me?

Taylor's mum arrives two days later. On the morning of her arrival, Taylor stays home and Sha gets up and goes to work, looking white and acting like an automaton, which I suppose means she's doped up on tranquilizers. I've got the spare room ready—on Taylor's instructions—and he's arranged something "special" for lunch. When he sets off to meet his mum from the Greyhound bus station he's acting nervous but happy, too.

Flossy doesn't want to wait for lunch, especially not for Babcia, who she announces she *hates*. I try to keep her sweet with potato chips.

At ten to two, Taylor's mum walks through the door with a cat-carrier in one hand and a gold-handled walking stick in the other. She's wearing gold ankle boots, and her white frizzy hair is scragged up on the top of her head with a huge, shaggy, gold dahlia. A vast purple tent dress sets it all off. Sha would have a *fit*, but just the sight of her makes me grin. I love the way she's themed her stick into the colour scheme.

Taylor dumps down two enormous, battered suitcases; Babcia plonks the cat-carrier on the floor and sets about unlocking it. There's kind of a tense atmosphere, as though there must have been words in the car. "Flossy," pleads Taylor, "come and kiss Babcia Stasia!"

I give Floss a push and she flounces huffily over, just as a tiny dog bullets out of the carrier, barking furiously. Flossy flees screaming back to me.

"*Quiet!*" commands Babcia, presumably to both of them. "Flossy—*come*!" She advances, scoops

Floss up in a big warm greedy hug. "Don't be afraid of Pompom!" she says, then she turns to me. "And who is this?"

"I told you, Mama," says Taylor, wearily, "that's Rowan—Flossy's nanny."

"Nanny!" scoffs Babcia, her mouth curling with disapproval at the word. "Why does Flossy need a nanny when she has her babcia here?"

"Mama, we *talked* about this," groans Taylor. "You can't run around after Flossy—all her ballet classes and swimming classes and—"

"Hah!" scoffs Babcia. "You never had any of that when you were small. And anyway, if Sharon didn't work such long hours—"

"Mama, *please*."

"All right, all right. I said I wouldn't criticize and I won't. Hello, Rowan. I'm delighted to meet you. Now—is lunch ready?"

Lunch is pretty hellish. Babcia criticizes Taylor's careful deli selection and threatens to warm Flossy's bottom when she throws her mug across the table because I wasn't refilling it fast enough. She chews gustily and noisily and feeds Pompom (who smells) tidbits from the table whenever he yaps. With something like desperation, Taylor tops up our wine glasses and says, "Here's to you, Mama. So glad you could come and stay."

"Even though there's nothing for me to do," she retorts.

"Mama—there's plenty for you to do! You can cook us some of your wonderful meals, for a start. So we can all eat together—spend time together like a real family."

"Hah! A real family! You want me to do the impossible, son?"

I lie very low that evening, and the next time I encounter Babcia is when I return after dropping Flossy off at school the following day. She's sitting up at the kitchen counter, Pompom asleep at her feet, and the kitchen has not only been tidied up, it's gleaming.

"Oh!" I exclaim. "You cleaned up—thank you—it's—"

"You've got enough to do with my granddaughter," she says. "I heard the fuss the little madam made, getting out of the door."

"She's not normally like that."

"I hope not."

"She's—upset. She's used to Sha waking her up, and for the last few days—"

"—Sharon's been in one of her *bad* moods so she left it to you. Typical." Babcia pats the stool beside her and smiles at me. Her teeth are a similar colour and condition to the string of old amber beads round her neck, but it's still a good smile. "Come and sit down. I made coffee—real coffee."

Nervously, I sit beside her, take a sip of the coffee she pours out. It's strong and creamy.

"Now," she says, "you tell me what's been going on with my daughter-in-law." And then, hardly waiting for me to say a word, she launches into how they never got on from the start, how Sha (who's really Sharon, which I think is hilarious) was always embarrassed because she wasn't smart or refined enough. "You know what they offered me last Christmas? A *facelift. Her* idea, of course. I told them—you just don't want people thinking your mother's really old 'cause that means *you* must be old. Well, too bad, I *am* old and you're getting that way." She mourns on about how she warned Taylor not to marry Sha. "She's like one of those damn mannequins in a shop window, all style, no bones, no blood . . . all she thinks about is *appearances*. Or how things look to outsiders. She's made my boy into a drunkard, and she's ruining that poor child. *Ruining* her."

I listen, drinking more of the wonderful coffee. I put in some of my views, about how Floss should just be allowed to *be herself*, not be bludgeoned and chivvied into doing things her mother thinks she should do all the time, and as I talk, I realize I'm talking about myself too, about my upbringing, and my eyes fill with tears. Babcia pats my hand, tells me I have a good heart, and one day I'll make a good mum. It all gets quite emotional.

We chat on in total agreement until it's time for me to fetch Floss again, and when we get back a delicious lunch has been prepared—fried potatoes and bacon and some kind of pumpkin. Flossy of course turns her nose up, but Babcia tells Flossy if she eats it all up she has a present for her. The present when it's produced is a pair of cheap safety scissors and some folded strips of pink paper. I hold my breath and wait for the scene, but before it can happen Babcia has picked up the paper and scissors and produced a twinkling line of pink ballerinas.

Flossy's enthralled. She dances them round the table while Babcia watches her with a kind of hungry, angry love. "Now," Babcia says, picking up the scissors again, "shall we make some teddies?"

"Ducks!" squeaks Floss. "Can you do ducks?"

While I write *Creative paper cutting and quality time with Babcia* in Flossy's Daily Diary, enjoying in advance the intense irritation this will cause Sha,

Babcia cuts out dancing pink ducks, holding each others' wings. Then she says, "And now my darling, it must be time for your afternoon nap. Isn't it, Rowan?"

I grin at her.

We're allies.

THAT EVENING, PROBABLY IN THE hope of distracting
Sha and his mother from their loathing of each
other, Taylor starts talking about the big dinner
party. "You make a guest list, Sha, and Ma'll get
some ideas about food—authentic Polish cuisine.
Fabulous."

Later that night I hear Sha gushing down the
phone that it's "*all* very last-minute and spontaneous but she *does* hope they can come 'cause
Mama is such a wonderful, traditional cook . . ."

I leave Babcia reading Floss her bedtime story,
escape up to the roof terrace and let Iggy out. "You
know—you look a lot better for all this exercise," I
say, as he clambers across a thick vine stem.
"You're getting leg muscles." He's faster, too, and
stronger as he climbs about. Which is great but
makes the fact that he's shut up in such a small
space most of the time all the more horrible.

"If I'm leaving, Iggy," I mutter. "I ought to go *now* while Babcia's here. So she can take care of Floss."

God, though. Just the thought of leaving makes me so scared paralysis sets in. Despite the fact that family units are—in my experience so far—proper hell, I'm terrified of going it on my own, of not being part of an organized set-up with a phone and a first aid box and a front door that locks and access to regular meals . . .

"I've got to get my head together, Iggy," I say to him, and he wags his jewelled head at me. "I've got to risk it—be on my own somewhere. Whatever happens I couldn't be more isolated and lonely and freaked out than I am here. Apart from you, of course, mate. Wish I could take you with me."

The next day I start my research. I start scanning adverts in the papers; I ask the unexciting nannies, Sara and Melanie, for advice; I call in on a couple of employment bureaus. Everyone seems to want me to get a different nannying job but I hold out against this. Some kind of hotel work seems best, 'cos it's residential. I get as far as phoning a big hotel complex somewhere in San Francisco and they sound promising but say I'll have to call in to have "employment confirmation." Fair enough—they've got to meet me face to face, haven't they? But I still feel like I imagine I'd feel if forced to jump from a plane without a parachute on my back. What is *wrong* with me—why am I such a coward? I've got money. Even if I don't get a job, I'll survive. I can go home, admit defeat—Nursery Sprites will pay the airfare. What is *wrong* with me?

Babcia's been here nearly two weeks now. The days are much better for me 'cos she does so much in the flat and with Floss, taking her out for walks with Pompom and so on, but the nights when Sha's home are horrendous. You couldn't cut the atmosphere with a knife—you'd need a chainsaw. They keep forcing me to join them for meals to use me as a buffer zone. The dinner party is on Friday, two short days away, and I have the strongest feeling Babcia will be packing her bags right after it. For Flossy's sake, I need to go while she's still here. I keep turning it over in my mind: do I just cut and run, do I face Sha and tell her I'm going? I'm immobilized by indecision. I need some kind of push.

And then it's the night of the Dinner Party, and I get that push. *Boy* do I get it.

CHAPTER
22

BABCIA'S BEEN COOKING SINCE SEVEN a.m. The smells and sights are wonderful—she's creating a real, traditional Polish feast. Twelve people are expected to the Dreaded Dinner Party—fourteen with Sha and Taylor. I'm getting paid twenty dollars to act as kitchen serf now, waitress later. This on top, of course, of coping with Floss, who's having a fine time helping Babcia beat eggs and rub butter into flour. Sha gets back from work early to set out the dining room, arrange the flowers she's brought. She's just this side of screaming hysterical as she squares up to her big social event. It's painful enough listening to her strangulated voice, so God knows what she feels like having it come out of her mouth.

Half an hour to go. Floss is in bed but refusing to settle. Babcia keeps a fuming silence as Sha queries this, nags about that . . . it's a big relief when the first guests finally arrive and Sha has to put her horror-clown smile on and hostess.

The first course—wonderful little mushroom parcels called *pierogi*—goes off without a hitch. I serve, pass round the sauerkraut, decork wine bottles for Taylor who's getting steadily rat-arsed. When it's finished I totter out of the room with an overladen tray of dirty plates and overhear Sha saying, "Oh yes, she's British all right. She's a sweetie—we're *so* lucky to have her. She adores Flossy, and she can't do *enough* for me . . ."

Choking, I hurry back to the kitchen. Just as I reach the door I hear an awesome crack. It's momentous—biblical. Like stone splitting.

I rush through the door and see that it is stone splitting.

Babcia's standing there, face crumpling in horror. "I thought these counters were heat-resistant!" she wails. Under a huge cast-iron cooking pot, the granite surface has cracked—a great, jagged split right across its width.

"Oh, my *God*," I mutter. I feel like I might throw up.

"I take it out of the oven, put it down—and it's fine! Then suddenly this terrible noise!" She's near to tears. "I'll have to tell Taylor, oh, the *expense*—this kitchen almost bankrupted him—"

I plonk down the tray, put my arms round her.

"Look—Mrs. Bielicka—it's OK. We'll tell him later, OK? After the guests've gone. Let's just serve this course, and—"

But then Sha's head appears round the door. Guiltily, we spring apart. "What's the delay?" she demands. "Is anything wrong—*OH MY GOD!*" She races to the counter, her face a mask of anguish, and shifts the heavy cooking pot. "Oh, you *STUPID, STUPID* old woman!" she raves. "That granite costs *thousands*—oh my GOD—I *told* you not to put cooking pots right down on it, I *told* you what could happen—"

Pompom's barking hysterically, making darting runs at Sha. "But Taylor—he puts frying pans on it!" Babcia wails. "Straight from the stove!"

"That's *different*! God, how can anyone be so STUPID! That cast-iron pot—it holds a *huge* amount of heat, far more than a frying pan could—don't you *understand* basic science, you *senile* old woman?"

Babcia bursts into tears. Sha stalks towards her with her fists gripped like she'd like to kill her. I'd like to kill Sha. I fling my arm round Babcia again, bravely gasping, "Oh come on, Sha—I know it's awful! But it's just a *thing*! It can be fixed!"

Suddenly it's very, very still and cold in the

kitchen. Sha turns on me, hissing, "What are you implying, Rowan? Are you saying I'm making too much fuss over thousands of dollars' worth of damage?"

"No—*no*! Look—it's awful, it's awful—I'm just saying it could be worse, it could be Mrs. Bielicka who was hurt, or *Flossy* . . . at the end of the day, it's only money . . ." Oh, Jesus, Ro. When you're in a pit, stop digging.

Sha's face could double for a mask of Medusa. I daren't look at her. "So you're saying I'm too upset about losing money?" she rasps. "You're saying—implying—I should only be this upset about my own daughter getting hurt?"

"Sha, that is not what I said—"

"You're saying I wouldn't *get* this upset about her, maybe? Only money?"

Listening to Sha's voice is like being injected with pure vitriol. Any minute now she'll grab a knife—no, it will rise off the counter by kinetic energy, and land in her hand—and—

"Hey guys, the natives are getting restless in there—what's happening?" Taylor's entered the scene. His wife and mother advance on him, screaming, complaining, sobbing. He takes in the shattered granite top and goes white.

Five minutes of very hard work follow. Taylor

gets a whisky down Babcia's neck and a tranquillizer down Sha's. I carry the wonderful goulash into the dining room and start dishing it out. Luckily, most of the guests seem to be too noisily sozzled to have registered what's been going on in the kitchen, and now they're too ecstatic over the sight and smell of the goulash to take in the fact that their hosts are still missing. Minutes later, Sha appears at my elbow, evil-clown smile at full stretch. "Sorry about disappearing like that!" she mews to everyone. "Poor Mama *burned* herself—such a shame!"

I flee back to the kitchen, find Taylor still desperately placating Babcia. He's bodily blocking her route to the phone, while she clutches Pompom to her breast and shrilly insists she's going to call a cab and leave right there and then. "Let's just get this party over," he pleads. "Let's just get through it, and then we can sit down and *talk* and—"

"You expect me to cook that woman's food for her, after what she called me?"

"Mama—*please*. For *me*. We'll sort it out when the guests have gone, *please*."

In the end, Taylor promises Sha will apologize, an event I hold to be as likely as the granite counter sealing itself up again, and Babcia (with another whisky in her glass) starts begrudgingly chopping

chocolate and walnuts to sprinkle on her stupen-
dous-looking walnut *mazurka*. I limp back to the
dining room, help serve out seconds, clear up and
crawl back. I'm about to expire of exhaustion
and tension. Part of my brain tells me I should
eat something; I find a spoon, and I'm hungrily
scraping the last of the goulash from the pot
when Sha—yet *again*—darts into the kitchen.
"Rowan? Dessert?"

"Er—I'm not sure it's ready—"

"Let's keep it coming, *please*. I'm *exhausted*. The
evening's been ruined for me, absolutely ruined.
Obviously."

Babcia looks up from her *mazurka*, murderous
hatred on her face. "Here," she spits. "Finished."

Sha barely glances at it. "Good. I want to get
rid of everyone so I can check out if our insurance
covers us for . . . for *that* kind of accident. You bring
the bowls, Rowan. Cream?"

Silently, malevolently, Babcia passes her a jug
of cream. Sha lets out a muted scream. "There's
not enough! This won't go around!"

"Yes it will," snaps Babcia.

"Suppose it runs out? Suppose it gets to the
next to last person and it's all gone, it's—"

"*Wheeesht!*" explodes Babcia. She stoops,
grunting, opens a cupboard, and emerges after a

few moments rummaging with a larger jug. "Rowan, pour the cream in here and whisk it up a little with the milk frother. Just enough to bulk it up, not to make it stiff, you understand?"

While Sha stands in front of me, wringing her hands, I tip the cream into the new jug, plunge in the frother wand, and turn it on. I rotate it, staring down into the foaming cream. Mustn't overdo it, mustn't whip it too much or Sha'll have another hysterical fit . . . oh holy *shit*. The unmistakable, gruesome shape of a spider's leg has swirled into view. Followed by another leg. Followed by a big blob of mangled body. *There must've been a dead spider in the bottom of the jug*! And I didn't check. And it's too mashed up to take out now and it's all black and hideous against the cream's whiteness. The only cream in the house. The cream that will surely tip Sha over the edge into breakdown. I keep rotating the wand, transfixed. What the hell do I do? The legs disintegrate; the body shatters. The spider turns into black dots. "Rowan, it must be ready?" squawks Sha, and seizes the jug.

I'm dead. She screams, "Oh my *Gaad*, what on earth's all this *black* stuff?"

Babcia peers into the jug. "It's vanilla," she says, firmly. "I crushed some vanilla bean to give some flavour to the cream."

Sha stares at her wildly for a second, then squawks, "Come on, Rowan!" and hurtles from the kitchen. Zombie-like, I pick up the bowls. Babcia glances over at me and winks.

She's guessed—she *knows*! Maybe she even *saw* the spider in there, and *let* me whisk it. Or Jesus, maybe she *put* it there—she had it up her sleeve, and dropped it in—I look back at her but she's already turned away from me. She's scooping ground coffee into the coffee maker, cackling like a happy witch.

CHAPTER 23

THE DINNER PARTY FROM HELL finally finishes. Babcia disappears off to her room as soon as she's made the coffee. And when I've served it up I cut myself an absolutely enormous slice of the wonderful *mazurka* (no cream), grab some raw carrot and the baby monitor extension and scoot up to the roof terrace. I let Iggy out, feed him the carrot, settle down on a lounger, and in between mouthfuls tell him all about my appalling night. I'm interrupted by the welcome sounds of people braying, *Thank you, marvellous evening sweetie, so clever, such wonderful food—goodnight, goodnight!* Then the even more welcome sound of the door shutting, and silence.

Then I hear Sha shrieking something, and Taylor yelling something back, then Taylor appears round the roof-terrace door. He looks so pitiful I feel almost sorry for him. "This has been," he whimpers, "the worse goddam night of my entire life." He decaps a beer against the side of the table, glugs most of it back in one go.

"D'you think you'll get the money back on insurance?" I ask, warily. I'm watching the distance between us. If he gets too close and tries anything I'm ready to fly.

"The money—? Oh, the kitchen. I couldn't give a shit about the *kitchen*. I just—I've had enough, OK? I can't take any more. I thought Ma would make it better—bring some sanity. But she just sent Sha over the edge."

While I rack my brains for something comforting to say, Iggy noses his way out from a clump of ferns. "There you are, you poor bastard," says Taylor, gloomily. "God, look at the size of him. It was all crap, telling us the cage size would restrict his growth."

"Are you going to get him a bigger cage?" I blurt out. I realize now is probably not the best time, but as he brought it up . . .

"No way. Too expensive. Anyway if we did he'd just grow some more, wouldn't he?"

"So what'll happen—if he gets too big—if he—"

"It's *gonna* happen," Taylor shrugs. Then he

makes a throat-slitting gesture and a horrible, throat-slitting noise. "They inject them. Just like dogs, the man said."

"The *man*?"

"Sha phoned this vet place up. He's coming Monday, to take him away."

I stare at him, stunned. "What d'you mean?" I croak.

"I mean poor old Iggy is cashing in his chips. Sha's been nagging on and *on* about getting rid of him, and now he's getting so big—"

I'm frozen, sick. *Oh my God, it's my fault*, I think. *I've made him grow, by letting him out so much, giving him all this exercise . . .*

"But he's so healthy," I wail, "it's *horrible* just to kill him . . . there must be something—wouldn't a *zoo* have him or something—"

"Zoos are overrun with people wanting to unload oversized iguanas. Jesus—don't look at me like that, kid! What does a fucking lizard matter when everything in your life's going down the drain?"

I can't move. I want to throw up. Suddenly, as though Flossy's dreams have picked up what Taylor's saying, the baby monitor gives out a terrified wail. I jump, leap to my feet.

"I envy him," slurs Taylor, as I hurry out of the door. "Fucking lizard. He's better off."

I settle Floss, heart pounding. Then, before I can have doubts about what I'm doing, I make two cups of cocoa because I know Babcia likes it as a nightcap, creep along to the guest room, and tap lightly on the door.

I'm expecting to have to wake her, but she calls out, "Who is it?" right away.

"It's me, Mrs. Bielicka. Rowan. I've brought you some cocoa."

"Come in." She's sitting up in bed, wide awake, Pompom asleep at the foot of the bed. "I thought you might be Taylor," she says sadly.

"Haven't you spoken to him yet?" I ask, handing her her drink.

"Thank you—what a kind thought. No, I haven't seen him. I heard him arguing with *her*, then he went off—he said we'd talk, but no. Well, there's nothing else I can do here. First thing in the morning, I'll get the Greyhound back home."

I plonk myself next to Pompom and wail, "Oh, Mrs. Bielicka—please stay a bit longer!"

She doesn't answer, just looks at me over the rim of her cocoa mug. Breathlessly, I hurtle on. "Thing is—I've got to leave. I can't bear Sha either. I'm going crazy here. But *Flossy*—"

"Poor little soul . . ."

"Exactly. Mrs. Bielicka—she loves you. Over the last couple of weeks, you've grown so close—she wants *you* to read to her at night now, not me."

Babcia smiles. "Maybe. But Rowan—I can't *live* here, can I? You resign, and they'll get another nanny to replace you."

"I know. But if you were here to smooth over the transition . . . so Floss didn't feel so *abandoned . . .*"

"But it could take weeks—for you to give your notice, for them to find a replacement . . ."

"Suppose I left now, though? Suppose I did a runner this weekend?"

There's a pause. "Are things that bad?" she asks.

"Yes. And there's something else. They're gonna have Iggy killed. They're sending him off to be put down Monday."

"The lizard."

"Yes."

"Horrible creature. It terrified my Pompom, he went up to its cage and it *lashed* its tail . . ."

"Look—you might not like him, Mrs. Bielicka. But he's alive, OK? He's happy and healthy and—look, how would you feel if it was *Pompom* being sent off to get a lethal injection?"

She reaches out, strokes the little dog's back. "I wouldn't let it happen!"

"Well, that's exactly how I feel about Iggy. He's so full of life, he's so excited when you let him out of his cage—I can't *bear* the thought of him just being *killed*. . . ."

"So take him with you."

Babcia and I sit and look at each other. It's a bizarre, mad situation, but somehow it's like we both silently decide there and then that I'm going—this weekend—and Iggy's going too.

"Do you have somewhere to go *to*?" she asks.

"Not really. I'm planning to head for a hotel in San Francisco. I'm pretty sure of getting a job there . . ."

I trail off, and Babcia leans forward and pats my hand.

"Pass me my purse," she says.

"What?"

"It's over there, on the dressing table. How much money do you have?"

"Look, Mrs. Bielicka, I'm fine, I've been saving—"

"Do as you're told, dear."

I fetch her her big, old-fashioned black purse. She opens it, counts out a hundred dollars. "It's not a lot, but it'll buy you a couple of nights or so in a motel."

I'm so touched my eyes start welling up. "It's

loads, Mrs. Bielicka, but I really can't take it—"

"Don't be silly, Rowan. If I'm not going home, I'll save at least that in food, won't I?"

"You're going to stay on, then?"

"Flossy will need me."

"You bet she will. Oh—you're the *best*!" On a sudden impulse, I reach forward and kiss the side of her face.

"Go tomorrow night," she whispers. "I'll tell them they need to get out alone together, I'll reserve the *restaurant* for them if I have to. And I'll offer to babysit. No one needs to know you've gone till far into Sunday. And then I'll act innocent and offer to stay."

"Mrs. Bielicka, I am so glad you're here! You're a fiendish plotter, you really are!"

"Go to bed now," she whispers, eyes gleaming. "Go quickly, before *that woman* gets wind of what we're up to!"

CHAPTER 24

AS SATURDAY'S MY DAY OFF, it's easy to start to put my escape plan in action. The first thing I do is corner Sha and ask her if I can have my wages. I should be getting paid at the end of each week but it can be Sunday before she finally coughs up, so I make a big deal of wanting to go shopping and, begrudgingly, she fetches her wallet and pays me.

In my room, I sort out my clothes, ready to start packing. I slink into the utility room and put all the dirty stuff through the washing machine, and fold the clean stuff in my case under my bed. Should anyone look in, it just looks tidier than usual, that's all.

As soon as Sha, Taylor and Flossy have gone out (for a doomed-sounding "relaxed family brunch"), Babcia tiptoes into my room with Pompom's cat-basket hidden under a towel. She's really getting into the whole conspiracy thing. "D'you think this'll work for the lizard?" she whispers.

I smile at her. "What d'you mean?"

"You can have it. It's too big for Pompom—he slides around."

I thank her profusely and examine it. It's a real deluxe carrier, all padded with closed-in sides and bars at the front, and its own little water bottle. "It looks perfect," I say. "But are you sure?"

"Sure I'm sure. I've been meaning to get him another one."

"Well, it's brilliant," I say, warmly. She's so sweet. I know it's fine for Pompom and the real reason she's giving it to me is to save me money. "Iggy'll be really comfortable in that."

Then a look of anxiety crosses her face and she says, "One thing really bothers me, though, Rowan."

"What?"

"It would be awful for you to leave without saying goodbye to Flossy."

"I know. But I daren't risk it. If she gets upset—"

She nods her head mournfully. "Maybe if you wrote her a letter, and I read it to her . . . we'll work something out."

My next job is to phone the bus company. I discover there's an overnighter, leaving at ten o'clock tonight, which is perfect as long as I can sneak my luggage out without being seen. I have to change buses at Sacramento the following midday, and then I arrive in San Francisco in the afternoon. Which gives me plenty of time to get to the hotel—or find a cheap motel if that doesn't work out.

It's all pretty daunting, and the old me would be juddering with panic. But something wonderful has happened: I've stopped worrying; I'm not trying to work out everything in advance any more. I'm about to embark on the riskiest, craziest adventure of my life and I'm actually able to take it a step at a time, to trust that—somehow—I'll deal with whatever happens. Well, I've got to, haven't I?

Next on my Escape List is paying a visit to the local exotic pet shop, where I've been sent before to get iguana feed. "Transporting an iguana?" says the long-haired youth in charge. "No problem. They're pretty docile in motion, long as you keep them cool. Here—this is our recommended carrier."

I check it over, see it's no better than Pompom's, then check the three-figure price tag and silently bless Babcia and her generosity. "I have a carrier," I say. "It's just—I'm going by Greyhound. Overnight. I'm worried about him getting distressed."

The young man flicks back his hair, turns to a

cabinet on the wall. "Herbal tranquillizers," he announces, plonking down a small bottle. "They're pretty mild, and real safe—that's how come we can sell them here and you don't have to go to a vet. You give one to three, according to the iguana's weight." I get a flash vision of me trying to cram Iggy on to the kitchen scales, gulp, and ask, "Anything else?"

"The thing with travel is balancing moisture and warmth. You don't wanna let an iggy dry out, or get too warm, so you have to spray him, but you don't wanna chill him down too much by *over*-spraying. Still, it's warm, so I'd say spray pretty regularly. Here." He plonks a slim water sprayer down on the counter, next to the pills.

"And that's it?"

"For the trip, yes. What have you got planned for him at the other end?"

We chat for a bit, and I'm vague but reassuring about the life of bliss I'm taking Iggy to, just in case the young man reports me to some scary Lizard Protection League and has me arrested for cruelty. He clearly knows all about iguanas, and he's keen to air his knowledge; I nod blankly as he rabbits on about iguana sexual maturity and incubating their eggs. Finally, I pay my twelve dollars and sixty cents, and leave.

* * *

Back at the apartment, after a whispered discussion with Babcia, I make a secret phone call to Nursery Sprites, the bureau that fixed me up with this job. I've got to make my leaving official, Babcia says, because if I don't, Sha will have to, and then Nursery Sprites will contact my parents and before I know it I'll be Officially Missing with my face on millions of milk cartons across the country.

When I get through to their office I tell the smarmy woman on the other end of the phone that my position here has irrevocably broken down owing to the dad hitting on me and the mum persecuting me. I tell her discussion is impossible and I'm leaving tonight. I'm taken aback by her concern, though. She demands to speak to Sha; I plead with her that I can't bear the thought of more confrontation. She warns me that they cannot be responsible for me if I do what amounts to a runner. I say I know that. Then she says that if I stay on until Monday they'll arrange a return flight for me. I say I've got another job almost in the bag, but I'd like the return flight if that goes wrong. She asks me if I've contacted my parents; I tell her my mother is pretty frail (*Hah!*) and I want to leave contacting her until I'm safe in the new job, so she won't worry too much. The smarmy woman finally agrees to let me ring off, promising me she'll phone my parents in the middle of next week to check that I've contacted them and told them I'm safe. It's all she can do. "After all," she winds up, as though rehearsing her defence for the police, "you *are* over eighteen. . . ."

Then I sit down and (slightly relishing the melodrama) write two letters.

To Mr. and Mrs. Bielicka,

Please forgive me for just running out on you like this. I've gone now because I hope Babcia can stay on and take care of Flossy until you find a replacement for me. It's been really hard for me to be here for a while now, for reasons that you know, but discovering Iggy was going to be destroyed was the last straw. I've taken him with me, I'll find him a new home. Please let Babcia take care of Flossy, they get on so well. Flossy needs less pressure in her life, and more fun.

Rowan.

I hesitate over writing that last word "fun," because what I really want to write is "love." But in the end I leave it as "fun."

The letter to Flossy is much more difficult to write:

Darling Flossy,

I've got to go away. I'm so sorry I can't be with you anymore, and I'm so sorry to leave like this without even a goodbye. But I couldn't stay forever, and I know Babcia Stasia will take very good care of you when Mommy and Daddy are at work. Iggy is too big to live on the roof terrace any more, and I've gone to take him to a new home.

Lots of love, Rowan.

P.S. I'll write to you.

I know it's weak, full of holes, but I can't tell her the whole truth about why I'm fleeing in the middle of the night, can I? As I sign my name, I comfort myself that it will be Babcia reading it to her, and Babcia will make it all all right.

Because Babcia's great. She's got it all worked out. She's booked the restaurant for Sha and Taylor—she's even offered to pay. She gushes on about how "everything got a little out of hand last night, but let's let bygones be bygones, and this is my way of saying sorry for the damage to that nice

173

granite counter." My only worry is she'll overdo the acting and blow her cover. I notice Taylor look at her a bit disbelievingly, but Sha, of course, takes it all as her due.

By five thirty, I'm all set to go. I've stolen some nuts from the cocktail cabinet and food and juice from the kitchen; I've crammed the stuff I need for the journey into my old college backpack. I practise walking in my room with my backpack on my back, case in one hand and cat-carrier in the other, and find I can just about move, although my arms feel like they're slowly detaching themselves from my body. I've ordered a cab for nine p.m. with strict instructions for it to park outside the apartments, and on no account to ring up.

And then it's just a question of waiting for the night. I let Iggy out for a long gambol round the roof terrace, so he's good and tired for the journey, and tell him all about our exciting escape and how he's going to love the deluxe cat-basket and how he's going to get funky and mellow on the herbal tranquillizers. "Although if you really are an enchanted prince, Ig," I add, "now would be an excellent time to throw the enchantment off. Especially if you're mind-spinningly sexy with a fast car and a fat bank balance. Although actually any kind of prince would do. Just so long as you can walk and I don't have to lug you around in a cat-carrier." Then I lean forward very gently and kiss the back of his head. He feels warm, smooth, like a living handbag, which I suppose to some sick people he is.

But my kiss has no effect. He stays lizard.

At seven thirty, I help Babcia put Flossy to bed. Between us, we give her the best time—duck and boat racing in the bath, stories, singing. Until Sha puts her head round the door and acidly asks, "I thought *Mama* was in charge tonight, Rowan?"

"She's just making the point in case you want babysitting money," hisses Babcia, as Sha's head disappears again. "But maybe it does look a little suspicious, two of us here . . ."

So I leave Babcia to settle Floss. I lie on my bed and try to get some sleep. I'll give you three guesses whether I get any.

At seven forty-five, Taylor and Sha leave the apartment. Flossy is fast asleep as I make my way through her room.

"I feel like I want to go *now*," I murmur to Babcia, who's hovering in the corridor. "Go and wait at the bus station. I mean—suppose they have a row and come back early?"

Babcia puts her arm round me and gives my shoulders a squeeze. "Come on, be calm. The cab'll be here before you know it."

At eight thirty I make my way up to the roof terrace, clutching the cat-carrier with an old (slightly damp) towel in it and two lizard tranquillizer tablets crushed in some peach (I'd worked out it was two Iggy needed by imagining him as bags of sugar). I haven't allowed myself to dwell for longer than a few nightmare seconds on the possibility that he might refuse to eat the peach and I'll have to somehow bundle him, protesting, into the carrier.

"Wanna get high, Ig?" I whisper. I open his cage and hold the peach out to him. He stretches his neck out, but he's clearly feeling lazy after all the exercise he had earlier—he doesn't want to leave his branch. I wave the peach under his nose, smear some round his mouth, and he licks it off and slowly, agonizingly slowly, clambers down the cage side. I daren't pick him up until he's off the mesh in case he just hangs on, but as soon as he's on the ground I throw the peach into the back of the carrier, pick him up, plonk him inside, and fasten the door.

Then I peer anxiously through the bars. He looks back at me, mildly surprised, then gets stuck into the peach. "Have a good nosh, Ig," I whisper, "and then *sleep*."

I unhook the cone-shaped heating light from his cage, threading the plug through the bars. It weighs a ton but I daren't leave it behind because I know he'll die if he can't bask. Then I lug it and Iggy in the cat-carrier at speed down the steps, leave them by the front door, collect my case and backpack, and cram the heating light into my case.

I leave the letter to Sha and Taylor propped up in the kitchen, then I creep back into Flossy's room with hers. "Goodbye, little girl," I whisper, as I lay it down on her bedside table. "I've got to go—I'm sorry I can't say goodbye properly. You haven't been the easiest kid to take care of, but you've been OK. And you'll *be* OK. You've got Babcia Stasia, and she'll—" I start back. Flossy's eyes are wide open and she's staring straight at me.

"Rowan—?" she falters. Her mouth's starting to go square like it does before she starts crying.

"*Shhh*, sweetie," I say desperately, "*shhhh*—go back to sleep—"

"*Where're you going?!*" she howls.

"I'm getting a new job, darling, in San Francisco—I can't stay here forever, can I?"

"*Yes! I want* you to!" She starts sobbing in earnest.

And then a warm hand's on my shoulder and

Babcia's saying, "Go on, Rowan—it's five to nine. Your cab'll be there. I'll stay with her."

"Goodbye, Floss!" I wail, peeling her hands from my neck. I stand up, feeling sick with what I'm doing, trying to shut out Flossy's crying. I walk to the door, without looking back. Then I do look back and Floss has been bundled into her Babcia's arms so tight I can't even see her.

CHAPTER 25

DIDN'T MY FORERUNNER JANE EYRE disappear in the night, too? After she'd discovered at the altar that her bridegroom already had a wife currently running amok in the attic? That thought comforts me as I totter out of the lift, arms straining out of their sockets. Although I don't think Jane took anything like this much luggage with her when she scarpered. Certainly not a great porky lizard in a cat-basket, that's for sure.

The next stage goes almost without a hitch. The cab is there, waiting outside; at the bus station, I pay for my ticket and find out the Greyhound's all ready for me. The driver's calling for our cases to be stowed in the undercarriage, and it suddenly hits me that it might be forbidden to take pets on board. In the kind of bravado borne of sheer panic I drape my jacket over Iggy's carrier and muscle my way with it right to the back of the coach, where I find a good seat with lots of leg room.

The bus sets off. It's blissfully dark; at my feet, Iggy is slumbering peacefully. I close my eyes and make myself revisit saying goodbye to Flossy. It makes me feel like hell, but I play over and over again that picture of Babcia swaddling her up in her arms and, slowly, I feel better. I know Babcia will take care of her.

With the steady droning motion of the bus, I can feel myself giving way to sleep. A wonderful feeling of emptiness, of freedom, washes over me. For the past couple of months I've been at someone else's beck and call for my every waking moment, and for most of my sleeping ones too. Now I'm cut loose, answerable to no one, floating like a piece of driftwood. I don't know where I'm going to wash up, and I don't care.

"You smuggled your pussykins on too, did you, honey?"

I jerk awake. *"Whaaa—?!"*

"Oh, sorry, honey—were you asleep? It's just, we'll be there in half an hour and I've been longing to see your little friend . . ." Before I can stop her, the elderly lady in the aisle beside me stoops down, peers into the cat-carrier—and starts back up again so fast she cracks her head on the luggage rack. *"Jesus Mary Mother of God!"* she gasps. "You've got a—oh, my *God*, it's *horrible*–"

"Sssshhh!" I beg her, desperately. People are staring round, wondering what the fuss is about. Soon panic will spread, they'll think I've got a boa constrictor under the seat, or a dismembered head. They'll demand an investigation, throw us off the bus . . .

"Shhhh!" I repeat, frantically, as she squawks, "What on earth are you carrying that around with you for?"

"I'm rescuing him," I plead. "He was going to be put down, he'd got too big—"

She fixes me with a ferocious, beady eye, and hisses, "You're not gonna let him go in the sewers, right?"

"What? *No!*"

"My brother-in-law Abe—he's seen 'em. They got alligators down in the sewers bigger'n twelve foot long!"

"Please keep your voice down!"

"People put'em down the toilet when they get too big. And they grow. And—" she adds disgustedly, *"breed."*

I lean towards her fervently. "Look—he's an iguana, not an alligator. And I promise you I'm not taking him anywhere *near* a toilet. I *like* him!

That's why I've gone to all this trouble to get him away!"

"What she got in there?" calls a man two seats ahead of me. A jury of twisted-round faces are glaring at me. My heart's thumping, waiting for the riot to start.

The old lady looks at me, sniffs, and says, "Nothing but an old stuffed alligator. Gave me such a shock. Thought it was a cat." Then she smiles at me, and moves on.

We finally draw up in Sacramento, and my heart's still going at twice its normal speed as I get off the bus. After the old lady landed me in it and then got me out of it I didn't dare check on Iggy, and I'm horribly aware I haven't sprayed him for several hours.

As soon as I've collected my case and I'm away from the disembarking crowd, I put down the cat-carrier, open it, and feel Iggy's skin. It's dryer than it was, and the towel feels dry too. Carefully, I spray him, all over, and he stirs, drowsily.

"Nearly there, Iggy," I promise, as I head for the bench that runs alongside the bus station wall.

"Iggy. That's original."

I look up. A beautiful boy is sitting on the bench a short way down, looking at me like he's waiting for an answer. He's got a face like one of those warrior masks you see in museums; strong and clear and symmetrical. But it's not a mask, it's very much alive, and his mouth is smiling all lopsided and one of his eyebrows has got this quirky twist in it . . .

Christ, he's *wonderful*! And I'm already a study for what lust and chemistry do to the body. Speeding heartbeat, dilating eyeballs . . . my palms are sweating so much Iggy is in danger of sliding—cat-carrier and all—straight out of my grip and hitting the floor.

I pitch my voice to sound husky and indifferent, fail miserably, and squeak, "What d'you mean?"

"Iggy," he scoffs, gorgeously. "For an iguana. Isn't very original, is it?"

His voice is a deep sexy drawl. Southern states, with something overlying it. 'Cos he's travelled, I bet, 'cos he's really seen the world. He looks like a wonderful sexy experienced romantic nomad. "How'd you know it's an iguana?" I ask.

"I was at the front of the bus. Saw the way that old lady shot back when she looked in your cat-carrier. Couldn't hear what was going on, but I was curious. And when you got off the bus, I had a good look and saw its snout. I think it's mean, cooping up a big lizard like that."

OK, OK, Iggy's the reason he's talking to me, it's Iggy he's interested in, not me. But I'm not giving up yet. It feels like fate that he's here at this terminal. It feels like my reward for all I've been through. And I could still be in with a chance, couldn't I? If Iggy and I came along as a kind of package, a joint deal?

"I know it's not nice for him," I say, defiantly. "But I'm rescuing him. We're running away."

"Seriously?" His eyes widen with interest. Gorgeous eyes, green-gold, like a lion. He turns his body further towards me, easy and relaxed. He's got long legs, great shoulders, great chest, all kind of rangy and relaxed . . . *Keep upright, Rowan, keep on standing up!* "Who are you running away from?" he demands.

"My employers. The bastards who were keeping him cooped up ninety-nine percent of the time in a tiny cage on the roof terrace, and who were going to have him destroyed 'cos he's growing too much. I was there as their nanny, and—"

"*Wow.*" He's looking really interested now. It could still be in Iggy, but . . . "*Bastards,*" he says, imitating my accent. "So you're a British nanny?"

"'Fraid so."

"Like Mary Poppins."

"Oh, bloody hell, now that's really unoriginal."

He grins. "I loved that movie. Didn't you love that movie?"

"When I was *five* maybe."

"Cor blimey, guvnor, want yer chimneys done?" he says in the most appalling cockney accent ever, and I burst out laughing. And he laughs too, opening his mouth all sexy and wide. He's got the most fantastic teeth, white and a bit wolfish.

We're connecting. We're really connecting. It's not Iggy he's interested in. Well—not only Iggy, anyway. "All right," he says. "Tell me how you stole the lizard. C'*mon*—sit down and tell me."

So, not believing my luck, I put Iggy's basket down and sit beside the beautiful boy on the bench and tell him my story. I don't embellish it much, apart from slightly exaggerating Sha's psychosis and dwelling on Taylor hitting on me. It's amazing, I'm just about poleaxed by wanting this guy, but I'm still managing to talk. In fact I'm on a roll, the words are flowing, and I'm loving revisiting all the crap that happened to me, it's like a weight's lifting as I tell it all to him. It's like—if I can tell it all to him—it's somehow OK that it happened.

And he *listens* to me, eyes on mine. He puts in the odd prompt and question—he *wants* me to talk. If only guys knew how seductive it is to be listened to, really listened to, they might do something revolutionary like turn the footie off once in a while.

Every now and then his gaze drifts from my eyes to my mouth, and stays there for a few seconds. I can't tell you how erotic it is. I wind up with a slightly false description of Iggy and me romantically boarding the first Greyhound that came along in the deep dark of night. "That is so cool," he says, shaking his head all impressed. "I love it. So where you heading?"

I shrug. "Nowhere," I lie. Suddenly, the possibility of a job in San Francisco is nowhere. Suddenly, it's vitally important to be free to go anywhere. "I mean—there's this hotel in San Francisco that might employ me, but—"

"You mean you don't have a connection? You're not waiting for a bus?"

Whoops—now I'm not cool anymore. I'm hanging around like an over-eager geek just to talk to him, while *he's* just filling in time till his bus comes. I shrug, spread my hands wide, try to look zany and vulnerable at the same time. "I didn't think further than just *going*," I say. "Getting *out*. I dunno what I'm going to do. I need to find somewhere for Iggy.'

And then the wonderful boy turns right towards me on the bench, so that if I turned towards him too we'd be practically hugging, and says exactly what I was only just daring to hope to hear. "You know what you should do? You should come with me."

CHAPTER 26

SUDDENLY, I BELIEVE IN KARMA. I believe you get the payback in this life for something you did in your last. And in my last life I must've done something indescribably wonderful and good and self-sacrificing. Something like drown while bellringing in a church tower to warn the villagers that the nearby dam had just burst. There's no other explanation for what's happening to me now.

"I'm going to Truckee," he's saying, deeply. "I have a job there, hotel work. The work is the usual shit but the place they let you *stay* is amazing. It's why I'm going. It's on a lake—not the hotel, the huts—"

"Huts?"

"They built these huts—more like cabins, really nice, with decks and everything. On a little lake on the hotel grounds. They were going to be for the more adventurous hotel guests to stay in, but it didn't work out. The guests didn't like the silence at night, didn't like the owls, the—isolation." He grins, gorgeously. "So now they let staff stay there. Unless they prefer to be in this shitty basement complex up at the hotel. Most of them do prefer that, 'cause they're as chicken as the guests."

We smile at each other, bonded over deriding the pathetic scaredy staff, and I say, "It sounds *wonderful*."

"It's why I'm going back. We had such a great time last year, just hanging around and swimming in the lake . . . you should come. Hey—I don't know your name."

"Rowan."

"Ro-anne. That like Roseanne?"

"No. It's a tree. It's the mountain ash. And it keeps witches away if you plant it on your land."

"Seriously? That's great," he laughs, and then he *puts his hand down on mine*. My hand's on the bench and he just lands his on top of it, all sort of heavy, like the way you clap someone on the back or something, and says, "I'm Landon."

Oh my God. I must have done more than just save a village in my last life, I must've saved a whole country, or the world maybe . . . his hand is still on top of mine, on the warm wooden bench.

"They'd give you a job," he's saying, and moves his hand away, but I can still feel it there. I look at my hand because I can't look at him. "Waiting tables or something. Or—hey! You could work in the nursery! They'd love a British nanny in the nursery."

"You really think I could just turn up?"

"Sure. You're with me. I worked out OK last season. And you're a looker."

I'm *with him* and I'm a *looker*. That's it, I'm going to die of pleasure. Right now.

"They love lookers. No one wants a freak serving them a beer, do they? That's how come I got the job." He smirks. And then he looks at me, and smiles. And I suddenly know it's not Iggy he's interested in at all.

I smile back but as my mouth upturns I can feel a frenzied squeak of excitement wanting to come out so I downturn it again, sharpish. Oh my God, what's happened to me? I've never done anything like this before, never—I've never pitched myself so hard at a boy before, just utterly brazenly plotted on an impulse to be with him. But everything in the last forty-eight hours has been so dramatic and surreal, it feels like the absolute right thing to do.

And oh my God—I want this boy! I want to walk along the lake with him and undress him and

have him undress me and swim and make love—
oh my God—and I want to snuggle up with him and
make him breakfast and eat out with him and have
him buy me things and wear his clothes and—

He's still looking at me, smiling. "I've never
been with a British girl," he says.

I want to pull down a blackboard, make him sit
upright on the bench and pay attention. I want to
point to all the definitions of "been with." Been
with as in—been alongside? Been with as in—
spent quite some time with? Or been with as in
slept with you jumping-the-gun bastard? *Oh God, let
it be that, let it be that!*

Composure, Rowan. You're getting wildly
overexcited. You're going to hyperventilate in a
second. Calm down—you're a British nanny, for
Christ's sake.

I take in a deep trembly breath. He's looking at
his watch. "Bus'll be here in twenty minutes," he
says.

"You got the money for a ticket to Truckee?"

"Yes. Well—how much will it be?"

"Not sure. Around twenty dollars?"

It's worth it. It's worth it. Even if I can't get a
refund on my ticket to San Francisco . . . oh, come
on, girl—it'd be worth it if you had to sell your
soul.

"You gonna come?" he asks. "Go on, come."

"Oh, why not!" I say, as though it's just a whim, as though I could just as easily *not* come. "Those huts sound perfect for Iggy."

"That's what I thought. He can run free there— sun himself on the deck. Hey—you go get your ticket, I'll watch him."

And I totter off ecstatic and dazed to the ticket office. The woman behind the desk is mid-thirties and hatchet-faced, and as I approach I don't hold out much hope for a refund. I put on a waifish, appealing look, and husk out, "I have a ticket booked through to San Franciso—can I change it?"

She barely looks up. "We don't change tickets on the day of travel," she raps out. "You need twenty-four hours' notice."

"So if I need to go to Truckee instead—I'd have to pay the full fare?"

"Sure. Thirty-two dollars from here."

Shit. I'll pay it, of course I'll pay it, but it's a big chunk out of my dosh.

"You want a ticket to Truckee?" she demands, and as she leans towards me I notice this tiny tattoo on her wrist, half hidden under the cuff of her shirt. It's the woman symbol, the cross on a ring. The symbol of sisterhood. *Try it!*

"It'll take all my money," I croak, then I look

fearfully and theatrically over my shoulder.

"You all right, honey?"

"I—*no*. No, I'm not. I think someone's follow-ing me. That's why I need to change my ticket. *He* knows I've got family in San Francisco. I should never've bought a ticket to San Francisco, he'll follow me there, he'll find me again, he'll—"

"*Hey*, calm down." She puts a hand over the counter, squeezes my arm. "This man—he your husband?"

"Boyfriend, my boyfriend," I gasp, my words coming out in a panic-soaked stream. "I ran out on him, before he got up, he said he'd *kill* me if I left him, I left while he was asleep, but I thought I *saw* him, just then, over by that line . . ."

It's her turn to look over her shoulder. But she's checking for senior staff members, not insane boyfriends. "OK, OK, I'm putting this through," she says, tapping at her console. "The San Francisco bus is half empty, and the Truckee one ain't full. No one's gonna check."

"*Thank you*," I sob.

"And look, hon—you stick to it, OK? Don't you go back to him. There's a five-dollar difference."

I shove the note across the counter at her; she takes it, pats my wrist again. "You stick to it," she says.

I walk away feeling a little bit ashamed but mostly absolutely bloody brilliant. I mean—sod it, the bus company loses nothing and OK, I played shamelessly on that woman's feelings but I bet right now she's feeling all glowy and good about helping me out, so where's the harm? And I have just saved myself twenty-seven dollars! I'm longing to brag and gloat about it but decide not to reveal to Landon just yet what a good liar I am. And anyway, I'm not about to freak him by telling him I've completely changed my plans just to be with him, am I? Aaah, it was good though . . . an Oscar-winning performance. I *knew* I had her when she squeezed my arm . . . round the corner, reliving it and smirking, and all anticipatory about Landon, and—

—and the bench is empty. *Shit!* I should've guessed it. *I should've guessed it!* Landon's only interested in Iggy after all, he's some kind of freakish pervert who gets off on lizards, he's been *stalking* me for my lizard, and now he's got him and gone. I'll never see either of them ever again. I feel sick, awful, like someone's just slammed a baseball bat into my solar plexus, partly for Iggy but mostly, it must be said, for *me*, me on my own again, me cheated of that wonderful, long-legged, gorgeous boy—

"Hey! Ro-*anne*!"

Hope floods back. I look around. And then I see him. Spread-eagled on a grass verge, Iggy's open cat-carrier beside him, and Iggy himself lolling sleepily across his blue-jeaned thigh (*Hey, get off, Iggy, that's mine!*) sampling a bit of sandwich that Landon is holding out to him.

"Hi!" I call out, all casual.

"Hi!" he calls back. "He likes coleslaw!"

PART THREE

EDEN

CHAPTER 27

THE JOURNEY TO TRUCKEE IS blissful. We get seats together at the back with a lot of leg space to put Ig's cat-carrier in, and settle in for the long drive, punctuated, of course, by regular Iggy spraying sessions. The effects of the tranquillizers are clearly wearing off and Ig's doing a lot of water-guzzling and shifting about, but he still seems quite happy.

While Landon tells me more about the hotel and what it's like working there, I try to decide just how much he fancies me. It's hard to tell, because he's so happy and laid-back that everything seems to please him—talking to me, yes, but also the scenery we pass, and the other people on the coach, and even the driver, who occasionally sings horribly in a cracked baritone.

Landon's physical presence is so overpowering I find it hard to concentrate on what he's saying, and the conversation falters. Then after a while his eyes close, spreading fabulous, long Bambi-lashes on the top of his cheeks, and he falls asleep. I'm a bit disappointed about this but it does give me a chance to study him in minute, fetishistic detail. He's perfect. So beautifully made it's almost freak-ish. Even the little snoring sounds coming from his mouth are gorgeous. Oh, Jesus—have I ever had it this bad? He's slipping against the seat back and his face starts to slide towards mine. For a moment, I fantasize I'm going to kiss him, then I nudge him gently, and he shifts and falls and then his head is on my shoulder.

Mmmmmm. I rub my cheek very gently against his hair. I inhale the fabulous, cottony, male smell of him. When the envious girl across the aisle who's been ogling him the whole trip turns to stare I give off *Yeah, this is my boyfriend* vibes.

Well, it's going to be true, isn't it? I'm going to make it true. I have to. I've never wanted anyone or anything as much as I want him.

It's only a matter of time.

The sun's going down as we get off the bus, and the air feels heavy and thick with moisture. Landon, who's slept for the last half of the journey, is quite refreshed and ready to go. I, who haven't, am not. But I'm still in a state of bliss and more than happy for Landon to take over. He gets us on another bus for a much shorter trip, and then we walk.

We set off on a deserted-looking road that stretches straight into the horizon. Landon carries Iggy, demonstrating that he's not only hunky but gallant as well. "We'll be there soon, Iggo," he promises, as Iggy, who's now wide awake, shifts bad-temperedly in his cat-carrier. "You'll love it, I promise." A few cars and trucks pass us; one truck slows and the driver asks us where we're heading but Landon thanks him, says we don't need a ride. "Not worth it," he tells me. "We're almost there." Five minutes later we reach some woodland, and turn off on to a track, sides overgrown with scrub. We're not talking much now, just the odd comment.

Landon seems preoccupied. "We're not lost, are we?" I ask.

"No way," he snaps. "Why do you say that?"

"Just—it seems a weird road for a big hotel to be on."

"It's a country club hotel. And we're going in the back way."

"There's an entrance near the lake?"

"Right."

I keep shifting my heavy case from hand to hand. We've been walking for over half an hour and the air is so heavy it's like wet wadding round your face; the sky's getting darker with purple clouds.

"There's a storm coming," says Landon. "Hear that?"

Thunder's growling somewhere in the distance, like a warning, like a threat. And suddenly the full implication of what I'm doing hits me like one of those huge swinging balls that demolish tower blocks at a single stroke.

Jesus, what was I thinking of?! Setting off into the unknown with a complete stranger? I know nothing about him! Just 'cos he looks like an angel doesn't mean he's not a sick psychopath. We're in the middle of nowhere here—not a single car has passed us since we've been on this track. Apart from the grumbling thunder, we're in complete silence. And no one alive has the slightest idea where I am, and I've got no phone, no weapon . . .

Any minute now we'll reach a cave stuffed with dismembered female body parts, and he'll drag me in. Or a hut—a hut inhabited by hideous, mutant uncles who send him out as bait to lure young girls into their depraved midst . . .

"Hey, Thoughtful," says Landon, "what are you thinking about?"

I decide not to tell him. "Nothing much," I bleat. "Just—it'll be night soon. Doesn't it get dark really quickly here?"

"Pretty much."

My legs feel too wobbly to move, but I stagger on.

The scrubby woodland on either side of the track is growing taller, denser, scarier; the darkness continues to thicken like treacle. Then suddenly there's a jagged flash of lightning, and a huge thunder boom, and right away the rain's here, violently here, a drenching, manic monsoon.

"*Come on!*" shouts Landon, breaking into a run. "We're almost there—I recognize those boulders!"

Hair streaming, clothes plastered against my skin, I follow him on to a winding path flanked on either side by tall trees. And then—weird and welcome as the lamppost in Narnia—there's a Moroccan-style light on a stand, shining at us through the sheets of rain. Underneath it hangs a board saying "Grand Sequoia Country Club." We forge on, past an arrow-shaped sign saying, "Sports Center" and then another, saying, "Lakeside Cabins."

And suddenly I know Landon's kosher. I know with sure instinct that he's completely on the line, he's told me nothing but the truth, and I can trust him.

Suddenly I feel absolutely great again.

"I CALLED," HE GASPS, AS we jog along, "before I met you—I told 'em I might be late—they said they'd leave a key out in front of the cabin, I hope to Christ they have . . ." We're crossing a cleared space in front of a huge lake, gleaming blackly in the dark. Rain's powering down on it and it's churning, seething—the noise could be a waterfall. Dimly, I can make out a broad semicircle of cabins, facing the lake some distance back. They're raised off the ground with wide wooden steps in front of them, and they look snug and welcoming.

Landon stops at the third one along. He roots around under a large stone on the ground beside it, and pulls out a silver key. *Hallelujah.* Come on."

We hurry up the steps and he unlocks the door and ushers me inside the cabin. Then he follows me in, snaps on the overhead light, and shuts the door behind us.

The dark's gone, the rain's gone, and we're standing very close together, breathing hard and dripping water. I'm absolutely overwhelmed, full of shyness and intensity. I turn away, but not before I see Landon grinning as though he knows what I'm feeling. He stoops down to open the cat-carrier door. "OK, Iggy, freedom," he says.

Iggy trundles out, looking none the worse for his drawn-out journey. He begins pacing the floor, tongue questing as he examines his new territory. I look around too. It's a really nice space—dead plain, with wooden floors, wooden furniture, a Native American–style rug, and matching blinds at the two big windows on either side of the room. Iggy mounts up the back of the blue sofa, claws scraping the canvas cover. "He needs to bask," I say, glad to have something distracting to do. I open my suitcase, emerge with the heating light. "Where could I hang this?"

Landon points to the floor-standing anglepoise lamp in the corner. "Will it hang off that? It's pretty solid-looking."

Together, we attach the heater to the anglepoise crossbar. My hands are shaking with how close he is. I daren't look at him. It's like he's radiating energy. Or is that me? "If I plug it in, could you move it over to the sofa?" I ask. "Not so close he could scorch, just—"

"Near enough so he can feel the heat," says Landon, positioning the heater over Ig. Who flexes sensuously into the warmth, refusing to look at me. Maybe he's sulking. Because of the journey, or because he suspects he's not my number one any more . . . Gently, I run a finger along his back, but he swishes his tail, so I move away.

"Tomorrow the sun'll be out," Landon announces. "It always is, after a storm like this. Tomorrow he can bask outside to his heart's content. Do lizards have hearts?"

"'Course they do!"

"To pump their cold blood, huh? Everything'll be all fresh and green tomorrow, Ig." He grins at me. He looks so great when he grins it ought to be illegal. "He'll love it here, it's paradise. So will you." There's a potent pause, then he says, "Now that the lizard's settled, can we get out of these wet clothes?"

"God, yes."

"You go in there—that's the bedroom. Bathroom leads off it. Get changed."

"What about you?"

"I'll just towel off in here."

I pick up my case and backpack and go into the bedroom, hesitating over whether to close the door behind me. I don't want to look neurotic and/or rejecting do I? In the end I push it and it doesn't quite click shut. Then, gazing about me, I strip down to my skin, dropping my sopping clothes on the floor. The bedroom's gorgeous, like a sexy little cell, just whitewashed walls, a cupboard and a chest of drawers. And, central position and covered in a beautiful, barbaric-art throw, a big iron bed. The rain's drumming on the roof, and the room feels secret and sensual. A vision of Landon peeling off his soaking shirt and jeans just the other side of the slightly open door flashes into my mind and I take a deep, wobbly breath. Then I pull a towel hastily out of my bag and wrap it round me. I rub myself dry, wrap the towel in a turban round my wet, tangled mane, rummage for knickers and bra and put them on, and come to a halt. What do I wear? Should I assume we're hunkered down for the night, get into my PJs? No—I'll look obvious. Worse—I'll look naff. My lovely old silk kimono? No—too wannabe seductress. Save that for later. Jeans and T-shirt? That'll do. The green one that brings out the copper tints in my hair.

I pull my clothes on, leaving my feet bare. Then I find my make-up bag, and hurry through into the bathroom. I snap on the light over the mirror, and peer, praying. Hmm—not too bad. The drowned-rat-in-a-turban look is partly offset by the glow from falling in love . . . With the help of some spray-on conditioner, I tug my brush through my hair. I rub in moisturizer, then I slick on some blusher and lipgloss. Then I put on a bit of mascara. Then eye pencil. Then—

"*Shit, Ro-anne, what are you doing in there?*"

"Nothing!" I squeak. "Couldn't find a T-shirt, that's all!" Hastily, I stuff my make-up back in its bag, so Landon doesn't discover later that I was tarting myself up and assume I'm after him, and scurry out to the living room. Iggy's still on the back of the sofa, ruminatively chewing some apple that Landon must've given him. *Aw!*

"In here!" calls Landon. He's standing in a large cupboard coiling spaghetti into a saucepan of boiling water. "I thought I'd fix something to eat," he says. "The rain's still pouring, and there's no point in getting soaked again getting up to the hotel."

"Great," I reply. "What a sweet little kitchen." To call it cramped would be generous. There's a skinny stove and sink on one side with a tiny chopping space between them, and a small fridge at the end under some shelves.

He grunts. "The kitchens are another reason why these cabins never worked out. Self-catering but kitchens for gnomes. Hopeless for Americans. We like to eat big. I mean, that fridge—that holds just a coupla hours' worth of *snacks*."

"What you making?"

"Pasta and sardines," he says, proudly. "Found a can on those shelves. And the pasta's only a few months past its expiration date."

I try to look enthusiastic. Sardines repeat on me—not terribly romantic. Still, I bet they repeat on him too—they repeat on everyone, don't they?—and I'm so hungry and I think it's so adorable that he's *cooked* I'm actually feeling quite enthusiastic. "I got some nuts in my bag," I say. "Really posh ones. Stole them from my boss's cocktail cabinet."

"Terrific. We can have a feast. Like the cabin?"

"I think it's wonderful!"

"You like it now, you wait till the sun's out."

"The hotel punters must be mad."

"The *who*?"

I laugh. "*Punters*. People who—I dunno—pay money for something. The . . . guests."

"Right. Hey, I like that. Punters. I'm gonna use that."

There's not room for me in the kitchen . . . not unless I want to get very intimate, that is, which I do, of course, but don't feel I can, not yet . . . so I go back into the main room. Landon's turned off the overhead light and only the lizard heater is on, slanting a warm glow across Iggy's back and the sofa. He's also opened one of the sash windows wide, and the sound of the rain beating down and splashing from a nearby gutter fills the room, along with a lovely, earthy, damp smell. I wander over to the front door, open it, and lean in the doorway, looking out and inhaling. It's warm. The lake's a great empty black space, a drumming sound in the dark.

"It's almost ready," Landon calls out. "You hungry?"

"Ravenous."

"*God*, I love the way you say that! Say it again!"

"Rrrrravenous!" I purr.

He laughs, picks up the saucepan of spaghetti and tips it into a colander in the sink, and my heart's thumping with how fantastic I think he is, but at the same time I feel amazingly relaxed. I mean—I'm here, he's here, there's no pressure, it's not like it's a party where someone else could steal him away from me . . . I smile, thinking back to how scared I was an hour or so ago, when it hit me what an idiot I'd been just taking off with him, not knowing if he was an axe-murderer or not. Of course he could still be an axe-murderer. My mother would think he was. She'd have a blue fit if she could see me now, all stranded in this cabin. Well, too bad. I feel far safer right now than I ever did with the Bielickas, and they'd been vetted and approved both sides of the Atlantic.

Landon swaggers out of the kitchen, a steaming plate in both hands. "Eat up," he says. "I made a kind of sauce—I mashed the sardines in the oil they were in."

Sweet. I head over to the table, leaving the door open, and we sit down facing each other, like lovers, and eat the first half dozen mouthfuls in silence, apart from me saying, "S'good!" (Well, it's just about edible, isn't it?)

Landon jerks his head at the silver sheet of rain outside the door. "Doesn't look like it's stopping, does it?"

"Not for a while, no."

"Look, Ro-anne . . ." He puts his fork down. "I've been thinking. It's late. There's no point in trying to make it up to the hotel tonight to figure out your job and everything."

"I s'pose not," I say. I feel a bit alarmed, a bit excited.

"Not in this weather."

"No."

"That means we both have to sleep here

tonight, OK?" He leans towards me. "Look, I know this is weird, we've only just met and . . . and stuff. I wanna tell you I am in no way gonna try anything, OK? I'll sleep on the sofa in here, you have the bedroom. OK?"

"OK. I mean—thank you. That's great."

We finish the pungent meal like we started it, in silence, while my brain is in overdrive trying to work out if what he just said means a) he doesn't fancy me at all, or b) he fancies me so much jumping me is uppermost in his mind but he's fighting it or c) somewhere in between.

"I'm still hungry," he says, scraping his plate clean. "What about those nuts you promised me?"

When I get back from the bedroom, two packets of Sha's cocktail nuts in my fist, Landon is rolling a joint. "You cool with this?" he asks, licking the paper.

"Um—sure."

"You want some?"

"Er . . ." I watch him as he lights the joint and inhales, closing his eyes in extreme pleasure, as though he's finally come home. For some reason, I'm disappointed—just a bit. Weed has never been my thing. I'll have the odd toke but I've never really got the hang of it. When people get stoned all around me I feel like I'm left out of a secret I'm not really sure I want to be let in on.

"Aaaaah, I've been looking forward to this," he sighs, drawing in deep again. "It's been one helluva long day. Here." He holds it out to me and I take it and have a quick, inexpert puff, then I hand it back, hoping he won't notice my crap toking technique.

He does, though. "Not really into it, huh?" he asks.

"Not really. I prefer getting pissed."

He frowns. "You like to get angry?"

I laugh. "In England *pissed* means *drunk*."

"Right. Well—I could use a beer now, too. Still—we'll stock up tomorrow."

We'll. He said *we'll*. I smile at him and when he offers me the joint again I shake my head, and tear open the nuts. And we sit there in silence, just the rain outside and the sound of smoking and chomping. His eyes are half closed and I feel safe just to stare at him, rake him with my eyes. Every now and then he reaches out and puts his hand in the bag of nuts I'm holding, and transfers some to his mouth. It crosses my mind to give him the other bag of nuts but I like him helping himself, I like the contact. Then he says, "I gotta get more comfortable," and moves on to the sofa.

I think about joining him. I think about him

saying, "I am in no way gonna try anything OK?" Maybe if I made the first move . . . maybe if we just *kissed* . . . I want us to kiss so much. A kiss would be like a seal on things. Like the start of things.

Then I realize the joint has died in the ashtray beside him, and he's fast asleep.

CHAPTER 29

WHEN I WAKE THE NEXT day the white room's criss-crossed with bright bars of sun like subtle search-lights and it takes several seconds before I can work out where the hell I am. When I remember, my heart starts thumping with nerves and excite-ment. OK, *Rowan, you wanted life, adventure, love even. Now get up and get into it!*

I shower at top speed, fling some make-up on, get dressed in the clothes I wore last night. Then I walk into the main room. The door's open, and Landon's sitting out on the porch, Iggy sprawled companionably beside him. "Hi," I say nervously. "Er—bathroom's free."

"Didn't wanna disturb you," he says cheerfully. "Took a piss outside. Well—whaddya think? Like it here?"

I gaze past him. He's right, the place is mind-blowing, fabulous in the sunshine. I thought of the roof terrace as Eden, but that was a cramped, closed-in fake compared to this. This is the *real* Eden, all lush and watered from the rain last night. The lake's shining, surrounded by its screen of big-leaved plants, shaded at the far edge by a canopy of trees. It feels secret, hidden. It's silent apart from birds calling to each other.

"It's beautiful," I breathe.

"Seriously, though. I love it. Any time of day or night. I *love* it."

"Look at Iggy. He's in heaven."

"Yup. Just sunning himself on the deck."

"Is there anyone else in the other cabins?" I ask, thinking how much more like Eden it would be if it was only him and me staying here . . .

"Not sure. Think that far one might have someone in it. It all seems pretty quiet, though. Hey—if you're all ready, we should head up to the hotel. I need coffee. Then we can sign you in, get you a job, get you your own cabin, OK?"

"Er—right." This is all a bit fast. He's jumping to his feet.

"C'mon then," he says.

"What about Iggy? Should I leave him out here?"

"Sure. He'll hang around the porch—maybe take a dip in the lake—"

"Supposing he runs off?"

"Well, that's his choice, right? I mean—you stole him to free him?"

"Well—that and save his life . . ."

"Don't look so worried, Ro! I think he'll stick around—he knows you're a good source of food. And he's tame. He likes people, right?"

"Yeah. Oh, God—someone could steal him. He could go up to someone, all friendly, and they could lure him into a box, and . . ."

"Now you're getting paranoid. The only way you can be sure of Iggy is if you keep him in a cage, like those weirdos in Seattle. You gotta relax—you gotta think—if it's gonna happen, it's gonna happen! OK?"

He grins at me. I reckon he's just stated his whole philosophy on life and for some reason it makes me feel uneasy. He sets off down the steps and I follow him. At the bottom, I turn back to see Iggy on the top step, wagging his head. "You stay here, Ig, OK?" I say, helplessly, then I follow Landon towards the lake edge.

The water looks cool, clean and inviting as we walk along beside it. "Soon as we're done, we'll take a swim, all right?" says Landon.

"Oh, yes," I say fervently, mentally tossing up between my slimming black bikini or the sexy red one with maximum cleavage. "The lake looks fantastic."

"It is. It's fed by a little spring, it's always fresh."

We walk on into the trees, on to a little path all overgrown with vegetation. At the edge of the path there's another wooden sign with the letters "and Wa" showing through the vines. "Woodland Walk," explains Landon. "This was the way to the hotel for the cabin guests."

"The non-existent cabin guests."

"Right. So now it's *ours*."

I smile and walk a little closer to him as the trees get thicker. "These are Magic Woods," he announces.

"Yeah?" I laugh. "That's a bit twee, isn't it?"

"Twee? What the hell is twee?"

"Oh—you know—cute, sweet, icky-poo—"

"*What?!*"

"Affected, prissy—"

"Yeah, yeah, I get the picture—"

"Like elves live here or something."

"Maybe they do, babe. All I'm saying is, it's magic. You walk back through here after work, and it doesn't matter how tired you're feeling or how irritating the . . . *punters* have been, halfway through these woods you start feeling *good*."

I smile, hearing him use my word. "Yeah?"

"Yeah. It's good to spend time in, too. I've had some amazing, *magic* times in these woods."

I suspect these times involve drugs, and possibly sex too, so I don't ask any more, and we reach the end of the path in silence. We come out of the trees, and the hotel is suddenly visible across a great stretch of lawn pocked with a miniature golf course. And I start to feel really nervous. "Who exactly have we got to see?" I hiss.

"Oh—the manager. Derek. Don't worry, he'll love you. They always need extra staff this time of year. It'll be cool, trust me. In fact—let's get it done right now. Then we can enjoy breakfast."

I tag along behind him as he lopes across the lawn and I'm thinking in sheer panic—*Supposing it isn't cool? Suppose there's no job for me? What the hell do I do then?* We cross in front of a huge glass-fronted gym, with a few fat, red-faced blokes on exercise bikes pedalling grumpily in the window. "Did a few shifts in there last year," says Landon.

"Yeah?" I say. "Doing what?"

"Oh, handing out towels. Adjusting the weight machines. Posing." He laughs, pulls open a door at the side of the gym, and we're inside the hotel. "Down here," he says, heading off down a corridor lined with photos of sportsmen. "Derek's office. Hope the bastard's in."

A black guy in shorts, carrying a pile of blue fluffy towels, emerges from a side door just ahead of us and stops theatrically. "Landon, my MAN!"

"Hey, Clint!" They clap hands together, half shake, half high-five.

"They said you was coming back here! You coming in the gym with me, or the pool?"

"Dunno, man. They said it was bar work when I called."

"Oh, forget *that*, man! Come to the gym! I'll turn you into a fitness trainer. You'll have *ladies* lining up around the block wantin' you to get 'em buff, wantin' you to rub 'em down in the sauna." He grins, showing a bar of brilliant teeth. I want to punch him. Great, so I'm *invisible*, am I? I don't *count*?

As if he's picked up on my angry vibes, he turns his grin on me. "Sorry, honey. You two together?"

"We just met at the bus station," drawls Landon. "We need to get signed in with Derek."

Clint spins his eyes skywards. "Good luck. He's been in this bad, bad mood. OK—see you guys. Look me up later, right?"

"Will do, Clint."

We walk on, me feeling all uneasy again, like I did when Landon came out with his "if it's gonna happen, it's gonna happen" philosophy. I bet he's a real *ladies' man*, lining 'em up and casting 'em aside—I mean, it wouldn't be surprising, with his looks, would it. In fact it'd be surprising if he *wasn't* . . .

"What's up, Ro? You look sick."

"Just scared," I mutter. "What Clint said about Derek—it doesn't sound too promising . . ."

"Too—promising? Shit, I *love* the way you put things. It's fine. Derek's always in a bad mood, don't worry about it. Hey—here it is."

And he raps confidently on a green door with the words *D. Sargeant—Leisure Staff Manager* printed on it.

"Enter!" croaks a voice.

We enter. A scrawny, balding man with hunched shoulders who looks a bit like a vulture peers at us across a cluttered desk. "Ah!" he rasps. "It's Landon, right?"

"Yes, sir. Landon Peters. I called, remember?"

"I remember. Glad to see you back. We had to let three of our summer workers go only last week. Embezzling. We're seriously short-staffed."

Screened by the desk, Landon reaches out and nudges my leg. Only it's not really a nudge, it's more like a stroke, a caress . . . I feel myself go kind of puce, like all my veins have dilated. Unfortunately, Derek chooses that moment to fix his watery eyes on me. "And this is—?"

"Ro-anne, sir. She's British. A British nanny."

"Is that so?" he demands, looking me up and down, probably wondering why I'm not in a starched uniform and silly hat.

"I was taken on by the Nursery Sprites Agency in London," I say, cringing, as always, at the name. "I worked for a family in Seattle but I left a bit suddenly, because—"

"Don't tell me," interrupts Derek, tiredly, "the man of the house made a pass at you. So I guess a reference is out of the question."

And then, wonderfully, Landon puts his arm round my shoulders. "She was treated real bad, sir. Shamefully."

The sudden contact with Landon just about blanks out my mind, but I manage to gasp, "I could give you the Nursery Sprites Agency number, and you could phone them—"

Derek waves a weary hand to shut me up. "That won't be needed. Half of these references aren't worth the paper they're written on, anyway. We'll give you a trial shot in the nursery. Maria will tell me *right* away whether you work out or not."

"Thank you," I blink, already terrified of Maria. "That's . . . that's great."

"And you'll be back at the bar, Landon," rasps out Derek. "We need someone with a little glamour up front. Soon as you leave here—get your hair cut at the salon. I need you to start right away. Midday shift. Both of you. OK?"

"That's cool," says Landon, and I manage to gasp out "thank you" although my insides are liquifying at the thought of being plunged under Maria's scrutiny quite so soon.

"Is the pay the same?" asks Landon.

Derek gives a wry smile. "I think it's gone up by seventy-five cents an hour since last summer. Tips are still yours to keep, not pooled." He looks at me, and adds, "Landon knows the ropes, he'll tell you the way things work here. Now—any other questions?"

"Er—sir?" asks Landon. "I've shown Ro-anne the cabins, she'd really like to stay in one . . ."

A weird clicking sound, that in retrospect I realize is a laugh, emerges from Derek's mouth. "Not up to your old tricks are you, Landon?"

"Sir, Ro-anne loves the outdoors and the lake, that's all."

"Well, there's still a couple free. You could end up having to share but it doesn't look likely." He stands up and pulls open the door to a little cupboard on the wall behind his desk, revealing several rows of hooks, some with keys on them. "You got your key, Landon?"

"Yeah, they left it out for me last night."

"OK." He drops a key with an amber-coloured tag with 3 engraved on it on the desk in front of me.

"There you are, Rowan," he says, "the key to your new home."

"See," says Landon, as I follow him along the corridor, "it really is simple, ain't it?"

"I'll tell you when I've met Maria," I say. "D'you know her?"

"I know who she is."

"And?"

"Mexican. Worked her way up. Rules the nursery with an iron rod. Has a little temper. You'll be fine."

"Oh great," I groan. But I'm not really thinking about Maria. My mind's revolving like a tumble dryer, wanting to know about what Derek called Landon's "old tricks," knowing I can't ask, knowing, if I'm honest, that I don't really *need* to ask.

"C'mon, Ro, I'm starving. Let's go get breakfast. Then you can watch me get my hair chopped, then I'll take you to the nursery by twelve."

We walk inside the hotel complex for what feels like miles, up stairs, through great plant-filled hallways, past doors to restaurants called The Fresh Catch or Cedar Tree Bistro. "This place is *huge*," I exclaim, "it's like a city."

"Yup. That's good, though. Means you can get away from people. You know—hide. Now, the deal is, staff eat free anytime at the two cheapest places here, as long as they're not more than two-thirds full. Which they hardly ever are, 'cause they're lousy. So you can get OK breakfasts, and all the burgers and pizza and salads you can eat. Last year I made friends with the kitchen staff—scrounged food to take back to my cabin. That's the best."

"If you get the food, I'll cook it tonight," I say, hoping to pin him down to a bit of a plan.

"Let's see how it goes," he answers, and turns into the Redwood Diner.

He ushers me into a booth at the side, and right away a pretty, plump waitress is standing by the table, beaming fit to bust. "*Landon!*" she squeals. "They said you was back!"

"Hi, Gloria. Gorgeous as ever, huh?"

She flips the top of his head with her notebook. "And you're as smooth as ever, boy! Now—order up. There's only me and JJ on this shift."

This time I'm not introduced—I don't really expect to be. But Gloria is friendly enough as she takes my order for eggs, ham and hash browns, cooing, "I'll bring you a nice fresh pot of coffee right away!"

As she trundles off, I lean across the table towards Landon. "D'you know *everyone* here?"

He shrugs, like he can't be bothered to answer, then he gives me a heart-stopping smile.

I wish I knew what he was thinking. I wish I knew if he's just gonna dump me soon as I've got the hang of it.

The coffee arrives, smelling delicious. Gloria pours it out for us and I take a mouthful, and as it percolates into my bloodstream my spirits lift. And then Landon reaches across the table and takes hold of my hand. "It's been a hell of a twenty-four hours for you," he says. "You must be beat. Just get through the shift with Maria and get back to the cabin and then we can relax and you can settle in and, I promise you, in another twenty-four hours you'll feel like you belong here."

Then he sits back, smiling. And the food arrives, and I start to eat, and for once I don't bother to mentally rerun what he said so I can analyse every word, I'm too busy just sitting there *glowing*.

AFTER WE'VE FINISHED EATING BREAKFAST I follow Landon through the hotel into this swanky little arcade full of shops with clothes, sports gear and beauty products on sale. "There's the hair place," he says, "I'm gonna see if they can sneak me in. Why don't you check out the shops, come back here when you're through."

"Sure," I say. I watch him go in the door and greet yet another hotel employee like a long-lost friend, then I take off and tour round the bijou little boutiques. I do that for just long enough to avoid Landon thinking I'm obsessed with him, then I pitch up outside the hairdressers again and stare at him through the plate glass window. I can see his back and profile, and his full-on face in the angled mirror in front of him. He's going to look good with shorter hair—sharper, tougher, more streamlined. And his *neck*—I've always found men's necks incredibly sexy. Bus queues for me can be an erotic experience. And Landon's neck revealed under the scissors is gorgeous, brown with a sweet white line just under the new line of hair, and quite muscly, but not too thick-set, and— *Shit*. His eyes in the angled mirror are right on mine. As I look, he puts up a hand and waves. I wave back, all casual, then I turn on my heel and go and sit on a fancy white bench under a potted tree on the opposite side of the arcade.

Five minutes later, he's in front of me. "Whaddya think?" he demands, rubbing his head like it's a small dog. "Too short, you think?"

"No, it looks fine." It looks fantastic.

"It has to be off the collar. You wait till you see me in my black bar-staff shirt. I look like a fascist."

"Didn't they wear brown shirts?"

"Really? I look like shit, anyway."

I stop myself saying I find that absolutely impossible to believe, and stand up. Landon checks his watch. "Ten to twelve," he says. "Come on, you gotta punch in at Kiddie Heaven."

The nursery really is called Kiddie Heaven. We approach it up a wide, stroller-friendly ramp flanked on each side with cut-outs of circus elephants and clowns. There's something deadly sinister about the cut-outs. The clowns look evil, the elephants mad. As we reach the doors (painted with the words *Kiddie Heaven* disappearing under a marauding plague of giant blue butterflies) I think I can remember what it felt like when my mum waved goodbye on my first day at school.

"I'd better leave you here, OK?" says Landon, nervously. "Maria won't want me in the way. Just go on in, and say your name. Derek will've phoned. He's mega-efficient."

"How long's the shift?" I squeak.

"Only four hours."

Only four hours?! It's a lifetime—how am I gonna survive?

"And I think you get a break," says Landon, clocking my terrified face. "Can you make it back to the cabins afterwards? Just head out of the hotel, across the mini-golf course, then into the woods—"

"And follow the path. I'll be fine." Then my memory jumps, and I blurt out, "*Shit*, Landon, I forgot about Iggy! I haven't checked on Iggy!"

He puts his hand on my arm. "I'll do it. I'll run back on my break."

"And will you let me know how he is—"

"Yeah, if I can. Don't *worry*! Now go on in. It's

almost twelve. And I gotta get to the bar."

"Landon, thanks," I say fervently, then on an impulse, I crane up to kiss his cheek. Simultaneously, he turns his face down towards me and we mash noses. It's embarrassing, *hideous*; we fall back, not looking at each other. "Goodbye!" I squawk, and dart through the Kiddie Heaven doors.

It's like stepping into an air-conditioned alternative reality. All paintbox colours and nursery shapes—beanbags, boxes, climbing bars, balls—and more evil circus cut-outs everywhere, of deranged tigers and rabid dogs in ruffs and serial-murderer trapeze artists . . . The loud, relentlessly jolly plinky-plonk music can't drown out the cacophony of screechy toddler voices. They've all been herded into the far end of the room where a manic girl is waving a stripy stick in time to the music, trying and failing to get them all to *sing* . . .

Oh, Jesus. I feel like a mouse who's escaped from its cage only to be shoved in a bigger one— one in a nasty experimental laboratory. Why do I have to be here? Why can't I be back at the lakeside with Landon?

Someone's marching towards me. A woman

with a tight, curvy figure and ink-black hair in a ponytail. It can only be Maria. "Rowan?" she barks.

"Yes—hello!"

"Mr. Derek phoned me to expect you. You have worked in nurseries before?"

"Er—not nurseries, but I've been a nanny—"

"Is quite different in nurseries," she snaps, dismissing all my previous experience at a stroke. "Here we have group experience, group caring . . . quite different experience. You are more like schoolteacher, but kind schoolteacher for infants who need much help. You have taught in schools?"

"Er, no, but—"

"You must keep balance between kindness, firmness, order, fairness. You must be as referee as well as aunt figure."

Maria has good but fragmented English that she raps out at breakneck speed, and when she finishes speaking I have to let what she's said sort itself out in my brain. This, I realize, gives the impression that I'm slow, a bit thick even. But there's nothing I can do about it.

"So!" she continues. "Today this shift we give you *trial*." The way she says it, racks and thumb-screws come to mind. "We see how you do, how you cope, how the children are at ease with you. First, you must be changed."

"Be changed?" I echo, stupidly.

"*Changed!*" she insists. "We wear uniform here. Is more efficient, more as professional carer." She executes a sharp military turn and taps off to a door at the side. I follow her into a small ante-room. "For your use!" she raps out, stabbing her forefinger at the last peg in a line on the wall. "Now—your uniform."

She casts a critical look at my body, pulls open a cupboard door, rifles through a rack of nasty pink dresses, comes out with one and thrusts it into my arms. "You need shower first?" she demands, rudely.

"Er—no—I had a shower before I . . . er . . ."

She points to a large wicker basket in the corner.

"For uniform laundry. Try to keep dress for two days. But accidents can occur."

"Accidents . . . ?"

"Paint. Glue. Urine. Be changed!" she says, and leaves the room, shutting the door with a bang.

It's a real physical relief to be on my own again. I exhale twice, loudly, then I start to take off my clothes, looking around as I do. The room's pretty well equipped, with a shower-cubicle and loo off it, a table with a coffee-maker on it and—oh, bliss—a large water dispenser . . . I head for that, half-undressed, and gratefully sink a couple of little paper cups of cold water. Then I carry on being changed.

It's a shame there's a full-length mirror on the wall opposite me, because I'm faced with the full horror of how appalling I look—like a candy-pink bolster with a cinched-in waist. The dress has *puff sleeves*, for Christ's sake. It has to be the nastiest, most unflattering dress ever made, *and* it's at least a size and a half too big. That bitch Maria misjudged—no doubt maliciously—my size. I consider going to the cupboard and fetching a smaller one but I reckon I'll be even more uncomfortable if it fits. So I give myself a last despairing glance in the mirror, take in a huge deep breath, and go back outside.

To my relief it's not Maria but a friendly-looking black girl who's waiting for me. "Hi," she says, "I'm LaToya."

"Hello! I'm Rowan."

"Ah know. You're the British nanny."

"Well—I'm British and I've worked as a nanny for a few months. Not sure if it's the same thing."

"Whatever, Maria's already spreading it around we got a Brit here. Sounds good."

"Well, great, if it helps me hang on to the job—"

"A week with these brats, girl, you may not be so eager!"

"Are they brats?"

"Most of 'em. You ain't gotta be poor to afford this place. Most of the kids—they're *spoiled*."

"Oh, God. And we still have to be nice to them?"

"*Very* nice. Now—I gotta show you the ropes. You're on cutting and sticking right now. C'mon." I follow her over to a long, low table, with eight tiny chairs lined up either side. On top are tubs of dinky scissors and crayons, and boxes of bright sticky paper and wooden shapes of fish, dinosaurs, trains . . .

"You gotta make pictures with them, any theme you like, up to you. Some of them can do lots, some are useless. Some just wanna lick the glue."

"Er—right."

"Rowan, I ain't gonna beat around the bush here," says LaToya in a low voice. "We keep the kids safe and happy, yes. But it's important that the parents think their little darlings is doing somethin' good with their time, somethin' *educational*. So when you help with pictures or models or anything—you gotta make sure it looks good, too, OK? To take out, OK?"

"You mean like—"

"Take over. Yes. Do the whole damn thing if you have to."

"But that's—"

"Cheating. Pointless crap. Yup. Welcome to Kiddie Heaven."

I decide I really like LaToya. She grimaces at me encouragingly and I grimace back. "Watch out," she murmurs. "Here's the boss."

We turn; Maria's in the process of marshalling eight mixed-sex infants over to the table. "Forty-minute session, then five minutes break, then two more sessions same number children!" she raps out, and stalks off, taking LaToya with her.

The kids—who were quiet and well-behaved under Maria's efficient direction—turn on me like hyenas.

"Who are *you-ou*?"

"What we gonna *do-ooo*?"

"That looks *bo-ooring*!"

"Don't wanna sit *do-owwn*!"

Oh, God. Sink or swim time. I put on a big,

bright, I'm-in-charge grin and say, "Who likes dinosaurs?"

"Hal does!" someone squeaks, nudging a small red-haired boy.

I turn on Hal and demand, "Want to make dinosaurs? In a big swamp, in a jungle?"

"Fighting each other?" he asks doubtfully.

"*Eating* each other! Tearing each others' heads off!"

"*Eeeow!*" go a couple of the girls in prissy fascination while Hal shouts, "*Yeah!*"

"OK, everyone, sit down!" I carol, clapping my hands. "We're gonna make the best dinosaur pictures *ever!*" I grip the shoulder of the oldest-looking girl. "What's your name?"

"Chelsea," she says, self-importantly. "What's yours?"

"Rowan. Chelsea—I bet you can draw round shapes really *well*, can't you?"

"Yes I can!"

"Here." I thrust a flat diplodocus, a pencil and an orange sticky sheet at her. "Who else is good?"

Another bossy-looking girl thrusts her hand up. She gets a pterodactyl and a blue sticky sheet. "Now—who's good at cutting out *spikes*?"

Within minutes, I've got a mini production

line going. Soon as Chelsea's finished her diplodocus I slam a tyrannosaurus down in front of her, then I put seven sticky sheets under her diplodocus and cut round it. The younger kids are enthusiastically cutting thick green spikes destined for the primal jungle. I seize big sheets of white paper, and cut them in half to make banners. I cut out eight blue pterodactyls. Then I squawk, "OK, let's get *sticking*!"

Everyone sets to and it goes brilliantly, thank *God*, 'cos I'm aware that Maria is keeping a watchful eye on me from across the room. Chelsea's picture is positively ace, with dinosaurs peeping out from jagged ferns, perched on shaggy trees . . . she's even cut one in half, and got its rear end emerging from one clump of green and its head protruding from another. Mindful of LaToya's warning, I sit near the youngest and dumbest and practically do their banners for them. Three minutes to go till my forty minutes are up, and everyone's got a banner guaranteed to make the most critical parent swoon with admiration. I sense Maria looming behind me. "OK—*names*!" I squeal. "Everyone who can—write your name on. If you can't—I'll do it for you. Then you can be sure to take the right one away with you!"

When we've added everyone's names, Maria claps her hands and the kids all stand up with their pictures. "Well done, my little ones!" she cries. "Put them in the Going Home Corner. Won't your mommies and daddies be so pleased with them, they're *super*!"

She turns to me and her beaming smile snaps off. "That was not so very bad at all, Rowan," she raps out. "Five minutes break."

I head off for the side room, and nearly collide with LaToya, who's heading out. "Coffee's hot," she says. "You just got time to burn your throat!"

I find a mug, rinse it out, and pour coffee from the coffee-maker into it. I discover a biscuit barrel behind the kettle and cram two fig-rolls in my mouth. I need *sugar*. That session went well, but I put out enough energy to supply a nuclear power station. I've got to adjust to having more kids to deal with. Maybe it'll be better when I get to know them a bit . . . The door swings open. "Your next group starts!" Maria barks.

Shit, is five minutes up already? I haven't even had a pee yet . . . I totter towards her and she snaps, "You planning to scald the children in your care?"

I look down at the coffee mug in my hand. I want that caffeine, I *need* it . . . Despairingly, I turn back to the table, take a last quick searing swig, and put the mug down.

CHAPTER 31

TWO THIRDS OF THE WAY through my third and last sticking session and I want to *die*. My head feels like someone's been playing football with it and I've never been this utterly, completely tired-to-the-bone ever before in my *life*. The second session went OK, with a couple of bright sparks drawing round dinosaurs and only a brief tussle with a kid who was cutting out huge red blood-splats for a dinosaur Armageddon. Then I had another *joke* of a five-minute break. Barely time to rush to the loo and down the mug of now-cold coffee I'd been forced to leave behind last time before Maria was shouting for me again. And now this third session is pretty much a total disaster. It's full of dumbos. I'm whizzing round the table at top speed doing just about every banner from scratch, while the kids try to escape or sit there chewing balls of sticky paper. Overworked as I am, I can't stop thinking about Landon, either, and his promise to check up on Iggy and let me know how he is. I want to know that Ig's safe, of course I do, but more than that I want Landon to care enough to come here to give me a report on him . . . I check my watch. *God.* Even when this session's over I'll still only be just over halfway through the whole shift . . .

I'm writing names on banners when Maria bowls over again. And this time she's got a genuine smile on her face. She dismisses the kids to the far end of the room, then she says, "So, Rowan, I throw you in the deep end, yes?" I giggle vaguely, and she says, "The green plant shapes—clever. And making the strip not the square. Tomorrow you maybe do something with fish, and seaweed shapes? Underwater scene?"

I force my mouth to upturn in the grim parody of a smile. Right this minute, I'd sooner hack off my hands than do more cutting and sticking. "Now—work with children not all fun things," says Maria, gravely. "You have long break—ten minutes maybe. Then I need you to wash painting things. OK?"

I totter off to the side room, and slump into a chair. There are only two fig-rolls left in the biscuit barrel. I take one. There's a kind of stone-like feeling in my guts, because of Landon. I know I'll feel horrible if it gets to four o'clock and he still hasn't shown by the time I'm free to leave . . . I make it back outside just as the ten minutes is up. I'm still on trial, and I want this job. Even if I leave here in a few days' time with a broken heart and shattered dreams and other assorted cliches, I want it for now.

Back in the main room again, LaToya collars me.

"How's it going?"

"OK. Well—I'm knackered, but—"

"You're doing great. She likes you, I can tell."

"Well, that's a relief. What's next?"

"You gotta wash that crap in the sink over there—*really* clean or Maria goes nuts—and lay it out to dry. Then it's *music*, before the parents pick 'em up. You good at singing?"

"No. I'm shit."

"Don't matter. Sing loud and *happy*—you know, all enthusiastic—and the job's yours—*who the hell is that*?"

I spin round. Landon's at the window, looking unbelievably gorgeous, waiting for me to spot him. I wave; I'm melting from the inside out, like a choc ice in the sun. He grins, gives me a thumbs up.

"Holy shit," breathes LaToya. "He's all right . . . You know him?"

"Yes," I swoon, giving him a thumbs up back.

And he goes into this weird mime; he wags an arm behind his back, opens his mouth and darts his tongue in and out fast, four times. Then he sticks his thumb up again and nods, grinning. I grin back, like my face might split, and mouth, "Thank you!" He points at his watch, mouths, "Later," and speeds away.

There's a slightly stunned pause. Then LaToya demands "What the hell was *that* all about?"

"It was meant to be my iguana. He was telling me he's OK."

"Your iguana—?! If you say so, girl. Didn't look like that to me."

"It *was*! He was miming his tail, and his—"

"Tongue. *Sure*. So—you two together?"

"We only met yesterday. He's why I'm here."

"I *bet* he is. How'd you meet? Hey—*watch it*—Maria."

Maria clicks over to join us. "LaToya—have you explained to Rowan about the painting things?" she demands.

"Yes, ma'am."

"I'll get started cleaning them right away," I say, enthusiastically. Right now I'd blissfully clean the boys' toilets.

"Good. That boy at the window—a friend of yours?"

"Um—sort of."

"Keep away from that boy is my advice. Boys—trouble. Now—the paint pots."

I spend the next half hour or so contentedly swishing plastic tubs and brushes in soapy water, rinsing them thoroughly, and lining them up to dry. My mind's full of Landon, full of how it's going to be when I see him again. I can't decide whether to go straight back to the huts, or drop into one of the little hotel supermarkets first and pick up a few supplies. My impulse is to race back to the huts, but I don't want to either a) look desperate, or b) starve if Landon doesn't show.

I think about the key with the number 3 on it, safe in my bag hanging up on my hook. I think about having my own cabin, my own sun-deck—and being able to sleep all night without being woken up by screaming. For a moment, I see Flossy's face in front of me, the way she looked when she came round after a nightmare, white and sobbing, and I get a great rush of remorse for the way I ran out on her. I call up a picture of Babcia folding Flossy up in her arms. I call up Iggy's image, think of him with a lethal needle going through his scales, then browsing peacefully by the lake. I fight off my demons. I tell myself I did the right—the only— thing. Then I go back to daydreaming about

Landon over the sink.

At ten past three, Maria claps her hands very loudly, and bellows, "All right, everybody, *music* time!"

A big blue box is wheeled out, overflowing with tambourines, little drums, and bells on sticks. The kids are marshalled together by the big window at the end. Then forty minutes of hideous brain-splitting noise follows. No one seems to want to sing the same *song*, let alone keep to the same beat. I'm checking my watch every two minutes, like someone trapped underground who knows they'll run out of oxygen soon. I discover it's quite possible to grin madly and sing loudly at the same time that you're screaming inside to escape. Which is a useful talent, 'cos Maria keeps looking over at me, checking I'm joining in.

Finally, *finally*, the big doors at the end swing open and assorted parents rush through, their love for their offspring boosted by the guilt they feel at having so much enjoyed their few hours of freedom.

"Get to know *whose* kid is *whose*," hisses LaToya, as she passes. "Take a special interest in a kid with its parents—'specially if they seem anxious. Act like that kid is your favourite, like you spend practically all of your time with it!"

"Right!" I say, obediently, then I add, "Why?"

"Tips, you dummy! *Tips!* They think you've been good to their kid—they slip you something at the end of the week!"

I watch as LaToya scoops up a surprised little boy, and bears him lovingly over to his mum and dad. I hover, smirking, amid the chaos, trying to commit to memory who belongs to who. When I see Chelsea march over to a tired-looking woman, I sidle up to them and murmur, "Chelsea was *so* clever and helpful when we made dinosaur pictures today!"

The woman throws me a jaundiced glance. "Bossy and know-it-all, you mean!" she snaps. *Fine*, I think. *No tip there, then.*

At last, the huge room is cleared of parents and children. I'm almost hysterical with eagerness to get out, back into the open again. But taking my cue from LaToya, I help clear up, putting tiny chairs on top of tables, packing away the instruments in the music box.

"So," says Maria, appearing at my side, "you think you like it here?"

"Oh yes," I lie, fervently, "it's great. The kids are *great*."

"No, they're not," states Maria, flatly. "They are spoiled, demanding and badly-behaved. But it's a job, yes?"

"Er—yes. I hope so."

"I think so. I think you will be fine. At the end of this week, I confirm with Derek. Now—shifts." Maria shows me the Shifts noticeboard, where, she assures me, my name will soon be added. It turns out I'm expected to do one four-hour shift one day, two four-hour shifts the next, with two days off a week. On the days I only do one shift, I generally have to put in some time on night babysitting. This, Maria explains, is where you man a whole panel of baby-listening devices, and if one of the kids starts crying badly you contact its parents, following the instructions left. Also organized are trips with some of the older kids, like swimming, sports and nature rambles, and if these trips overrun your shift you get extra pay. When she's told me everything, Maria says, "You look surprised."

"Do I? I s'pose I'm just amazed at what an . . . industry it all is. The childcare here, I mean."

Maria smiles grimly but proudly, like a general who knows he and he alone is protecting his land from enemy invasion. "This hotel," she says, "*depends* on my nursery. For its reputation—and its survival. We are just as important as the *kitchens*. Don't you forget that."

"I won't," I promise, solemnly.

"So. Tonight—babysitting switchboard, yes? Eight till midnight, the room next to this—I show you now, on our way out. Come—get changed back."

I get out of my uniform, hang it on my hook. I'm too gutted to say anything as Maria points out the little room where I and one other helper are to be incarcerated for four long hours tonight. I thought I'd be free now—free until the next day, at least. Suddenly, the Bielickas' luxury apartment seems like not such a bad place to be after all, and the phrase "out of the frying pan" is rotating in my head . . . I glance at my watch. It's half past four already. I need to eat, get my head down for a bit, shower, check on Iggy, and Landon, what about *Landon* . . .

I zip into a small shop called, nauseatingly, Woodsman's Provisions and buy some very basic stuff like apples, bread, beer, cheese and chocolate at very fancy prices. Then I speed along the corridors and hallways, following the signs to the gym. After only two wrong turnings, I'm racing across the miniature golf course, heading for the trees.

But when I reach them, I stop. They're dense, impenetrable. I can't see a path, I can't see a sign. Cursing at myself for not paying more attention—

for not turning round to place where Landon and I were when we exited the woods—I pace up and down, panicking.

It's hopeless. There's no way in. Like a forest in a fairy tale, Landon's Magic Woods have closed up against me, and won't let me in.

I check my watch. Five past five. At this rate I should forget getting to the cabins, just head back to the nursery switchboard. Who needs a life anyway?

Iggy, that's who. He's depending on me.

OK, Rowan, you unbelievable braindead thicko, THINK! Think where you were when you first saw the hotel! I swivel round, jog along with my back to the woods, pummel my brain to remember what angle the hotel was at when I got my first sight of it . . . *that's it, that's it. I was further over, to the right—yes. Here!*

I turn back to the trees. What could almost be a path is winding through a dense group of young saplings. I weave my way into them, kicking through the ivy covering the ground, stubbing my toe on something. I look down—it's a short plank of wood, all rotten, and just visible through the ivy are—*letters*! It's a broken sign! I scrape the leaves aside with my foot, read *o the La . . . To the Lake!* YES!

Like some wired-up Native American guide, I

speed on triumphantly into the wood, tracking the path. A broken stem here, flattened grass there . . . it's all I can go by 'cos I don't recognize any of it. Not even that very distinctive dead tree that looks like an evil dwarf. I plunge on, and the tree canopy gets denser, and the way is gloomier and darker, and I start to think I've been in here longer than I was this morning. Then I'm sure I have. A lot longer. Oh, God, let me be on the right path. Oh, God, I should've taken more notice of my surroundings instead of ogling Landon. I'm a slut. A sex-crazed slut. If I get out of this wood and safe back to my cabin I swear I'll renounce men for ever, I'll become a nun, a nun who never goes out, one of those nuns who get themselves bricked up behind a wall . . . the trees have started to thin, the path widens. I race on into daylight.

And there's the lake, there's the cabins . . . !

Now all I have to do is find Iggy, and let Landon find me.

CHAPTER 32

"IGGY! IGGY, BABE!"

Silence. Just the stirring of leaves, the chirring of crickets in the long grass. The peace, the stillness, after the afternoon I've had, is wonderful. I'm a mouse escaped from the laboratory, free in the fields again. The sun's low in the sky, full of heat, and the lake's shining, cool and beautiful, but I can't enjoy it till I know Iggy's safe. I dump my shopping and hurry over to the lakeside, anxiously scanning the surface for little floating iguana bodies. "Oh, come on, Iggy," I call. "What've you gone all moody for?" I walk anxiously along the lake's edge, peering at the undergrowth. Nothing. "Is it Landon?" I call, more quietly. "Are you jealous? You had your chance to turn into my prince, didn't you? I couldn't wait forever."

Absolute silence. I start shouting Iggy's name. I'm not certain iguanas can hear—they don't seem to have ears, for a start—but it makes me feel better. And then I spot something very green on a half-submerged log a short way away, flexing sinuously in the sun. It's a lizard tail. "Iggy, you *toad*!" I erupt.

He turns his head, registers my presence. Everything about him—his grin, his lazy body, the shine on his scales—says he's had the best, the freest day yet in his life. Something that could be an insect's leg is sticking out of the side of his mouth. "Been hunting, have you mate?" I ask, pulling my shoes off and splashing my feet in the water. *All it needs*, I think, *for things to be absolutely perfect, is for Landon to turn up*.

I sit there for a while, soaking up the beauty, until it dawns on me how ravenously hungry I am. The late-morning fry-up I had with Landon feels like it was light years ago. I check my watch. In just over two hours' time I've got to be walled up in the nursery switchboard cupboard, listening to kids wailing over the intercom. "OK, Ig," I say, getting to my feet. "You've had hours of freedom, and the sun's going down. I'm gonna shut you up in the cabin for the night." I reach over, hoist him two-handedly off his log. He hangs there compliantly, but when I start to walk with him he suddenly twists towards me. For one scary moment I think he's on the attack. His claws take hold of my arm, he clambers up, twists and shifts until he's hanging, perfectly balanced, across my shoulders.

And suddenly I know what it's about. "You did this with your last owner, didn't you?" I breathe. "The nice one. Aw, Iggy. He used to take you about with him, didn't he?" Tentatively, I start to move forward. Iggy remains balanced, riding me like a sultan on an elephant. His claws gripping through my T-shirt are a little bit creepy, but it's so cool to have him balanced like this I don't care. In my head, I'm making a grand entrance into the bar where Landon works, Iggy round my neck like a stole.

We glide across the ground towards the huts. It's the first time I've had a really good look at the outside of them, and I'm charmed. Because they aren't used for hotel guests any more, they've been allowed to get a bit dilapidated, go back to nature. The paint on the wood is curling off like bark-strips in the heat; vines are overgrowing the steps and decks unchecked.

Number Three cabin is only one away from Landon's. And it's not until I'm excitedly pushing the key in the lock that it dawns on me that all my stuff—all my clothes, make-up, washing stuff, towel, *everything*—is locked up in Landon's cabin.

"Oh, *God*, I need a shower, Ig!" I wail. "And what about your light—you need to bask under your light when I'm gone!"

I'm so pissed off I pull the key straight out again, head straight over to Landon's hut, Iggy still perched on my shoulder. Maybe he forgot to lock it, I think, or maybe he put the key back under the stone . . . I reach the door, shove it—and it swings open. *Brilliant*. As long as someone hasn't nicked my stuff while we've been gone.

Quietly, we go in.

I STEAL ACROSS THE BARE-wood floor towards the bedroom and my neck prickles as though I'm being watched, as though I'm not alone. "Hang on Ig," I whisper, to give myself courage. "We'll just grab my bag, and your light, and we'll be off . . ." I push the door to the bedroom open. And there's Landon, spread gorgeously and probably nakedly under the duvet I slept under last night. I'm suddenly so turned on I have to steady myself against the door frame. One beautiful strong brown arm is flung out behind his head, his profile is all in relief against the white pillow, his mouth is slightly open, he's breathing deep and steady . . . I want to get in beside him. I want to dump Ig and all my clothes right here on the floor, and climb in beside him . . . Iggy butts his snout disapprovingly at my chin as though he knows what I'm thinking. And over in the bed, Landon stirs, shifts, brings his arm down . . .

"Hello?" I quaver. If he's about to wake up I don't want him to think I've been lurking here ogling him as he sleeps, like some kind of pervert stalker. Especially as that's what I have been doing.

"*Mmmmm,*" he goes, pleasurably.

"Landon?" I squeak. "I just came by to get my stuff—"

"Hey, babe," he says, in a slurry, sleepy voice, then he lazily raises his arm towards me and kind of *beckons* me towards the bed. This is almost too much to handle. He can't mean it. He can't mean *me*. Can he? I glance across at the bathroom door, dreading a naked girl emerging . . . "*Wrrrrgh* . . ." moans Landon, blissfully. He rubs at his eyes, focuses. And double-takes. "Where the hell did you come from?" he demands.

"You left the door unlocked. I needed my bag, my clothes . . ."

"Oh, wow, that is *cool*. The lizard . . . that is so *cool*. You train him to do that?"

"No—not me. His previous owner, I think. He just kind of . . . climbed up on my shoulder."

"It's the way to travel!"

"Iggy obviously thinks so."

"So—Ro-anne! You OK? Your nursery session went OK?"

I lean against the doorjamb and tell him about

257

my day. He really is a good listener. At least I think he's listening. He's looking at me and smiling, anyway, and that's enough. "It's working out," he says. "Right? I got my bar shifts worked out. Shit, though—" he checks his watch—"I got to be back there in two hours."

"For eight o'clock? Me too. And I need a shower and I'm *starving*. I—"

"Dinner is all set," he interrupts proudly. "I got a load of stuff free from the kitchens. Babe—you go shower. Dinner will be ready for you when you're done."

I'm going to be shut in a cupboard with a switchboard for four hours. There is absolutely no need to put on mascara, blusher, eye pencil, lip-liner. There is no call for my favourite low-cut T-shirt. Or cleavage-enhancing bra. But I put them all on, with my favourite neck chain, and squirt on loads of perfume for good measure.

I've sort of settled in—I've tipped my bag out on the bed, hung some clothes up, put my stuff in the bathroom. But the pleasure of having my own cabin—which normally would be just about *overwhelming*—is a very poor second to the anticipation of seeing Landon again.

"He's *cooking* for me," I swoon to myself in the

mirror. "*Again*. And before, when I asked him about tonight, he was all non-committal. He's decided he likes me, he must've done, *really* likes me. He called me *babe*. Twice. So maybe he *did* know it was me when he was half asleep in bed, maybe that was his subconscious wanting me to get in next to him . . ."

"Pull yourself together, Rowan," snaps my sensible side. "Back home, if a guy called you *babe*, you'd a) puke b) laugh or c) punch him in the face."

"I know. But here—from him—it's great. It's absolutely *great*."

Half an hour later—having settled Iggy on the back of the sofa with his light attached to the big angle-poise lamp, just like in Landon's cabin—I sashay through Landon's door. "Hey—you look good!" he exclaims, instantly making all my hard work worthwhile.

"Thanks!"

"How's Iggy?"

"Flaked out. *Blissed* out. Thanks for checking on him, earlier. I was so relieved when you let me know he was OK."

"No problem. You didn't need to worry. He was just chilling out at the edge of the lake, happy as a pig in mud—"

"He must love all this *freedom*. After being in a cage."

"That's how we all feel, babe." (*Three times! THREE times!*) "But bring him inside for the night, eh?"

"I have done."

"Good. You get all kinds of hungry wildlife around here after dark."

He grins at me, showing all his wolfy teeth. It's so sexy I unfortunately let out a shrill giggle, which I try to cover by asking, "So what've you cooked?"

"A kinda chicken stir-fry. With mushrooms and stuff."

"Wow. Wow, Landon, I am *so* impressed. The guys at home—their idea of cooking was maybe beans on toast if you were really in luck, or dialling for a pizza or something . . ."

"So did you leave lots of guys at home?"

He almost sounds like he could be jealous. *Fantastic.* I shrug nonchalantly, say, "Oh—you know—friends. Mostly."

"Right."

"When can we eat? It smells wonderful."

"Now. Let's take it outside, sit on the deck." He heads into the tiny kitchen, re-emerges with two steaming platefuls.

"That looks as good as it smells," I enthuse.

"Hey, Ro, what's with all the compliments? You want something?" It passes through my mind to tell him exactly what I *am* after, so I clench my teeth shut. "Tomorrow night maybe," he goes on, as if he's read my mind. I'm stunned till he carries on, "I'll get some steaks, and cook 'em outside. I love lighting a fire at night."

"Cowboy," I tease, my heart thumping, 'cos if he's telling me, I must be invited too, and that'll be three times he's made me a meal, which must mean he's passionately in love with me, mustn't it? "But doesn't it attract all that hungry wildlife?"

"Nope. They're too scared of ending up on the grill."

We sit down side by side on the deck as the sun starts to drop in the sky, and begin to eat. I tell him the stir-fry tastes infinitely better than the sardine spaghetti he made last night. He grins, repeats infinitely better in his awful English accent. I laugh, tell him to sod off, and he mimics that too, so I bat him one on the arm. He catches hold of my hand. Then we both kind of stop, like we're not sure what to do next, and he lets go of my hand and we begin to eat in earnest.

And I think—what we were doing just then was *serious flirting*.

In between mouthfuls he tells me about the subculture of the staff here, the whole soap opera going on as people make love or war "in this microcosm of what's going on outside" as he calls it. I'd be really interested in what he's saying if I wasn't so fixated on him physically. The way his mouth moves, the way his eyebrows draw together and make this sexy little crease when he's concentrating, the way his jaw looks when he chews. Suddenly, he nudges me, and points to the far side of the lake. I look up and see a small, slender deer stepping out from the trees and nervously trotting towards the water.

"*Ooooh*!" I breathe, thrilled.

"You ever seen a real deer before?"

"Only in parks—"

"They're just cattle. Shhh. Watch."

Another little deer appears out of the trees, followed by another. They join the first deer at the lake's edge. Then they all stoop their long necks, and drink. One deer lifts its head, listening; the other two copy. And then the three of them turn as one and race back into the cover of the trees.

There's a silence, and I feel all bonded and close to him, 'cos of seeing the deer together. "That was *magic*," I whisper.

"Moonlight's the best way to see 'em. If my

brother was here, he'd have his gun ready."

"Oh *no!*"

"*Sure.* Venison stew—delicious."

"He *couldn't've* taken a shot at them. They were too gorgeous." I sigh happily, stretch my legs out on the deck and gaze around me. "You know—I really don't understand why the guests at the hotel won't stay down here. If they're into being outdoorsy and stuff."

"Outdoorsy? Is that more British slang?"

"No, I think I just made it up. You know what I mean, though. It's so idyllic here."

"Yeah, but the *punters*—they're not really into being *outdoorsy*. It's all fake. What they want is the idea that they're outdoorsy—"

"Stop nicking my word."

"No, I like it. They want to think they're all healthy and gutsy, having adventures everywhere. They go on a coupla bike rides and hike for a while up in the mountains and see possums and raccoons running around and feel *great* about themselves, getting back to their roots and all. Then they play golf and sit around in the bar."

I laugh, really liking what he's said. Without exactly meaning to, I'm leaning in quite close to him. And he's not drawing back. "Thank you for dinner," I murmur. "When can I cook for you?"

"Tomorrow?" he says, all low and sexy. "Or maybe we should get a fire going?" The air between us—all half a centimetre of it—is shaking, shimmering. Then he suddenly jerks up his arm, checks his watch, and blurts out, "Holy *shit*, it's a quarter to eight!"

Within seconds, he's locked his cabin door, and we're heading into the gloomy Magic Woods. "It's not *fair*!" I wail. "We shouldn't have to work—we should just be *free* like Iggy!"

"You said it, sister. The lizard is a privileged little bastard."

"We could live like him. You got that food free."

"Yeah, but only 'cause I work here. And I had to buy the cooking oil. And I need toothpaste—"

"I s'pose so."

"And shower gel and shampoo . . ."

"Washing-up liquid. Magazines."

"Shorts. Shirts."

"Chocolate. More chocolate."

We hurry on, into the center of the wood. It's really dark in the middle, where the trees are thickest. And a sudden thought hits me. "Oh, *shit*, Landon—it's going to be pitch black when I get off work!"

He glances at me and laughs. "You're not

scared of the dark, are you, Ro-anne?"

"I am in these woods, yes. Bloody terrified. I'll get lost, I'll get attacked by wolves or witches . . ."

"Bears, maybe."

"What?"

"We have brown bears around here! Hey, keep your shirt on—they won't attack you. They come up to the trash cans sometimes."

"Oh God, that's *amazing*!"

"Look—come and find me at the bar—I finish up around twelve thirty. The Crescent Moon Bar—it's right by the diner we had breakfast at. I'll get you back safe, OK?"

I thank him, and float euphorically out of the wood and onto the golf course. That's as good as a date, that is.

CHAPTER 34

I'M HOPING IT'S GOING TO be LaToya on the grave-yard shift with me, but it isn't. It's someone with a mousy bob who introduces herself limply as "Sam," and sniffs a lot. But she's happy to show me the ropes even if she does go over the same thing about a million times like it's the most major job in the world.

Every hotel room that offers the babysitting service is represented on the huge switchboard by its number and a little light bulb, and those that have signed up for tonight's session have their little bulbs lit up. Sam and I divide the rooms between us (twenty-two each), put on our earphones, and start to plug in. Twenty minutes is supposed to be often enough to check on each kid, which gives us a very brief breather after we've finished all twenty-two before we start on in again. Just long enough to get a cup of tea.

So I sit there and listen to baby after child after baby snuffling and snoring and shifting about, waiting for one of them to start wailing. My stomach's screwed up into the old familiar knot, the one I always got waiting for Flossy to have a nightmare. Poor old Floss—I must write to her. Tomorrow. And—*God*—I must phone Mum too, and let her know I'm safe—it's just I've had so much to organize. OK, lech over. But I've had so *much*!

"I got a screamer!" Sam breaks into my thoughts, voice full of grim satisfaction. "Room 524 . . ." She checks her list. "Mr. and Mrs. Stanton at the Oasis Spa." Efficiently, she dials through to the spa, giving instructions to the desk to inform the Stantons that their infant needs them. And then she's back to plugging in, plugging out again.

As the minutes tick by (forty-five seconds on average on each kid) I increasingly feel I've entered a surreal, parallel universe. Quite apart from the weird effect on your brain of listening in on the sleep of twenty-two infants, it's become clear that Sam views this as a kind of competition. When I have three "screamers" one after the other, she glares at me like I'm winning all the prizes at a raffle. I get the message through to the parents in their restaurants or bars, but I have to fight down a real urge to plug back in to the crying kids again, to share their pain. "It's awful, isn't it?" I say to Sam. "I hate hearing them cry."

Sam shrugs irritably. "Hearing them cry is what we're here for," she snaps. Then her face clears. "Another screamer!" she gloats, and reaches for the phone.

As midnight and the end of the shift approaches, the little lights start to go off as parents return to their rooms. At five to twelve I have two lights left on, and Sam has three. "What happens if they're late?" I ask, anxiously. The last thing I want to be is late.

"We wait for fifteen minutes. Then we check with where they went. I'll do it if you like. Last time, this woman felt so guilty she gave me a big tip."

In the end, there's no need for either of us to stay. All the little lights are safely out by 12:05.

"Wanna hot drink?" Sam suggests unenthusiastically. "We earned it. They make a good hot chocolate with melted marshmallows at the diner next door. Puts you right to sleep."

"Sounds wonderful," I lie, sleep being the last thing on my mind, "but—I'd kind of arranged to meet someone."

"OK," she shrugs, with the air of someone used

to being turned down, and trudges off.

I fly along the corridor, heading for the Crescent Moon Bar, stopping off briefly at a restroom to have a quick pee and titivate. I reckon I look twenty-one and I also don't look too bad considering the stress I've been under during the last four hours. Nothing that a quick slick of lippy can't fix, anyway.

I'm feeling pretty nervous as I enter the bar—I'm surprised at how glitzy and elegant it is, for a start. I might've been overdressed for the babysitting cupboard, but here I look distinctly downbeat. Everywhere, there are low-cut dresses, spindly shoes, sparkly jewellery . . . and there behind the bar, looking strange but debonair in his uniform of jacket and dicky little bow tie, is Landon. Two women seated on stools at either end of the bar like griffins on gateposts are gazing at him fixedly. They look a lot older and a lot richer than me.

I summon up all my courage, and walk over to him. "Ro-anne!" His face lights up, fabulously. "You found me!"

"Obviously!"

"*Obviously*. What you having? On the house."

"Oh, thanks. A cold beer, please."

"This is America, babe. It don't come any other

way." He plonks it, grinning, in front of me and one of the griffins hails him with a flash of red talons from the end of the bar. I watch him as he serves her, automatically charming and flirty. She tells him to keep the change. The clock on the wall says 12:20. Ten minutes to go.

Landon zooms past, dealing with another order, and when he returns he slams another bottle of beer down in front of me.

"I haven't finished this one yet!"

"You will. Bet you need it, after the shift you just did."

"Too right. My ears are still ringing from all the squawking. I—"

But he's off again, serving someone else. He's not exactly elegant as he serves—not like the skinny Puerto Rican guy serving alongside him— but I can't keep my eyes off him. I watch his hands moving over the dark mahogany of the bar, finish my first beer, start on my next one. I watch his arms work. I keep thinking ahead to our walk through the woods. How it'll be so dark I can justify holding his arm if not his hand. I'm starting to feel really good.

At twelve thirty on the dot, Landon turns to the burly black head barman and says, "OK, Jacko, I'm off."

"OK, man." And then Jacko smirks and says, "So, man—you disappointed or relieved she didn't show?"

She, *she*. Who is *she*? Something cold flows into me as Landon laughs. He's not *taken* already is he? "Maybe a little of both," he says, then he disappears through a door at the back of the bar.

I know I ought to act cool and unconcerned but I just *can't*. The best I can make myself do—when Landon's appeared beside me in jeans and T-shirt again and we've started to walk towards the door—is sound as casual as I can as I ask, "So who were you talking about just then? With Jacko?"

"What?"

"The she who didn't show?"

"Oh, that. There was . . . someone I thought might be here. Someone I was with last year."

"Ah. And isn't she here?"

He shakes his head. As we head along the corridor, I'm scanning his profile like it holds the key to the mystery of existence, but I can't read anything there. I'm formulating more questions in my head, questions that won't make me sound like a predatory female, but I veto them all. Then Landon suddenly announces, "Her name's Coco. She worked at the bar too, last summer. We had a—you know, a vacation thing. And because we were both off to college—different colleges—we broke up at the end. We'd kinda kept in touch—she said she was coming back here—but no one at the bar's heard from her. So I guess she ain't gonna come."

The Sherlock Holmes part of my brain is in overdrive. I work out it must've been during his first shift that he found out that Coco (*crap* name!) hadn't come back to the hotel this summer. Because before that shift, when he dropped me off at Kiddie Heaven, he'd acted friendly but all kind of cool, non-committal, wouldn't get tied down about meeting up again that night. Then, *after* the shift, he was suddenly much more friendly, making me food, saying he'd walk me home . . .

I decide for once in my life not to over-analyse. OK, maybe I'm second best, who knows, who cares. He's so clearly the first best *ever* it kind of cancels it out if I *am* second best.

And he's free now. *Available*.

"Look at all the Grey Staff," he mutters. I look up, focus on the outside world again. Everywhere there are grey-boiler-suit clad cleaners, polishing floors, buffing glass, emptying trash cans. "That's what Management calls them," he goes on. "The Grey Staff."

"God, that's weird," I mutter back. "And the

way they all come out at dead of night to keep everything going."

"Best time. Otherwise the guests have to see it, don't they?"

"Yeah, but why *shouldn't* they see it? This place, it's like a . . . *castle*, or something. The guests are the lords and ladies. All pampered and everything. And the Grey Staff—they're like the serfs."

He laughs. "Ro-anne, you are one *strange* girl! If they're serfs, what're we?"

"People who want to get out of here as fast as possible?"

"Definitely," he says, and then—*miracle*—he takes hold of my hand and starts speeding along the corridor to the exit, towing me along behind him, and soon we're out in the cool night, running across the moon-streaked miniature golf course lawn towards the trees.

When we crash into the wood it's like entering a dark, secret room. Suddenly, we're closed in, private. And as if he's acting on this, he turns to me, puts both his hands on my arms, says, "You know what? I thought I was disappointed. About Coco. But I'm not sure I am."

"Why not?" I croak. My heart's thumping. Not from the run.

He stoops down, I crane up. And we kiss, the

kind of kiss that's been building for a while, longing to happen. We're mashing our mouths, out of
sync—it's not expert. Even with my dire lack of
experience I can tell that. But it's ecstasy, it's *him*.

"Hey," he says, as we draw back for air. "Come
on."

And he tows me further into the wood.

CHAPTER 35

WE HURRY WORDLESSLY THROUGH THE trees. I feel almost delirious with excitement and pleasure. There's this triumphant chant inside my head: *I've done it, I've got him!* I want to stop again, kiss again in the still dark, but Landon seems intent on getting through the wood as quickly as he can. We hurry on, barely stumbling. He keeps to the path and his hand feels strong and fantastic round mine.

Soon, we've reached the other side of the wood, and I can see the lake all silvery in the moonlight. Landon turns to me. "So," he says, eyes half shut, seductive as hell, "whose cabin we going to?"

I push down the thought that he's being too efficient about all this. I push down the thought that he thinks we're going to make love right away. I look at his face and say, "Mine, of course. I gotta check on Ig, haven't I?"

"The lizard! Of course. Come on."

Inside the cabin with the light from Ig's lamp glowing, it suddenly feels awkward. Iggy's still basking sleepily on the back of the sofa; I make some stupid comment about him looking like he hasn't moved since I left him. Landon flicks his tail a couple of times and I squeak, "D'you want a beer? I bought some earlier . . ."

"Yeah—but you don't wanna buy beer, I can get it for you."

I hasten off to the tiny kitchen, fetch a couple of bottles from the fridge and decap them. When I return, he's lounging on the sofa, Ig still stretched out behind his neck. I hand him a beer and he takes a swig and grins at me over the rim. "I've never made out in the same room as a reptile before," he says. Then he puts his beer down on the table and holds out his hand. "C'mere, Ro."

Awkwardly, I kind of crumple down beside him. He puts his arm round me, takes my beer off me, puts it beside his on the table. Then he starts to kiss me again.

I put everything I can into that kiss. I try to respond, try to show him how much I want him, but he's going at my mouth so hard I'm not sure he notices. His hands slide from my back round to the front. One of them dives up my T-shirt. And all the time he's pushing me backwards so that soon I'm going to have to lie flat or start pushing him back like some kind of stupid wrestling match . . . without really meaning to I gasp out, "Hey—slow down!"

As soon as it's out of my mouth I regret it. It sounds like a criticism, a complaint. But he just sits back from me, shrugs and says, "Sorry." Then he reaches out for his beer again.

There's a pause. *Shit*, have I blown it? I study his profile. *Shit*, why did I stop him? What's so wrong with being . . . overwhelmed like that? I force myself to act all cool and experienced and reach a hand out to his neck. "Sorry," I murmur, wriggling my fingers into his hair. "Sorry. Give us another kiss."

This time he lets me lead. For about three seconds. Then he's into mouth-crushing again. I decide I don't care. I decide he's so fantastic I'm going to play it his way. He moves from my mouth to my neck and starts nuzzling it. Then he starts pulling my top up. I hold his hand still. His other hand moves to the fastening on my jeans. The memory of Boring Billy—who I went the Whole Way with about seven times—infiltrates my mind, and I think—*Why not?* I know what it's all about. I want this, I want him, he's such a turn-on . . .

That's just the trouble. I'm not exactly turned

on. I want to feel passionate, open, fantastic . . . but that's hard to feel when the *fast forward* button is being held down hard. "Wanna move on to the bed?" he murmurs. "It's kind of inhibiting having the lizard watch."

"Landon," I blurt out, "we only just kissed for the first time ten minutes ago!"

He pulls back from me, sits up. "Oh," he says. "OK. Sorry. I thought—"

"What?"

"I thought you wanted to be with me."

I'm desperate to ask, "*Be with*—is that American for shag?" but I don't have the guts. "I do want to . . ." I mutter. "I really like you. It's just . . ."

"Going too fast for you?"

"Yup. A bit. I mean—" I fall silent, knotted up with squirming embarrassment. As much for what he's saying as anything. The practical way he's talking, like I'm a car he's warming up. But then I look at his face again and decide I'd forgive him just about anything. After all, looking like that, he's probably used to women *being with him* about sixty seconds after they first set eyes on him . . .

"OK," he says. "No problem." And he picks up his beer again, and takes a swig.

He's not aggressive, I tell myself. He's not one of those bastards who try and manipulate and bully you. He's just pushing his luck and not . . . *reading* me right.

"What shifts are you doing tomorrow, Ro?" he asks. And his arm comes down round my shoulders, all warm and relaxed.

I think. "Oh—the first one. Eight till twelve. Then the graveyard shift again."

"So you got the afternoon free? Hey—that's cool! I'm off too—we can take a swim in the lake?"

"That'd be great!"

"It's gonna be hot tomorrow. Hotter than today. You wanna meet for lunch? I'll show you the other diner staff can go into for free. We can eat, and come straight back here . . ."

This is *much* more like it. I snuggle happily under his arm, and then I twist to face him and put my arm round his neck. My skin brushes against Iggy's scaly skin and I let out a shriek of shocked laughter and Landon moves in fast for another kiss while my mouth's still open. Now that is a turn-on. And the kissing—it's better. Like we're starting to learn each other. But when he starts trying to undress me again I break in with, "Is it safe? To swim in the lake?"

"What, snakes and stuff? I've never had a problem. Hey—you gonna get me another beer?"

Normally, asked this, I'd say something along

the lines of, "Get your own, dickhead!" but now I find myself jumping to my feet and trotting happily off to the kitchen, from where I call out, casual as all hell, "So—if you were in touch with Coco, you know, after last summer—how come you didn't know if she'd be here or not?"

There's a silence, like he's considering this. I'm half expecting him to tell me to mind my own business, that it's all too painful to talk about. But instead he says, "I don't think I wrote enough for her. She wanted me to be *definite* all the time—about weekends, and if I was coming back or not. I got this letter saying how she was fed up I'd never commit for dates and stuff. So—meeting up again here—it was kind of open."

Oh, *bless*! I think, gleefully. "Kind of open"? It was slammed shut, sweetie! You were *dumped*!

WHAT WITH ME BEING ON an early shift tomorrow, it's fairly easy—after we've finished our second beers and smooched a bit more—to evict Landon from my cabin, both of us promising to meet at 12:1 pm outside Kiddie Heaven so we can go to lunch together.

I go off to bed in a state of advanced bliss, to rerun the evening, relive the best bits, anticipate tomorrow, and analyse it all to death. After a nice time spent writhing about gloating and calling up his face and body in my mind's eye, I reach my *Things to face*:

1: Now this takes a bit of admitting to, but—he doesn't kiss as well as Boring Billy. Boring Billy was actually quite good in a clinch. Which is why I ended up going all the way with him, even though he didn't excite me that much to look at or talk to. Or anything to. I've got a thing about kissing. In my opinion kissing should be like a dialogue—responsive, interactive. Not tongue-thrashing and mouth-mashing.

2: He doesn't seem—face it, Rowan!—nearly as excited as I am about getting off together. He seems—face it!—almost practical. As in—how far and how fast can I get this to go?

I let these two downers of thoughts sink into my skull. Then I lie as calmly as I can and move into my *Think Positive* phase. And what I come up with is this:

1. Give it time. He needs time to learn how fabulous and interesting I am. And anyone can learn to snog. And:

2. I have pulled someone who looks like an angel. Who exudes sex from every pore. WHAT THE HELL AM I WHINING ABOUT?

I'm up and ready bright and early the next day. Iggy clambers down from the back of his sofa and makes a run at the shaft of sun streaming in through the window; then he waddles over to the door and waits, like a little squat dog.

"Now stay close, Ig, OK?" I nag him, as I open the door and let him out. "Don't go getting lost. Or drowned. Or killed. OK?"

My skin tingles as I walk past Landon's cabin. He's in there, I think, asleep and gorgeous. Some day soon, I'll be bringing him breakfast, waking him up.

I positively float into Kiddie Heaven. Maria shrilly reminds me of my promise (what promise?) to cut and stick underwater banners and I serenely get down to that with the first group. My seaweed is a triumph, my drowned anchors (created without the aid of a wooden shape) stunning. After that, I lie on the floor and patiently play cars and garages with half a dozen wired-up little boys currently refusing to join in anything else. In short, I'm a saint.

Through the huge windows, I can see how hot the day is getting. I'm longing to get out there, feel the real air on my skin. I keep thinking of the lake, and swimming with Landon . . .

"*Sssssss!*" LaToya breaks into a particularly good fantasy about an underwater clinch.

"Hi! You all right?"

"I'm great. And you are too, girl, right?"

"More than. *More* than."

"Lizard man? The looker with the tongue?"

"That's it. Although, actually—he's not that brilliant with his tongue."

"You found that out *already*?"

"Kissing! Jesus, Toya—*kissing*!"

And we go off into muted shrieks of laughter. Maria is well over the other side of the room—LaToya ducks down and makes like she's playing cars too. "Well I scored too!" she squawks.

"Really? Who?"

"New waiter. *Beautiful*. And when I say scored—I *almost* scored. This bitch Sophie—works in hairdressing?—she thinks she has, too. But I know I'll get him. Told him I'd see him at the Coconut Club later, when I get off the Graveyard . . ."

"No kidding! I'm on that shift tonight!"

LaToya grins. "Aw, that is *great*. I'll smuggle in a bottle, we can have some *fun*. Now tell all—what's lizard-boy *like*?"

As we shift toy cars about, we salivate over the merits of the guys we've pulled. LaToya's so frank and open it's hard not to be the same back, and I enjoy myself immensely. I realize how much I've missed this, laughing with another girl, swapping obscenities . . .

The little boys grouped round us listen in awed silence, eyes glued on our faces. "I hope they don't understand what we're saying!" I snigger.

"Ah, s'good for 'em," says LaToya. *"Educational.* Maybe they'll pick up a few tips, be better lovers when they're older . . ."

Our giggling is cut off by a pair of dominatrix shoes clicking into our line of vision. "Since what time did it take two to supervise a game of cars?" Maria barks. "LaToya—go check on the table with finger-painting."

LaToya pulls a face at me, grins, and hurries off.

I'm getting better, more relaxed. My guts only start knotting up in fear at being stood up about half an hour before Landon's due. And since he's only ten minutes late, that's only forty minutes of stress . . .

And it's worth it. Forty *hours* of stress would be worth it—forty *years*. I stand and gawp as he lopes up the Kiddie Heaven ramp. I keep forgetting how good-looking he is, as if I'm mentally censoring it for not being possible.

"Sorry, babe!" he calls out, breezily. "I went to the gym, got talking to Clint . . ."

"S'OK. I'm starving, are you?"

"Yeah. Let's go."

And he takes hold of my hand, and we swing off along the corridor. Deeply fantastic.

It's like I'm his *girlfriend*.

We almost don't get into the pizzeria, as it's really full. But Landon pulls his charm offensive on the waitress (tactically letting go of my hand first) and she ushers us into a cramped table by the tills.

Over pizza and salad, I try to get Landon to talk, but conversation doesn't flow. When I ask him about his day, his life, him*self*, his take is along the lines of: "Yeah, I work. Yeah, I work out. So what?" It occurs to me that he's probably a good listener because he doesn't have a lot to say. Well—maybe he's right with his *so what*? The physical stuff between us is growing all the time, and right now he's working his leg against mine under the table and running his fingers up and down my bare arm . . .

"C'mon, you finished?" he says. "Let's go swim."

CHAPTER 37

ON THE WAY BACK TO my cabin, I decide on my slimming black bikini rather than the sexy red one with maximum cleavage. Partly 'cos I feel less conspicuous in it and partly 'cos my skin hasn't tanned yet so black is more flattering. As I leave the cabin, I've got a towel wrapped self-consciously round me, but I needn't have bothered. I can see Landon at the far side of the lake, front-crawling like a maniac. He's not going to notice my entrance.

I don't think of myself as a genius swimmer. True, all the practice in the Bielickas' apartment pool has helped, but I still feel nervous of this great stretch of natural water. Natural as in—full of savage fish, and worms that burrow into your skin, and weeds that grab your ankles and drag you down . . . but the desire to be submerged when Landon spots me overwhelms my fear, and I wade in.

It's deep. And *freezing*. I throw myself forward, and start to swim.

Halfway across the lake, and I'm loving it. Once you're used to the cold, it's great, a real fix. I breaststroke slow and leisurely, not wanting to seem too eager to get across to him, looking around at the hot light on the trees and plants, casting branch shadows, leaf shadows . . .

"Hey! Ro-anne!" Landon waves from the other side of the lake, then puts his head down and starts powering towards me. I tread water a bit nervously. And suddenly he's bursting like a seal right up in front of me, all gorgeous and dripping. Not even plastered down hair can detract from him. He takes hold of my arms, gives me a chilly, wet kiss. Then he says, "C'mon!" and starts swimming off again.

I follow him to the far edge of the lake, the side that's nearest the woods. Here, great prehistoric-looking trees droop their branches and snake their roots into the water, making little caves and seats . . . a huge flat stone, submerged in the water like a tiny island, glints in the sun. Landon takes hold of an overhanging root and hauls himself on to it. I goggle at his back and think, *Shit, shit, shit.* I'm going to be fully exposed, now, aren't I? No way round it. Maybe that's why he's doing this.

He wants to size me up.

"C'mon, Ro," he says, holding out a hand to help me clamber up, "this is the best sunbathing spot on the whole lake. Trust me, this rock is *hot*. You'll be dry in seconds."

I remind myself of how good I looked in the multi-mirrors of the Bielickas' shower room, owing to all those sessions in the gym and the excess of health food I ate. Then I take hold of his hand, and scramble as elegantly as I can onto the great stone. "Hey," he says, grinning. "Hi."

He likes me. He does. He likes what he sees. I make a big deal of raking my wet hair back off my face with my fingers, so that my stomach stretches out all taut and sexy. "I love this rock," he says. "I *own* this rock. C'mon, let's lie down, catch some rays."

Gingerly, I lower myself on to my back. The stone's hard, but warm, like he promised, and worn smooth by the lake washing over it. I shut my eyes against the sun's glare; the water's drying on my skin in hundreds of tiny pleasant prickles which mesh in with the hot feeling from lying right next to him. Just our arms are touching. His skin's warmer than the stone, and smoother . . . I can feel him breathing.

Then suddenly my face is showered with cold

water. I snap open my eyes; he's right above me. "Hi," he says again, then he manoeuvres in and kisses me.

Our practically naked bodies collide. My shoulder blades graze against stone as he covers me, mouth grinding on mine. The hot feeling's vanished. I'm awkward, threatened. He's holding my head like he's trapping it, slotting one leg between mine . . . I jerk my head away, push him back, wriggle out from under him."What's *up*?" he says.

I turn on my side, face him. I can't think what to say. He looks so good. I *do* want him, I do—just not right away, and not out here on this *rock*. I crane forward and kiss him on the mouth. "I don't understand you," he says, but he's smiling.

"What d'you mean?"

"Why don't you just . . . *go* with it?"

I take a breath. "I am going with it. I'm going with it . . . the way *I* want."

"OK," he says, shrugging. Then he stands up, and dives off the stone.

I sit and watch the great plume of water that closes round him and I feel hurt, upset, angry, confused, the works. "*Screw* you," I mutter, slithering off. I'm halfway across the lake when he draws up beside me.

"Hey," he goes.

"Talking to me now, are you?"

"What?"

"Why'd you just—*piss off* back then?" I snarl.

"But you pretty much told me to!"

"No, I didn't."

"Well, that was the message I got," he says, and speeds off again. He's waiting for me in the shallows as I wade out of the lake. With total confidence he whams his arm round my shoulders and says, "You're so *British*."

"Yeah? What—'cos I like to finish conversations?"

"How d'you mean?"

"You keep wandering off halfway through!"

"No, I don't!"

"Yeah, you do." My anger's gone, I can't help it. Being hugged by him feels so good. "Anyway—why am I *British*?"

"'Cause you're such a *prude*."

"Oh, fuck off. I am not."

"Prove it."

"I just told you to fuck off, what more d'you want?"

"Come back to my cabin."

There's a silence. Half of me wants to knee him, the other half's thinking—why *not* sleep with him? I mean, what exactly are you doing here,

Rowan? Ticking off a few boxes to say you've developed some kind of a relationship with him before you think it's OK to have sex? So what if he's pushy—maybe that's good. Maybe if we sleep together now we can kind of *relax* with each other, relax into each other, we can—

A sudden shout interrupts my silent, frenzied justifications. A guy (tall, brown-haired, wearing nothing but a pair of shorts) is heading off the deck of the cabin the other side of Landon's, waving energetically. And when Landon spots him, his arm *whips* off my shoulders and he's running towards him, yelling, "Ben, you asshole!" and then another guy appears out of the cabin and Landon yells, "Rick!" and the three of them bosh into each other in a kind of big, buddy-buddy group hug, and they're all talking excitedly all at once about when they arrived and where they're working and the great time they're all gonna have this summer and saying, "Hey! *He-eeey!*" a lot.

I walk slowly towards them feeling horribly left out. Trying to push down the fact that Landon's showing more enthusiasm now than he did all the time he was having lunch or swimming or even *making out* with me. Trying to push down the fact that I *might've* been about to go back to his cabin with him and make love, and he must've known this, and yet he's not showing the slightest, *tiniest* bit of irritation that this has been interrupted . . .

In fact, he's not even showing he remembers I exist.

CHAPTER 38

IT'S BEN WHO SPOTS ME lurking up to them. "Landon, you bastard," he grins. "Should've known you'd have someone hot already!"

Immediately, I warm to Ben. He's no way in Landon's league but his face under its three days' stubble is friendly and comfortable-looking. Finally, Landon turns to me. "Hey—Ro! Come and meet my friends!"

Fine, I think acidly. I slink up to them, all self-conscious in my black bikini.

Me joining them is an excuse for them to recap on their buddy-buddy bonding past. They tell me they met last year, and had such an ace and epoch-making great time they all promised to come back. Ben and Rick (shorter, white-blond hair) kept in touch and travelled here together, but Landon didn't return their calls so they weren't sure he was going to make it. Ben's got work in one of the bars; Rick's waiting on tables, just like last year. They both find it hilarious that I'm in the nursery. Then Rick, with a sly glance at me, asks, "And what about the other member of the group?"

"Coco?" says Landon, all offhand. "Dunno. Not here."

There's a pause, during which I agonize and fume. So she was in a *group* with them, was she? *Nice*. And I'm doubtless a poor substitute. I'm inadequate, second best. While I'm agonizing and fuming, Ben draws a package out of his back pocket, which Landon and Rick greet with roars of approval.

"Yeah, c'mon!"

"Let's do it!"

Dope. Of course. The three make their way back to the deck of Ben and Rick's cabin, and flop down. Half-heartedly, I follow them, hover on the wooden steps. I'm starting to feel dead conspicuous on account of having hardly any clothes on. Especially as Rick keeps sliding his eyes over me.

Ben starts rolling up; Landon's already got his eyes half-closed in lazy anticipation. "Hey, Ro," he says, "Come and join us—c'mon, sit down."

Part of me wants to. Part of me wants to huddle down beside him, just to *be* with him, be near him. To see if he treats me like his girlfriend with his mates there, for a start.

But another part doesn't. Another part is running on *pride.* "I gotta work, later," I say. "I can't go getting stoned."

"We've all gotta work," sneers Rick, who I decide there and then I hate.

"Anyway, it's an advantage, being stoned when you're serving," says Ben, genially. "Makes it easier to deal with all the shit." Then he puts the joint in his mouth, and lights up.

"I've got stuff to do," I say. "I've got to make some phone calls, write to people . . ."

"Party *on,*" jeers Rick. *God*, I hate him.

I hover for a moment, *willing* Landon to remember that he'd talked about getting a fire going later and cooking some steaks, but he doesn't. All he says is, "OK, babe, see you." And his eyes are not on me but the progress of the joint.

I turn around and walk away.

I feel absolutely gutted. *Dismissed.*

As I let myself in my cabin, I remember with a jolt of panic and guilt that I haven't seen Iggy since I got back. I grab a long, cotton shirt, sling it on, and head for the lake, scanning the edge where I found him before. Landon spots me, which is something I suppose, and calls out, "What's up, Ro?"

"I'm looking for Iggy!"

"Hey—relax! He's fine!"

And so saying, he returns to his joint. I march round the lake, willing him to get up off his dopey arse and come and help me look. He doesn't move though. Instead, I hear snatches of him explaining to the others who Iggy is, and their responses: "No kidding? Weird! A big green one? Cool!"

When I'm on the far side of the lake, Landon and Ben start waving, like they're beckoning me back. "Sod off," I mutter under my breath. I'm starting to feel really wretched. No sign of Iggy anywhere. I carry on round the lake, peering into the undergrowth, scanning the water surface, praying . . . Nothing.

I draw up near the cabins again. And Landon calls out, "Hey, Ro—why didn't you come back? We tried to tell you—he's here!"

I examine the deck. A blunt green snout is visible the other side of Ben's leg. My relief is spoilt by a feeling almost of *betrayal*. Iggy—what are you doing here? With *them*?

"Guess he was attracted to our voices," says Landon, complacently.

"And the smell," slurs Ben. "He's a real dope fiend. Look." And he exhales a long spume of smoke around Iggy's gently nodding head.

"Don't do that!" I snap.

"Hey, it's OK!" says Landon. "Iggy's lean. He's mellow."

"Yeah, well, I don't want him—*kippered*."

Ben's the first to start laughing. "Kippered," he sniggers. "Kipp-*ered*!" Then the other two join in, inanely.

"C'mon, Iggy," I say. "Home time."

"We-like-the-lizard!" chants Rick in a silly voice. "Leave-him-here!"

"Yeah, leave him, Ro," chips in Landon. "The sun's still hot. And it's *his choice*."

I push down a very strong desire to punch Landon in the face and stomp off. If Iggy had any loyalty at all, he'd follow me, but he stays on the deck, buddy-buddy bonding.

And then just before I reach my cabin Landon calls out, "Hey, Ro—aren't you on the Graveyard tonight? I'll meet you after. So you don't have to go through the woods by yourself?"

"Yeah," I call back. "That'd be great."

OK, so I'm weak. OK, so I should have said, "I'll see myself back, thank you!" in a Grade A snotty voice, instead of gratefully seizing on his half-baked offer like it was some kind of *prize*. The trouble is, any kind of offer from Landon feels like a prize. And although I still feel pissed off with him, now it's a kind of niggling, wriggling little stream instead of a great, ferocious tree-tearing current.

I shower and dress, and head through the Magic Woods to the hotel to phone Mum.

I brood massively on the way through the wood, and decide Landon is just a total hedonist. I mean, Christ—he even likes to cook! I've got nothing against the pleasure of the appetites, but not when it's all you're living for. And not when it means you treat *me* as just another bit of pleasure.

Especially a possibly passing one.

As I head across the golf course, I'm hit by a real bout of loneliness. I wish I could talk to Mel, chew everything over with her, get her opinion. Which part do I go with? The part that's gagging to rip Landon's clothes off or the part that's saying, *whoa*, slow, take it easy or you'll get hurt . . . Mel would *know*. She'd say—

I know exactly what she'd say. She'd say—get some time on your own with him. Somewhere where ripping each other's clothes off is not an option. Time to talk, time to let things develop, time to see what he's really like . . .

Great advice, Mel. Except now Ben and Rick have arrived, how am I supposed to do that?

The phone call to Mum goes off pretty well. I start at the end, telling her I'm in Truckee now and it's fabulous and I'm *fine*, I've got a place to stay,

I've got a job. Then I backtrack to why and how I left Seattle, with much emphasis on my decisiveness, bravery and good sense. She listens, gobsmacked. She keeps saying, "Oh, darling!" and "Well done!" I tell her the hotel address and contact number; she promises to transfer more money into my account. I don't actually need it as I'm better paid now, but I reckon it'll make her feel good to do it so I don't argue. She asks me if I'm feeling nervous about the A level results, out in a few weeks' time; I avoid telling her I'd forgotten all about them. We finish the conversation on the best of terms, saying *love you*. As I put the phone down I register I may actually have succeeded in impressing her at last.

Glowing with daughterly achievement, I spend a while wandering round the enormous hotel complex, and realize I'm really beginning to get my bearings in it—where the shops and restaurants are, where Landon's bar is . . . it feels good, like I'm beginning to settle in. I bump into Clint, the flashy black guy from the gym, and spend five enjoyable minutes flirting with him. He tells me any time I want to use the gym for free—"The sauna, the pool, anything!" I've just got to give him a shout. I tell him I will.

Then, chuffed and refreshed, I walk back

through the woods. I've got a couple of hours before the graveyard shift, and I need to eat, and write to Babcia and Flossy.

Unless Landon's there wanting to barbecue me a steak, of course.

CHAPTER 39

Dear Flossy,

How are you, darling? I hope you're well and happy. You'd like it here. It's hot and sunny and Iggy loves being free to roam about. There's a big lake he paddles in! I've got a job working in a nursery with lots of kids your age but none of them is as good as you at drawing or dancing! Much love and kisses,

Rowan xxxx

After I've written to Flossy, I write more lengthily to Babcia. I thank her again for all her help, for the money and the cat carrier. I tell her about the "nice helpful boy" *(ha!!)* I met, the job, the beauty of the surroundings and my cabin. I wind up begging her to let me know how things are with Flossy.

As I push both letters into an envelope

addressed to Babcia, I utter a quick spell over it. *Cursed be Sha if she opens this. Cursed be Sha if she looks within* . . . I've just got to hope Babcia is still there and first to the post in the morning.

After that, I go outside to reclaim Iggy. The three dope-smoking musketeers have disappeared, but Iggy's still traitorously drowsing on Landon's top step. *"Wrong* cabin, mate!" I tell him reproachfully, as I stoop to pick him up. He's too sleepy—or dopey—to protest.

I lock him up in the cabin and set off in the waning light for the babysitting room. And I'm suddenly overcome by sheer triumph and pleasure that I've done it, I've pulled it off, I've moved to America and survived, I'm *surviving.* Sod Landon. I'm all right on my own. I've got this great place, I'm dealing with it all, getting to know people . . . As I walk through the wood I take my emotional pulse, decide I'm OK.

Truc, if Landon stands me up tonight, it's going to all come crashing down, but as it is, I'm OK.

Over the next few hours, LaToya and I share a bottle of sweetish white wine and perfect the mind-boggling technique of simultaneously talking non-stop and plugging into sleeping kid after sleeping kid. Our in-depth discussion of the failures of the male sex is put on hold only when one of us gets a screamer. LaToya's as wound up as a steel spring—she's sure Sophie's going to pull out all the stops tonight to beat her to the fabulous new waiter. As midnight approaches, she applies fresh make-up and curses her.

At five past twelve, we're left with one switch-board light bulb each. Then, with an almost audible ping of relief, my bulb extinguishes. "*Shit*!" LaToya wails. "When are mine gonna get back? If I'm not at the club soon, that *bitch* Sophie's gonna make a real move on him, I know she is . . ."

"You go, Toya," I say. "Go on. It won't be much longer."

"Oh, Ro—you're the best! You sure?"

"Sure I'm sure. I can't stand seeing you so tensed up. You're gonna explode in a minute!"

She plants a big warm kiss on my cheek, squeaks, "I owe you, OK?" and darts out of the door.

Alone in the cupboard, I sit and glare at the last light bulb.

Go on, you stupid little isolated fairy light, give up, die! No one likes you!

It continues to glow, stubbornly. I check my watch. Twelve fifteen. OK, *Room 347, time's up*. I reach for the sheet of parents' details, and discover that Room 347 belongs to Ms. Debbie Arbuckle, and her place of escape is the exclusive Shivers restaurant at the far side of the hotel complex.

Bet she's on her way back to her room. But still, I'll call just in case.

The maître d' at Shivers is excessively snotty with me. He tells me to hold the line and then leaves me hanging on for hours. I'm poised there, waiting for the light to go out, waiting for the phone to be picked up. Neither happens. Then a breathless, urgent female voice is gushing into the receiver. "Honey—can you give me another hour? I'll pay you! I'll pay you well! Fifty? Fifty dollars till one a.m.—well, say one fifteen? Is that a deal? Honey?"

"Er—"

"Oh, say *yes* for Chrissake—this is—I *need* this time! He's almost—he's gonna—I'll make it a hundred. A full hundred dollars. Honey? Is it a deal?"

Sheer greed kicks in. "Ycs!" I squawk. "OK, I'll stay. Until one fifteen, OK? You'll come to the babysitting room then?"

"Yes!" she squawks. "I know it! I've done this before!"

I bet you have, I think, as I say goodbye.

Next I dial the Crescent Moon Bar, and Landon picks up. "Hey, babe! Thought you forgot me!"

I tell him what's happened. He crows, congratulates me, and I beg him to wait for me. "I can't walk through that wood on my own," I trill, all girly-girly frail. "Not at one thirty in the morning. I just can't."

"Sure," he says. "I'll come over to you. Soon as I'm finished up here."

I fall over myself thanking him. Then, with a flash of plotting genius, I tell him I'll use the loot to treat him on his next day off.

"No need for that, Ro," he replies, genially.

Yes there is, you idiot, I want to get you on your own for a day! "Look, Landon—I couldn't *do* this if you weren't gonna walk back with me! The money—it's morally half yours!"

"*Morally!*" he scoffs.

"We can go out somewhere. Have a good time."

"OK," he agrees. "Great. Hey—you seen a baseball game yet?"

My heart sinks a bit. I'm not into sport at the best of times and baseball games on TV always look so comprehensively naff. "Er, no, but—"

"You got to. Seriously, you can't come to the US and not see a game."

"OK, let's do that!" I say. Face it, I'd happily

visit a chicken-processing factory as long as it was alongside him.

"This guy I know at the bar? He was talking 'bout getting tickets for the big game Saturday. I told him I didn't have the money, but if you're *serious* . . ."

"Sure I'm serious. Tell him you want two. Will a hundred dollars cover it?"

"More than. We can have a blast . . . spend the whole day there. I can get Saturday off, what about you?"

"I'm sure I can," I say happily, savouring the phrase *whole day there*. "I think I'm down for Friday but I'm sure I can swap."

"That's great," he says. "I'll be right over."

Blissfully, I put the phone down.

Around twenty to one the door handle turns, and Landon's suddenly there in the dark little room with me. "Hi, Ro-anne," he murmurs, sitting down on the edge of the switchboard.

"Hi," I say, trying not to squeak.

"You OK?"

"Yeah. Thanks for coming. It's creepy in here on your own."

"Let me listen." I watch him as he puts on the earphones, grunts, tosses them down again and says, "Still snoring." Then, like it's the logical thing to do next, he leans forward, puts an arm round my neck and kisses me. Maybe it's the way we're spaced out but it's better, less mouth-mashing. Just as I'm really getting into it he pulls away and groans, "This is gonna kill my back." Then he grins at me, takes hold of my arms and pulls me up from my chair. He's sitting, I'm standing between his spreadeagled legs, my face just a little higher than his. I wind my arms round his neck, and kiss him again. And then we're off, and I'm thinking how much better it's got, how much more in tune, my mouth on his, our tongues moving, his body pressed close . . . "This isn't the best place to be making out," he breathes.

"Why?"

"No lock on the door . . ."

I smile at him like I'm agreeing, but inside I'm not. That's exactly why it's a great place. You can't just jump into good intimacy, you've got to take it slow. And over the next half hour or so, we take it wonderfully slow. Talking a little, laughing. Kissing, hugging, cuddling, stroking. As he'd say— *making out.*

Then like a slap the door's yanked open. I spring back from him, grab the earphones that I'd totally forgotten. Thank *God*—gentle breathing.

"Still asleep!" I gasp as nonchalantly as I can to who can only be Ms. Debbie Arbuckle. She's got big, *big* peach-coloured hair and an equally gigantic cleavage, and she's already rummaging in her glossy handbag.

"Thanks, honey!" she raps out. "Here—*damn*—only got seventy. Seventy OK?"

I'm about to bleat, "Of course," when Landon breaks in with, "But you said a hundred."

She glares at him. "Who the hell are you?"

"Her manager."

"Her manager my ass! You two look like you've been enjoying yourself in here, and you wanna charge *me*—"

"*Charge* you? You made a deal! Now come on—why don't we just walk along to the shopping concourse where the ATMs are?"

"I can't leave my baby that long. I have to get back to the room."

Blank-faced, Landon holds the earphones out to her. "Here. Listen. Like she said—fast asleep. You can get the cash and be back at your room within twenty minutes if we move it. Twenty minutes is the time left between babysitting checks, isn't it, Ro?"

"Yes, but—"

"So come on—let's move it."

She glares at him, but if she delays to argue it'll look like she's not putting her kid's needs first, won't it? So she swivels round on her terrifying pink stilettos and stomps ahead of us to the concourse.

Ten minutes later, I'm giggling slightly hysterically as we romp our way over the golf course and into the trees. "You were so rude back there! I'd've taken the seventy!"

"Aw, come on—did you see the bag she had? And the *jewels* on her neck? She was *loaded.*"

"I s'pose—"

"For all *she* knew you gotta pay me for getting you back—"

"I *am* going to! Hey—take the money now."

We've reached the end of the woods. A half moon has risen and it's shining over the lake, giving me just enough light to delve into my purse and come out with the hundred dollars.

Landon takes it. "You sure?" he says.

For a brief moment, I'm not sure. I'm not sure I'll ever see the tickets. Then I say, "Sure I'm sure."

He puts his arm round me and smooches into my hair. "No point in asking you back to my cabin, I guess?"

For a few seconds I'm seriously tempted, but I

shake my head. "What is it with you Americans and *pressure*?"

"Sorry. *Sorry*. You just really turn me on." Then he kisses me above the ear.

Tonight has been the *best*.

CHAPTER 40

My Dear Rowan,

How very nice and reassuring to get your lovely letter. I'm so glad things have worked out for you, and you have a good place to stay. Flossy is doing well now, although we had the most awful tantrums when Sharon discovered you were gone. I persuaded Taylor to let me take Flossy away for a little vacation at the beach. She had a lovely time, paddling and making sandcastles. When we got back things had calmed down, and they asked we to stay for a while longer. Sharon says she can't trust nannies any more.

I put a stop to half the things in Flossy's ridiculous schedule—I can't manage it at my age. And I must say she seems a lot calmer and happier as a result. Hardly any nightmares

*now! I'm teaching her to knit and bake, like
a real Polish granny!
With love to you, dear,
Stasia Bielicka*

Also in the envelope—which I collect the next
day from the hotel mail center on the way back
from eight gruelling hours in the nursery—is a
great drawing of a sandcastle manned by turquoise
crabs with *To Rowan from Flossy xxxx* on it. As I take
it into the kitchen to stick it up, I reflect that the
disappearance of Flossy's nightmares might have
something to do with her life being less busy, but
it's also got everything to do with Babcia being
there.

Stay on, Stasia Bielicka, I think, as I pin Flossy's
picture to the wall. Stay on with your grand-
daughter.

Two days go by, and I don't see Landon. Our
free time just doesn't coincide. I'm going crazy
with wanting to see him. I hang around the lake,
walk past the gym, go into his bar. No sign. I can't
bring myself to ask about him. Or leave him a note,
tucked into his doorframe. I don't want to look
that desperate. And I want him to come after *me*.

"Jesus, Rowan—you with him or not?" nags

Toya, when I wail to her. "Didn't you make any *arrangements* to see each other?"

"No. Making arrangements—that's not really his thing. It's all about—you know—spontaneity."

"Oh, brother. You gotta start laying some ground rules. You tell him you gotta start organizing your shifts so you can see more of each other."

"I don't think he'd know what I was talking about. I don't think he knows what *organize* means."

"Then you explain it to him, girl. Or you'll *reorganize* his face."

The trouble is, Toya's kind of no-nonsense thinking just doesn't work down at the lake. The way Landon and Ben and Rick talk about it, people just drift together, have a good time, go with the flow. Everyone acts as unlike the pulsing efficient mega-organization that is the hotel as possible— they don't plan *anything*. I don't want to break the unwritten rules, do I? I don't want to look uptight and over-anxious.

I spend the early evening sitting with Iggy by the lakeside, eating crisps (or chips as I should call them now) and an avocado pear. I try and make myself enjoy the absolute stillness and beauty surrounding me, but my brain's on a fast-spin of tangled-up longings, plots, analysis and fears. And I'm trying not to look too closely at the fact that the baseball tickets still haven't appeared. In the end, I head up to the gym for one of the free sessions Clint promised me, and work very hard on the rowing machine and the weights. It exhausts me, but it doesn't stop me feeling uptight and over-anxious, or looking at the door the whole time, praying Landon will walk in.

The next day is Friday, and I have a gruelling double session at Kiddie Heaven, easily the nastiest shift combination. There's never time for a proper lunch break; Toya and I have had to get skilful at stealing tiny sandwiches and cakes from the kids' buffet lunch. I promise myself that today, the last day before the baseball match, Landon will appear with the tickets. From eight o'clock on, I'm scanning the windows, fixated on the door. As the day crawls to its four o'clock close, my stomach feels as though it's set in concrete. I race back to my cabin, sure he'll be by the lake, or there'll be a note on the door—*something*.

Nothing.

I limp into my bedroom and crawl between the sheets, wanting oblivion. I gaze at the light skidding across the whitewashed wooden walls, at the twisty vine making its way through the half-open window, trying to empty my mind of all of it.

The next thing I know I'm waking with a start, heart racing. It's almost dark and I feel like I've been asleep forever, and for a moment I don't even know where I am . . . then I realize what's woken me up.

Outside, there's a party going on.

I pull on my kimono, speed over to the open window, and peer out. A fire's flickering down by the lake, flashing reflections across the water. A little CD player is cranking out sounds but you can hear joshing and laughter above it. I count nine people—sitting around, moving about, beer bottles in their hands.

Landon's sprawled on the ground talking to a girl I've never seen before. He's got a joint in his hand. He looks like a fallen angel, smoke wreathing about his head. Rick's next to them, chatting to a guy I don't recognize. Ben's poking at the fire. Clint's there, arm round a stunning Japanese girl.

And I feel so left out, so forgotten, I want to cry.

No, I don't. I want to get a machine gun and splatter them all with bullets . . .

Calm, it girl. Cool. But why didn't Landon come and knock for me, why didn't he tell me this was going to happen, why didn't he invite me . . . ?

Right.

Fifteen minutes later I've done my face, brushed my hair, pulled on my favourite summer skirt and a casual but sexy top. The long sleep has done my looks good. I approve myself in the mirror and sashay out, barefoot. My heart's thumping but I'm acting calm, indifferent. No one notices me. I walk on across the sandy ground towards the group. At last, Ben glances up from tending the fire. "Hey, Ro!" he calls.

I don't answer him. I'm looking at Landon. Whose head has lifted at the sound of my name and who's looking straight at me . . .

"*Ro!*" he calls, all enthusiastic surprise, which could be genuine or guilt-fuelled. "Hey—you *were* there! I gave you a shout a while back but I thought you were out . . ."

"I was," I say. "Out for the count. I was knackered."

"Well—come and join us, babe! We got steaks—I promised you a steak, right?"

"Yeah, you did," I say. *Except*, I think, *I thought it was just going to be the two of us.*

I'm right up there now, near the fire. The girl on the ground next to Landon glances at me, face full of hostility. I'm waiting for Landon to stand up,

or pull me down next to him—to *claim* me.
"Wanna beer?" he asks, breezily. "Over there. We
got a case."

"Perks of being a bartender," slurs Ben.

"Right. And the perks of being a waiter—"

"Free steaks!"

"*Yeah!*"

They're off again with their sick-making
buddy-buddy bonding routine. Ben hunkers down
beside Landon, takes the joint off him. Frozenly, I
fetch myself a bottle of beer and inexpertly knock
the top off on the side of the box. I won't sit down
beside them, not with hostile-girl there. At last,
Landon gets to his feet. "Better check the fire," he
mumbles, heading over. "Think it's hot enough?"

"Yeah, I do," says Ben, exhaling. "Slap 'em on."

From the corner of my eye, I can see hostile-
girl scrambling to her feet too. With viper-speed,
I'm at Landon's side. "Want any help?" I murmur.

And *hallelujah* he puts his arm round me, hugs
me to him. "Sure," he says. "You wanna unwrap
these?" He picks up a bleeding, paper-wrapped
parcel and hands it to me. I take it, reverently. And
like some cheesy cooking duo on the telly, we work
together, oiling the steaks and laying them out on
the grill. "Where've you been?" he says. "How come
you never came up to the bar to see me?"

The concrete in my stomach melts away. "I didn't know when you were working," I reply, casual as all hell. "How come you never came to the nursery to see me?"

"The nursery? I knocked on your cabin a couple times."

"Yeah? I was out."

"Thought you were avoiding me."

The concrete in my stomach has been replaced by clowns and jugglers. I flash a triumphant grin at hostile-girl, who lies on her back, stares at the sky and gives up all hope of Landon. Whose brow is furrowed gorgeously with concentration as he rubs salt into the meat. It's already starting to brown over the flames, give off a good smell—I realize I'm starving. I take another swig of beer and lean towards him. "Looking forward to tomorrow?"

"The game? *Yeah*. Hey—I got 'em!" He rummages in his jeans pocket, pulls out some dog-eared tickets. "Haven't let them outta my sight. I've *slept* with them."

"You hang onto them," I laugh. "They're safer with you."

"We need to go at nine. That too early for you?"

"No. I'll be ready."

"It's gonna be terrific. The Giants have really

upped their game since last season, they're—"

He breaks off. Dope-induced hysteria has broken out on the ground, centerd round Rick. "No, I'm telling you, man," he's gurgling. "It's next to the women's johns and it's called a *Baby Changer*."

"It's a room for changing *diapers* in, man!"

"Nah, nah—it's where you trade your baby in for something else! It's like—like a *money* changer!"

"So whaddya change 'em for?" interjects Landon, forgetting about telling me about the Giants.

"You change 'em for—I dunno, man."

"Maybe a baby something else."

"A piglet!"

"A squidlet!"

"What's a squidlet, man?"

"A baby *squid*. Everyone knows that!"

They're all nearly pissing themselves now, they think it's so funny, and they go over the whole thing all over again, with further embellishments. I glare at Landon as he snorts and guffaws. *If you weren't so great-looking, mate . . .*

I feel like I'm falling in and out of love with him the whole time. It's exhausting.

At least he's the first to stop giggling. A steak spits, and he turns back to the grill and starts turning the meat, rubbing on more oil . . . I look at the side of his face as he works, and it comes into my head that tomorrow will be the Final Test. OK, when other people are around, when there's loads of stuff going on, he's going to get distracted, isn't he, and because with every fibre of my being I want him to be totally focused on me, I get upset, and hate him for it, but if we had something more real, more solid going underneath, then tonight would be fun, tonight would be *great* . . .

Tomorrow, I'll have him all to myself. Tomorrow, I'll find out what's he's really like.

Tomorrow I'll find out if we're on or off.

We drink more beer, eat the steaks, put more wood on the fire and lounge about on the forgiving ground as the night gets black and stars come out above us. The fire keeps spurting up showers of sparks and the dope-heads *ooh* and *aaah* over this like it was a firework display. Landon stretches out beside me on the ground, and without warning kind of gathers me up, and starts kissing me, flowing into it all relaxed as though we'd last snogged three minutes ago, not three days.

Tomorrow, it's all hanging on *tomorrow*.

WE GET TO THE BASEBALL stadium after a long bus ride (one change) at around eleven in the morning. Ben has agreed to look out for Iggy so we can stay as long as we like. Both of us have got Sunday off too. Everything's in place for it to be the best weekend of my life.

The bus ride isn't exactly thrilling, mainly 'cos Landon sleeps for most of it, but five minutes after arriving at the stadium, I decide I've seriously underestimated baseball. It's like one huge friendly party—like a fiesta. There's crowds of happy people milling about, buying beer and hot dogs, claiming the same-team supporters as friends, the others as enemies; there's loud music, fireworks, cheerleader displays . . . "This," I announce, "is a lot more fun than being forced to watch rugby in the freezing mud." Landon laughs, takes hold of my hand, and we find our seats. There's only ten minutes to go till the first pitch and the stadium is seething with excitement. The sun's beating down on us; I lather suncreen on my face and arms, stretch out my legs to deepen their tan. And then, to a great roar from the crowd, the teams run out.

The way to enjoy baseball, I decide, is vicariously. I love Landon explaining it all to me, I love the way he's excited by it. Most of all I love being this close to him while he's so involved in something else—a something else that isn't another person, that doesn't exclude me. It's a bit like he's in a cage, a cage made by his involvement in the game, and I can reach him through the bars and touch him and stroke him but he's not going to suddenly turn and focus on me. It's *dead* erotic.

At the seventh inning, the Giants are three points up, and Landon's on a high of tension and excitement. He fetches more beer, and then he looks at me properly for the first time since play started, and says, "Ro—this is awesome. I can't believe I'm seeing this live. Thanks for this—seriously." Then he kisses me on the mouth, and asks, "Are you enjoying it, babe?"

"Yes," I answer, with total honesty. "I'm loving every minute."

The Giants win, 9–3. We join the triumphant army leaving the stadium, find a bar that isn't quite full to bursting point, and squeeze together on a bench in the corner. I put my hand on his leg and realize that something's happened to me. Before, I was mad about him—his looks, his voice, the way he moved—I was excited by him, seriously after him. But now, spending a whole day like this, touching him, holding hands, our mouths always close together, relaxing into each other . . . now I'm addicted. I'm addicted and I've got to have him and I don't even want to think what cold turkey would be like.

But it's weird, we've stopped talking. After the excitement of the match finishing and pushing through the crowds to get here, we've both fallen silent. I feel awful about it. In the end I pluck up courage and croak, "What's wrong?"

"What do you mean?"

"I dunno, it's gone all awkward, it's—it's like we've got nothing to say to each other any more."

"That's because we don't wanna *talk*," he says, staring hard at my hand on his leg. "We wanna do other things together than—*talk*." I go hot red. He won't look at me. "I know what you're thinking," he mutters. "I know you think I've been trying to jump you beginning from the beginning and now you're thinking that's the worst line you've ever heard. Well, it's not a line, it's *true*. Right from the beginning, when we first met—I thought you looked great, I really wanted you. I can't always think of things to say when I want you this bad. There. I said it."

He turns his full concentration on his empty beer bottle; he looks almost grumpy. I want to fling myself at him, bite his ears, hug him half to death. Instead, I go and buy him another beer.

What is it that makes you decide to sleep with someone? Has anyone ever analysed this? Has he changed, have I changed? Whatever, everything's changed. On the bus on the way back we're wrapped round each other. We still don't say much but it's kind of understood that we're not going to go into separate cabins when we get back.

The note tucked into Landon's door is written in red lipstick. Which when you think about it tells me all I need to know right there and then. All it says is: *Guess who's here?* The "o" in who is drawn like a little heart. And there's a single cross. A single kiss.

"SHIT," BREATHES LANDON, "SHIT."

I can't bear the way his face has changed, his whole face. I've never seen him look like this before. Kind of scared and happy and awed and excited and God-knows-what, all at the same time. "It's Coco," I mutter, "isn't it."

"Yeah. Shit—*yeah*. This is so like her. Saying she's not coming, then showing up—"

Why aren't I fighting for him? Why don't I say—but you're with me now?

"Where's she likely to be?" I ask.

"At the bar. She would've gotten a job there. Cocktail waitress."

"You'd better go and see her then," I say. "Hadn't you."

He turns towards me. "Look," he mumbles, "I have to talk to her. Ro—I meant what I said, in the bar. And today has been the best. I—"

"Go and sort it out," I mutter. Then I turn away, and walk to my cabin.

I spend the next three hours sitting alone on my cabin floor, face resting against the back of the sofa. Iggy's tail swishes occasionally; apart from that everything is still. As the minutes tick by and Landon still doesn't come, I feel like the pain is slowly dissolving my heart.

Around ten thirty, there's a knock at the door, and I open it. If I had any hope left at all, it withers away when I see Landon's face. Wordlessly, I turn, and he follows me into the room.

I don't recognize him. He looks high, elated; but he also looks small, somehow. Shifty, dirty. His eyes keep sliding away from me.

"Ro-anne, I feel terrible," he mutters. "Leaving you like that, after the great day we had."

"S'OK," I lie. "So—was she there?"

"Yup. She's back."

"And you're—"

"We're . . . we're back together, yeah. We've been talking all this time, and . . . Look, I feel terrible. You and me—we could've had something together, I know that. I'm just glad we didn't get further than—you know—fooling around—"

Inside, I flinch. If he's that stupid—*if he's that stupid*—I don't want him near me any more. I'm so

327

hurt I want to hurt him back as hard and as bad as I can, but all I can think of to say is, "Look, it's OK. It's no big deal."

I can't tell from his face if he's even registered what I said. He's backing towards the door. "I hope we can be friends, Ro, yeah?"

And, God help me, I say, "Yeah."

CHAPTER 43

I ONLY HAVE TO WAIT another twelve hours to meet Coco.

When Landon leaves I anaesthetize myself with a couple of beers, howl and sob myself quietly into exhaustion, then sleep. The next morning I let Iggy out and go for a long swim in the lake, crossing it three times. If I'm crying or swimming I'm not thinking, and the one thing I don't want to do is think. I want to feel numb. I can't bear to analyse, go over what-might-have-beens, what-I-should-have-dones . . . not yet.

Out of the lake, I scurry back to my cabin, get myself ready for the afternoon shift. I make myself swallow some toast and tea in lieu of both breakfast and lunch. I'm longing to get in among the brats, and let their demands and chatter fill my head.

I turn from locking up my cabin to see Landon and a girl heading out of his door. She's very slim, very gorgeous, very blonde. She looks far too polished to be roughing it down by the lake; she's even wearing heels. I look at her and know what Landon and I had really is over.

I feel sick with jealousy and hurt. I make myself walk forward.

Landon's staring at the ground. "Hi, Ro," he mutters. "Coco, this is Rowan."

I hate her. I greet her, acting warmly. She greets me back. And then she's off; explaining how she got here, how she decided at the last moment "to give this guy just one more chance," how Landon and she have this weird love-hate relationship but they can't keep away from each other . . . As she speaks, her hand is running up his arm, snaking round his shoulder, touching his face . . .

I make my face into a pleasant listening mask, block out what she's saying. I wonder if she has any idea who I am, how I got here. I think she must have because what she's saying is so pointedly possessive.

Her face is round, kind of sensual, wide-lipped, and it never stops moving. She changes expression the whole time. On some people it might look mad; on her it's compulsive, fascinating. Her energy is extraordinary: strong and hot and exciting. Landon's bewitched, I swear he is. He's gazing at her and he looks—*enslaved*.

". . . but we're not gonna stay down in that cabin, are we, Lando? That was last year. You can't repeat things. That hippy scene, by the lake and everything—"

"I *liked* that scene," says Landon, in this cutesy, reproving, lovey-dovey voice.

"Aw, *baby*. That was last year. You have to move on—do *fresh* stuff. Anyway, it gives me the creeps, just the *owls*. I want more than *owls*. There's some really great people staying around where I am—really *fun* people. And you should *see* my room!"

"But babe—it's in the basement!"

"They're *all* in the basement, Lando! Anyway—it's *huge*. And I sweet-talked my way into a suite."

"Only 'cause the manager's got the hots for you."

Coco shrills out a laugh. "You're jealous! Sweetie—you're jealous!"

At this point I break in, because I can't bear any more. "I have to go," I croak. "I'll be late."

When I tell her what's happened, La Toya is furious with Landon and kind to me. Even Maria is kind when she finds me crying in the side room later that day. She tells me I'm far too good for "that stupid boy" and lets me off early. La Toya makes me come out with her that evening, even though she was planning at having another crack at the beautiful waiter. "C'mon," she says, "we both need to meet new *guys*. We need to start over!"

I feel weird, disembodied, that night, like I'm acting badly in a bad film. I go through with it, though, because Toya is being such a good mate to me. I even dance. She tells me how she admires me, how well I'm dealing with it.

Three weeks go by, and I carry on acting like I'm dealing with it. I don't see much of Landon. He's living pretty permanently with Coco now, in her basement suite, although he still spends the odd night in his cabin, sometimes with her, sometimes on his own.

We're well into August; the sun blazes down and there's a haze of heat over the lake. Iggy's taken to spending the nights as well as the days outside, which he achieves by the simple method of refusing to be found at sunset. I unhook his lamp heater from over the sofa and stow it away, and the room looks better. I love my cabin. I love just being there, sitting out on the deck, waking up to the streaming light and the bird calls.

Ben and Rick kind of close round me, filling the gap that Landon left. Ben's sweet to me— inviting me over when he's cooked something, rounding me up to go cycling, or into town to the movies. For Ben, Landon's a taboo subject, but Rick likes to talk about him. He tells me what Landon and Coco are up to. He particularly likes dropping hints that their sex life is something else.

More young hotel workers move into the cabins round the lake, and we form a good, changing group; we go swimming together, and have barbecues at night. The day I learn from home that I've got the grades to get into Warwick University, we have a big celebration going on half the night. I work hard in the nursery, I party, I work out in the gym, courtesy of Clint. I make friends with a lovely girl called Kay in the spa and she lets me relax there and gives me free manicures, free leg-waxes. I'm looking good and I know it and several guys make a move on me and I think about going out with them but in the end I turn them down. One of them—a barman, Charlie—really likes me. He flatters me, gives me free drinks.

All in all, my life's pretty sorted. I'm the British nanny, the one with the wacky pet iguana who rides on her shoulder, the one who lives by the lake and knocks about with La Toya. All in all, it's a pretty good way to spend a summer.

Except sometimes I think it's not how I'm really spending it. Sometimes I think I'm just dealing every hour, every minute with a jealousy so hungry it's threatening to eat me up. Just the sight of Landon in the distance sends my heart thudding and crashing. When I'm with other people I'm fine, but when I'm on my own, he comes in again. Then it's like I'm living in what-might-have-been. I keep thinking back to the time Landon tried to make love to me in my cabin, or on the rock in the lake. I keep thinking what I'd do now.

One memorable Saturday I'm eating in the Redwood Diner and he comes in on his own and walks across and joins me. He acts shifty, guilty. He mumbles about how he hopes we can still be friends; he says he misses me. He says he regrets what a pushy idiot he was, at the start. Then he says he's "glad it never really turned into anything" with me or he'd feel he acted like a real shit. I make out everything's cool, what we had wasn't important and it's water under the bridge, just friends now, blah blah. I'm not at all sure why I do this. Then I look at his face and think I'm going to start crying so I say I have to go, and I get up and leave.

After that, I act like his friend, and I act like Coco's friend, even though I hate her. They come down to the lake occasionally, join in a barbecue. Sometimes I bump into them at the hotel. Coco partronizes me, puts on a sexy display with Landon in front of me. I don't know if he's told her about us or if some sixth sense warns her how much I like him, but she really rubs my nose in what they've got together. I watch her flirt with other guys, on a mission to get Landon jealous, and I watch her succeeding. I watch them fight, then make up again, publicly and passionately. One night she throws a glass at him, and he ducks and it drops and smashes on the floor. She storms out and my heart's in my mouth—and then he rushes after her.

It makes me mad, that I'm like this, so obsessed still. I unburden myself to Mel in long, angry, anguished letters. She answers every one, telling me I'm worth twenty of Landon, telling me to move on.

I know I'm waiting, though. Waiting for something to happen.

And then one day, it does.

PART FOUR

ESCAPE FROM EDEN

IT'S A DAY THAT STARTS well. Rick collides with me as we're both on our way to work and tells me Landon and Coco have had another massive bust-up. "*Really* serious this time," he says, watching my face. "*Mega*."

I pretend to be indifferent but I'm not. And even though I'm on a double shift, and the kids are dreadful, all day I feel weirdly excited, kind of powerful and predatory, and they don't get me down. I walk back through the Magic Woods, and feel good. I think of all the people back in London, squeezed on to the Underground with their senses shut down, and I want to laugh out loud. Grass is swishing past my legs, grasshoppers jumping around my feet. Shafts of sun light up my arms, and there's a strange bird calling in the trees ahead of me.

I skirt round the shining lake, all cool and

alluring with its soft fringe of big-leaved plants. The midday sun's just reached the steps of my cabin deck and it's spreading like honey over the wooden boards. There's no sign of Iggy. I call him a few times, kick my shoes off, and walk across the warm wood to the cabin door. Once inside I stand there for a moment or two, just lapping up the freedom and the silence. *All mine*, I think, *all mine*. I wander into the bedroom, strip off my clothes. I'm going to pull my bikini on, and get a cold beer, and sit out on the deck in the heat, and then maybe swim . . .

The mirror in the corner is showing me my reflection, head to toe. I advance on it, smiling, liking my body more than I've ever liked it before. I look thinner, fitter, tanned. My arms—they've got shape now. Gym-shape, swimming-shape. I lift them, admiring the way my silver bracelets clash across my skin. My tits look terrific. More swimming-shape. And why aren't there elegies to the beauty of pubic hair? Mine's gorgeous. Sunlight from the low window is streaking across it and it's *glinting*. I think—the guy who gets you, Rowan, is blessed among men. Oh, yes he *is*.

Wake up, Landon! Ditch that bottle-blonde bitch and come to me!

I pull on my red bikini, and head for the fridge.

I grab a beer and a nectarine to tempt Iggy with, go out on to the porch and subside on to the warm wood. The sun's still hot, full on my face. The silence is absolutely absolute, apart from a faint, soothing rustling from the shady trees growing on the far side of the lake with their thirsty roots snaking into the water.

Oh, God, I want him. Oh, God, it's not fair. Why did that psychotic cow have to come back to claim him?

I open the beer and as I slurp I spreadeagle my legs and admire them, all shiny since Kay's free leg-wax. I wonder if my toenails need repainting, decide they'll do another day. Self love—is it a substitute for real love? Nope—it just makes you feel more cheated if you haven't got it.

There's a familiar scritching sound, coming from the side of the deck. "Iggy!" I call. "Iggy—*you* love me, don't you, baby?" He plods into view, lizard-smiling, and canters towards me. "You're *beautiful*, Iggy. Look at your scales all shiny in the sun." I take a big bite out of the nectarine and hold the rest out to him, and he nuzzles into it, slurping up the juice, scoffing it luxuriously. He's looking older. His head—it's fiercer now, more mature. "You *sure* you're not under a spell, Iggy?" I murmur. "Like the frog prince? About to turn into a gorgeous bloke totally in love with me . . ." I plant a quick kiss on his cool head.

"Hey!"

I look up, and with a thump to the heart see Landon. He'd padded up on bare feet and I hadn't heard a thing. Oh lord, he's beautiful. Hair spiked up, still wet from swimming. Sexy grin, white teeth, White T-shirt over scruffy shorts showing a tan like mahogany.

I want him so much I'm melting into the deck, I've got a hot core inside me right down from my throat that's melting into the deck and I can't move.

"Hey," he calls again. "Girl and lizard. You two look great."

"Hi," I call back, faintly. I scan past him for Coco, but she's not there.

"You just finished your shift?"

"Yup." I take a sip of beer. "Been for a swim?"

"I've been floating," he says. "It's so amazing. The sky . . . and the water . . ."

"You've been smoking too, haven't you?"

He laughs. "A little. You going in the lake?"

"In a while. Want a beer?"

"You got enough?"

"Charlie gave me another couple of six-packs."

He comes nearer, right up to the deck steps,

and laughs up at me. "Ro-anne, Charlie *wants* you! He's crazy about you! I can't drink beer that he gave you as . . . as some kind of *love* token!"

I laugh back, preening. "Don't have any then. But it's great. Ice-cold."

He's loping up the steps towards me. I remind myself to breathe. Even his *feet* are sexy, for God's sake. Brown and flexible. "If I join you," he asks, "will Iggy get jealous?"

First Charlie, now Iggy, getting jealous. He thinks men *want* me! Well—a man and a lizard, anyway. "Iggy'll be fine," I say, "as long as you don't want any of his nectarine."

"Just—I saw you making out with him. Thought I might be interrupting something."

"*Making out* with him!" I scoff, hoping like hell he didn't hear all the stuff about frog princes. "Go on, get yourself a beer."

He wanders into the soft gloom of the cabin. I shut my eyes, waiting, and in my head a film's unrolling—me following him into the cabin, him turning and us just *knowing*, and then melting together, falling together, magically shedding most of our clothes on the way to the floor, kissing like crazy, like those first times only hotter, much hotter, and then, *then*—

"Ro?"

I snap my eyes open. "Yeah?"

"Nothing. You looked kind of weird."

I gulp. "Just—thinking."

"What about?"

"Oh—the day I've had. You know." My mind flips hastily back to the day I've had, decades away now. "How I *hate* kids some of the time. *Most* of the time."

"*All* of the time?" He flops down beside me, and prods Iggy, who ignores him. Then he pulls the ring on his beer, and lounges full length on the deck, propped up on one elbow. I get this huge compulsion to lie down beside him and stretch out face to face, but I stay sitting, back against the warm wooden wall. "You should get a bar job, Ro," he says. "You should. The tips you'd get—seriously. Just put on that fancy accent, and *wham*."

I laugh, and go into the accent. "Kin I get yew another beer, sah?"

"Yeah. *Yeah*!"

"Maybe some bar-snecks? Peanuts, sah? Eow—*sorry*—I tipped them deown your trisers!"

"God, it's so sexy! You should talk like that all the time!"

"*Pervert*. What—you into upper class English-women or something? Riding crops, and . . . and bugles?"

"*Bugles*?"

"For fox hunting."

"That's *beagles*."

"*No*—that's dogs—bugles are the *horns*!"

"*Horns?* English women have *horns*?" He rolls on to his back, guffawing.

"Only the very posh ones!" We're both laughing now, and it's weird, it's like we're back before Coco turned up, or even better, and I know he's half-stoned, but even so . . . "I might just do it," I gasp. "Go for the bar job, I mean. Or I'm gonna end up killing one of those little kids. Especially Jordan."

"Bad, huh?"

"Yes—he's horrible. He hits me to get my attention. Like—really whacks me, with a toy car or something. Or if he's near enough, like across the table from me? He reaches out and slaps my face."

"*Jesus*. You *should* kill him. We could bury him out here, in the woods."

"Or row him out to the middle of the lake and throw him overboard."

"Yeah! With a stone tied around his waist. So his skeleton doesn't float up one night and *point* at you, all, like, *accusing* . . ." He talons his fingers, makes a spooky *wrrrrgh* noise right in my face, so

347

I'm looking straight into his mouth. It's quite a turn-on. Iggy starts up from his doze, waddles bad-temperedly off to the deck railings, and scales them. "I love the way he does that," says Landon, as Iggy straddles the top bar with his tail and legs dangling, and closes his eyes again. "So laid-*back*. Iggy, you are one cool critter." Then he turns back to me. "Do it, Ro. Work with me in the bar. We can have a blast."

I take a deep breath, and risk it. "Won't Coco be a bit pissed off if I'm in the bar with you?"

There's a silence. Landon's looking down at the deck, twisting his beer can in his hand. *You've blown it, you prat,* I think, all anguished.

"She is anyway," he says.

"What?"

"Pissed. At me."

There's another silence, a golden one full of potential. Then I shrug, casual as all-hell, and say, "Why?"

"Dunno. I'm not . . . doing it right for her. *Being* right."

"How d'you mean?" I'm treading carefully here, half expecting him to shy away and want to drop the subject.

But he doesn't. "I dunno," he mutters. "I keep saying the wrong things. I keep really messing up."

"Oh no," I say, thinking, *Oh yes*. "What are you doing?"

"*Christ* knows. I'm not—into her enough, or something. Oh—you don't wanna hear me whining."

"S'OK," I shrug. "What're friends for?"

He smiles, all rueful. Then he goes on. "Like— she was waiting for me at the bar the other night, waiting for me to finish up. There was this guy sitting at the bar near her, a few seats down. He moves up next to her, tries to get in a conversation. She tells him to get lost—he gets lost. So fine, it's over, right?"

"Would've thought so, yeah."

"Not according to Coco, it's not. It's not over and it's *my fault*! I should've stepped in, I should've told him to get out. I should've been more *protective* or something . . ."

"But he hardly did anything! You just said—he left when she told him to!"

"Yeah, he did."

"And you couldn't be rude to a customer, could you?" I say, piling on the treachery to Coco. "I mean—not unless he tried to grope her, or something. It could be your job on the line."

"That's what I said to her," Landon says, looking straight at me again. "And she comes right back at me and screams that I'm being all—what was it?—superficial. Two-dimensional."

"Two-dimensional? What did she mean?"

"Beats me. Thing is, she wanted me to be jealous, or something. She's got some kind of mind-fuck going on, and she wants me to join in."

FanTAStic! This just keeps on getting better! Now—calm it, Rowan. Play this down. Don't show him you're desperate for Coco to screw up. "You'll get in her good books again," I say, aiming for a light tone.

And just as I'm kicking myself for the goody-two-shoes phrase, he mutters, "I don't think I want to. Not anymore."

I DON'T THINK I WANT to. *Not anymore.*

Those eight words, they're precious, like diamonds dropped into my open hand. I store them away in my mind so I can gloat over them later. So I can gloat over why he said them to *me.*

Landon stretches his arms out behind his head, a lovely, muscle-wrenching stretch, and mutters, "We're in Eden here, absolute fucking paradise, and she gets stressed and upset the whole time. She won't spend time down here—she says she wants to be up where the action is. She won't just—relax! Let it happen! I just *don't know* what her problem is."

I do, I think, *I know exactly what her problem is. You're absolutely drop-dead beautiful and she's on guard for every red-blooded female in the place falling for you. If I hadn't fallen for you myself I might even feel sorry for her.*

I take another slow sip of beer, all sympathetic but relaxed, casual. "So," I murmur, "what are you gonna do?"

He scrambles to his feet. "Go for another swim," he says, and strolls off down the steps without a backward glance. *Arrogant prat*, I think, begrudgingly admiring his retreating shoulders. He pulls his T-shirt over his head and drops it by the lakeside; I stare at his back as he just sort of tips over into the water, arms at his sides, like a tree being felled.

"Come on, Ro!" he splutters, as he comes up for air. "Get that fancy bathing suit wet!"

I feel embarrassed about standing up, walking towards him as he watches me. It's too much like the first time we swam.

He's standing up, facing me. The water's lapping round his waist. "Come on! What are you waiting for?"

Slowly, I get to my feet. *Remember your reflection*, I think. *Remember how great you looked in that reflection*. I start to walk down the steps towards him, holding my head up and my stomach in. *Take your time*, I tell myself. *Don't scuttle*.

He's watching me. I keep going towards him, and his eyes are glued on me. They're trying to stay on my face but they keep moving down, all over my body.

I'm starting to enjoy it. I walk on, reach the edge of the lake. "Come on in," he says. "Aren't you gonna get wet?"

Something's shifted in his voice, it sounds tighter. It's lust, I know it is. A great lovely burst of lust has shot up from his groin and got him by the throat. And it was me and my body that did it to him. He lifts an arm, slices a great splash of water towards me, and I dive through the plume and start swimming.

And he follows me. I cross the lake doing a furious crawl, heading for the trees at the other side of the lake. When I get there I grab hold of one of their snaky roots and pull myself out. I'm perched on a huge root, legs dangling in the water, by the time he reaches me. "You're like Iggy, sitting there!" he calls up, out of breath. "Iggy on a branch!" Then he grabs the end of the root and starts rocking it.

"Pack that in!" I squawk. "Pack that—" I break off as I fall, inelegantly, and hit the water shoulders first. I twist underwater, and as I'm plunging down, green water and weeds shooting past my open eyes, I'm thinking, *A mate would get him for this. He wants us to be mates—I'm allowed to get him!* I beat against the water, swim upwards, break the surface less than a metre away from him. He turns at the sound, and as he's turning I launch myself and land on his shoulders. I force his head under water, then I fall back, and swim clear before I can get totally overwhelmed at having grabbed him like that. "Got you!" I scream, as he comes up spluttering, "*Great* duck!"

"All RIGHT!" he roars, and starts pounding towards me. I turn and swim too, but he's on me too fast; he grabs me by the leg. I kick, trying to get free, and he lets go but lunges at me and gets hold of both my arms, right at the top.

Oh, *Jesus*. Suddenly we're face to face, tussling a bit, treading water in the lake. One of my straps has come down and it's caught on his thumb and he's pulling it away from my skin. Being held by him again—it's too fantastic to cope with. "*Pax!*" I gasp.

"*Pax?* What's that?"

"It's very posh English. Well—Latin. It's what posh kids say when they want to stop play-fighting."

He flexes his thumb again—the strap slides further down. "What if I don't wanna stop?"

Our legs have got entangled under the water. We're starting to sink. He lets go of my arms and on an absolute instinct I turn and start swimming for the other side again. That was enough, I say to myself, for now. *Jesus*, was that enough! I speed up a bit. I can remember the feel of his hands on my arms like they're still there. Oh, God, being face to face with him like that again. Body to body. I should've stayed. No, I shouldn't. It was *enough*. For now. He'll come after you, if he means what you want him to mean. He'll come after you, catch you up again.

I stop swimming, tread water again. I'm halfway across the lake and I can hear a girl shouting, shrill and furious. I scan the lakeside—and see Coco. In a short scarlet frock and matching sandals, hands on hips, leaning forward, shrieking . . .

"Oh, *shit*," Landon breathes, behind me.

He's drawing up beside me.

He came after me!

CHAPTER 46

"YOU FUCKING **BASTARD! THIS IS** why you couldn't come out to the *mall* with me? This is what you do when you get a really bad *headache*, you lying BAS-TARD?" Coco's hardly pausing to draw breath. Her face is all screwed up and she looks like a nasty little pug dog having a fit. *Fantastic!*

"Oh, holy *shit*," mutters Landon, again. "I'm in for it now."

"*Come out!*" screams Coco. "Come out of that water! How long has this been going on? *Landon!* How long have you and that British *bitch* been seeing each other?"

This is getting *wonderful*. If she doesn't scream her way into a total seizure and die, at least her hideous hysterical mad-lady act should put Landon off her for good. He starts to swim towards the shore and I catch him up and swim beside him, knowing that this will enrage her even more. "We were only having a *swim*," I murmur to him, sideways. "What's she on about?"

"I told you—it's the *jealousy* thing."

"Well, don't get all guilty about it, Landon, for God's sake. You've done nothing wrong."

"I got out of shopping with her—said I had a headache, a killer one."

"Which a nice cool *spontaneous* dip has helped fix, OK?"

He grins at me through the waves we're making. "OK! Wanna be my defense lawyer?"

We stop talking as we swim into the shallows, and then we both start wading towards Coco. She turns on me, spitting. Her face is as red as her dress and she looks satisfyingly ghastly. "What did you come with him for?" she shrieks. "I wanna see him *alone*!"

"Hey, calm down, Coco," I purr. "This is just the way out of the lake. I'm off to my cabin—you can see him on his own."

"Yeah, babe, *relax*," says Landon. "We were just swimming."

"That's not what it looked like from where I was standing! You—*lying shit*!"

"Oh, come on, Coco—cool it! Look—what's the point of trying to talk if you're like this?"

And he stops wading towards her, as if to

underline what he's just said. So I stop, too. Coco glares at me; her face looks like a boil that might suddenly burst. I turn a little more towards Landon, wrapping my arms round my body, holding my arms where he was holding me, making this brilliant cleavage.

"*Stay away from him, skank!*" screeches Coco "*Slut!*"

"Jesus, Coco—calm it!" says Landon.

"*I saw you back there!* You were *kissing*! You had your arms around her and you were kissing!"

"No, we weren't. We were just goofing around."

"Oh, *great*! How great for you both! When you *lied* to me about feeling too sick to go shopping—"

"The cold water helped my head. It made me feel better."

"Oh, what shit. *What're you smiling at*?" Coco turns on me.

"Coco—leave it," says Landon. "C'mon, let's go."

"Just because she's the hotel mattress doesn't mean *you* have to try her out!"

"Oh, I've heard *enough*," I interrupt loftily, adopting just a tinge of the posh-English that Landon said was so sexy. "You're going to be *so* embarrassed about this when you calm down,

Coco. Absolutely nothing was going on." I wade as elegantly as I can towards the shore, and Landon follows me.

"*I saw what I saw!*" she screeches, idiotically.

"Well, get your eyes tested, then."

"You—*fucking whore! Slut!*"

"And get tested for Tourette's syndrome while you're at it." She gawps—she's got no idea what I'm talking about. "And don't go around accusing *me* of being a slut," I add, forcefully. "You're a far bigger slut than I'll ever be!"

"*What is that supposed to mean?*" she screams—and breaks off. There's a rustling, dragging noise by her feet.

Iggy, roused by the commotion, has chosen that moment to stroll down to the lake to join us for his early-evening dip. Coco looks down just as Iggy looks up, straight at her, his wide lizard-mouth leering all friendly. He takes a step towards her, really close; his long reptile claws scrape against her toes in their pretty open-toed sandals. And the scream that exits her gob reverberates round the lake loud as forty firecrackers going off all at once, but not quite loud enough to drown out the snort of laughter at my side. I look up at Landon, and we exchange a brief conspiratorial grin.

"Didn't you *tell* her about Iggy?" I hiss.

"No!" he hisses back. "She doesn't like to talk about stuff that doesn't involve her."

Nice, I think, and wade on to dry land.

"*Get it away from me!*" she's wailing. "*Kill* it! Get a big stick or something!"

I leave it a few seconds more, hoping she might actually pass out or pee herself in fear, then I stoop down and scoop Iggy up.

"It's OK, Coco," I say, settling him across my shoulder, "it's only my iguana."

"You . . . you *sicko*!" splutters Coco, "you sick *bitch*!" but I'm striding off by the time the last obscenity is out. I can just imagine Iggy's wonderful green tail swishing stunningly on my brown back. I hope Landon's watching us.

"Thank you, Iggy, my mate," I whisper, as we reach our cabin. "That was brilliant." He stirs a bit, his claws rasping on my skin. "You can go for a swim later, promise. Just bear with me. This is called a *very—dramatic—exit*."

AFTER THAT, ALL I HAVE to do is wait. I wait first for
the screeching to die down by the lakeside, then I
wait a bit longer, for safety, then I let Iggy out for
his dip, as promised. Then I go back to the cabin,
pull on a flimsy white dress, go out to the porch,
and wait again.

Quite a bit of the time I spend reliving all the
delicious details of the afternoon. Such as when
Landon held on to me, when he swam after me.
And how horrific Coco was. How Landon *has* to be
in the throes of dumping her, right now. Dusk falls.
I'm starting to get restless. Where's Landon? Why
isn't he pounding up my cabin steps, maybe with
the marks of Coco's over-manicured talons on his
face, wanting sanity and sympathy?

To fill the time, I fix a big salad to share with Ig,
who doesn't eat much of it, possibly because he
stuffed himself to bursting point grazing by the

lake. I wait on. I make coffee. I make more coffee. The stars come out and glitter over the still water; the owl floats by, hooting mournfully.

I'm on my fifth cup of coffee when I finally see Landon weaving back to his cabin. He looks dazed, drunk maybe. *Shit!* This wasn't how it was meant to be! I stare at him, following his unsteady progress through the undergrowth, willing him to look up and notice me. But he doesn't. He reaches the steps to his cabin; I think, I can't bear it if he just disappears inside without a word. Then a few seconds later I crack and call out "Hey—Landon!"

He looks up. "Hey!" he calls back. For a horrible moment I think that's going to be it—I think he's going to carry on up the steps, go inside and shut the door. Then he adds, "You still up?"

"No, I've been asleep for hours."

"Oh yeah, ha ha. British sarcasm, right?"

"Right."

He ambles over towards me. And as he crosses the lozenge of light from my cabin window I see his face and I know without any doubt that not only has the bastard made it up with Coco he's almost certainly been spending the last few long hours having sex with her. He looks all kind of dopey and satiated and smug.

Shit, *shit*, *SHIT*! I want to throw a wobbly like Coco did back on the lakeside, I want to scream and rant and cry. I feel just as torn up, just as hurt as her—more hurt, probably, because I've got a fully functioning brain. But I can't throw a wobbly, can I—I've got no right to. She's the girlfriend; I'm just *someone*, someone he picked up on a Greyhound bus and *fooled around* with.

I've got to find out what happened, though. Maybe it's pure masochism, wanting the details— whatever, I want them. I squash down my hurt, plaster a smile on my face, lean one elbow on the porch rail, all carefree, and call down, "So did Coco forgive you then?"

"Guess so," he chuckles, smirking up at me. Briefly, I want very much to stab him. "Jesus, though, she's intense. *Wow*. She's like—over-powering."

"And you like that?" I croak.

He shrugs. "I told her I needed a night by myself. Figure stuff out." He starts climbing the steps towards me. "You look like a ghost in that nightie."

"It's not a nightie," I snap.

"Whatever. You're all kind of white in the night. You gonna give me a beer, Ro? I could kind of use one."

Keep on like this, I think savagely as I stomp into the cabin and get a couple more of Charlie's beers from the fridge, *please do keep on being an idiotic insensitive bastard like this. Then I'll get over you really fast and stop feeling like my heart's being minced in a meat-grinder.*

I walk back out on the porch. Landon has settled himself down comfortably on the deck. He looks wonderful, all spreadeagled and leggy. I hand him the beer with a big lump in my throat.

"I've been thinking about what you asked," he says.

"What?"

"Whether I liked her being all intense. Thing is—I don't feel like I've got a choice, you know? I mean—she rides over me. She stops shouting and takes me off to her room and first she cries and then she tells me she gets upset in *exact proportion* to how much she loves me. And then she shows me. She's all over me."

I leave a silence, trying to protect my mind's eye from seeing Coco *all over* him. Then I say, "I thought you were getting fed up with the games she plays."

"Games?"

"That's what you called it before. You know—mind-fucking."

He smiles, shakes his head lazily like he can't be bothered to answer. It's not mind-fucking he's full of right now, it's the other sort. I feel like I could cry again and this time I'm not sure I can hold it down.

"Anyway, I'm glad you sorted it," I mutter. "You convinced her we weren't screwing in the middle of the lake."

He takes a swig of beer. "No," he says, smiling. "Just friends. Although I dunno what she'd say if she could see me here now. She's so *suspicious*. You know—of *anyone*."

Great. Not even just of me. Of *anyone*. "Better go then, hadn't you," I state, dully.

"Yeah," he says.

And he stands up.

And goes.

AFTER THAT, SOMETHING HAPPENS TO me. After thinking Landon was coming back to me and having him snatched away again, something inside me goes into meltdown. My good sense and common sense and sense of reality—they all fuse into this heat-seeking missile aimed straight at him. I stop seeing the bigger picture. I just see him and how much I want him—and I see Coco in the way. Coco drugging him and enslaving him and bewitching him.

I think about how she does this. I think about the way she looks, acts. Up till now, I've just watched and waited and behaved myself.

It's time for that to stop.

Just two days later, I get my big chance. There's a big gala-type event planned for the ballroom of the hotel, and the events manager is going round recruiting some of the young, good-looking staff to go along and rev up the party atmosphere. Naturally, LaToya and I are invited. Coco and Landon—the Prom King and Queen of the hotel staff—are bound to be there too, aren't they? "Free tickets, free food and a couple of free drinks," the events manager promises. "We need to fill that place."

"Sure," I say. "We just go and have fun, right?"

"Right. Look fabulous, girls," he gushes, as he hands over the tickets. "And *dance*. I need you to start the dancing."

"I'm not dancing with any old dribbly guy just 'cause I'm getting in free," snorts LaToya.

"No one's asking you to," says the events manager, tiredly. "Just don't be horrible, OK?"

I've always had a real battle with blatantly sexy clothes. I worked out at quite a young age that what was so soul-destroying about stripping was that for the men watching, you stopped being a real person and just became boobs and bum. What's insulting is not that they *like* your boobs and bum—just that they don't connect them to *you* in any meaningful way. The kind of men who find it hard to look into your eyes if you're showing any cleavage fall into this category too. You feel they wouldn't notice if your face suddenly underwent a complete metamorphosis. Or fell off. Just as long as the bits they were interested in stayed in place.

Attraction that involves eye contact and conversation and interaction—attraction that involves the whole person—that's a whole level up on the evolutionary scale. It's a lot more complicated and a lot harder and scarier, and ultimately it's the only sort worth having. That's what I reckon anyway.

So—to get back to sexy clothes—I've always had the feeling, almost the superstition, that if I give in and wear really revealing, hey-look-at-my-body gear, I'm signing on for men to view me in a stripper way and not a real person way.

But this was different. This was war.

At first, LaToya's not a bit keen on my plan. "Dress up to impress *that* loser?" she squawks. "Girl—haven't you moved *on* yet? There are so many other guys around! And if he's so stupid he prefers that crazy poser-bitch to you, he ain't worth *spit*!"

But I talk her round. I tell her I'm motivated by revenge and lust and I outline what a laugh it'll be.

And LaToya loves a good spending spree, and she can't resist the chance to dress me up. "Well, like I say, you're *wasting* your potential, Rowan! Always in shorts, going barefoot . . ."

We head out after the afternoon shift finishes and catch a bus to the nearest mall where the stores stay open till nine. Under LaToya's critical, inspired direction, I get a dress that screams glitz and sex, sandals that make my legs look like a star's. "I never," I say, examining myself in the mirror, "thought I'd look this good. At least I think it's good."

"*Sure* it's good!" exclaims Toya. "You got the body—you should flaunt it more!"

I swivel unsteadily on my killer-heels. "To be honest, Toya, I feel like a real poser."

"Don't take it so serious! You're just playing, right?"

Playing. Acting out a role. LaToya's right. Anyway, who cares? I'm not the old me any more. I've become kind of honed and whittled down to this obsession that's taken me over. There's no room for the old me any more.

I want Landon. I'm not giving up. Maybe he treated me badly and he's an idiot and a loser and everything else LaToya says about him, but I want him. And in some weird way I want him more, now I've seen how hooked he is on Coco. If she can get him hooked—so can I.

I've got the clothes; I need a date. I settle on Charlie, the barman who gives me free beer. I come on to him mightily, all change of heart, and ask him to the gala. I don't feel too mean about setting him up because he's a bigheaded prat. Luckily for me, he's tall and OK-looking, and very into what he wears.

Charlie practically orgasms on the spot when we meet that night outside the ballroom. "Rowan, you look amazing!" he exclaims.

"Yeah, well don't sound so *astounded*," I reply, preening.

"No, no—you usually look great, but that dress—if you can *call* it a *dress* . . . !"

"Yeah, ha ha. C'mon." I put my arm through his, and we flaunt our way through the wide arched doorway. By the huge entrance mirrors, we pause and unashamedly check ourselves out. I meet his reflected eyes, and laugh. "Yeah, you look great too," I say.

"The best couple here," he gloats. "We should get a prize."

We walk on, down the wide blue-carpeted stairs, into the heart of the ballroom. It's huge, high-ceilinged, and decked out like the hotel's own private fantasy. Golden statues of deer and falcons loom out of swathes of fake corn, piles of fake stone. Strings of purple lights glimmer over a long bar with bottles cooling in a splashing fountain. It's magic, but I hardly notice it all. My radar's out for Landon.

Already, the room's half full and beginning to buzz. As we move towards the bar, the events manager pounces on us. "OK, kids, three free drinks and that's it!" he hisses. "And *circulate, circulate.*"

We move off. "Welcome to the Grand Sequoia Country Club, where fun is work," I say drily.

"What?" says Charlie.

As soon as we've got drinks in our hands, I drag Charlie off on a tour of the ballroom. I sparkle, I scintillate; I exchange smiles and gushy comments with the guests. "Don't go overboard," Charlie grumbles.

"I'm just singing for my supper, like the events manager wants—" Coco's making her way across the room, towing Landon like a tame dog. She's looking good but not much different than usual.

371

Landon's in his bar-suit, looking deeply fed up.

I fling my arms round Charlie's neck. "You feel neglected, don't you?" I coo into his astonished face. "C'mon, let's *dance*."

CHAPTER 49

THE NIGHT MOVES ON. MOST of it blurs and speeds past, irrelevant; some of it stands out like it's lit up by laser. Landon's face when he first sees me, kind of amazed, awed—confused?—and Coco's jealous sneer. Dancing near them on the dance floor, opposite Charlie but feeling like my ghost's left my body and gone to wind itself round Landon. Gleefully watching Landon watch me as I smooch into Charlie's neck. Gleefully watching Coco, hands on hips, face nasty, shouting at Landon; heart sinking as he puts his arm round her, and she lets him. Standing near them at the bar, trying to eavesdrop on their scratchy conversation, over-powered by the feeling that it's crazy, mad, *unnatural* that I can't just move in and kiss him. Thinking I might just do that, I might. Because he's *mine*, he's imprinted in me, in my DNA, he's *mine*.

More dancing. More senseless moving about,

shouting above the noise, laughing. Then, just before midnight, Coco suddenly erupts past us, dabbing at her eyes, pushing her way through the crowds, and totters at top speed out of the room. I radar scan for Landon and I can't see him. He's not here—but for once, he's not following her either.

It's my chance. It's my *chance*. "Charlie?" I say. "I gotta go."

"Go? Go where?"

"Look—just go. I'm sorry."

"*You're* sorry? You've been weird all night. Hot, cold. Crazy."

"Yeah, I know. I'm—*sorry*." I speed off.

Outside, I search like a lunatic. All along the corridors, past the gym, outside. To be faced by a shape on one of the benches on the terrace. A hunched, embracing, in-love shape. A Coco and Landon shape.

That's when I wake up. That's when it finally all comes crashing down; the heat-seeking missile inside me falters and fizzles out. *He's right*, I think, *Charlie's right, I am mad, I'm MAD. What am I doing? They're hooked on each other—they're never going to split up.*

I take my killer-shoes off and make cold dew-prints across the grass towards the wood. I walk through the trees with my hands outstretched, blindfolded by the pitch black. I skirt the lake, and inside my cabin, I take off my stunning sexy dress and hang it in the wardrobe, wondering when I'll ever wear it again. Then I sleep like I never want to wake up.

I've got the next day off and it's way past ten when I walk out into the hot sun. Somehow, I'm not surprised to see Landon there, stretched out by the edge of the lake. I think he's asleep till I notice that one hand's in the water, trailing to and fro, to and fro. The other hand's holding a joint.

"Hey," I say. "You OK?"

"No."

"Why?"

"Just—I'm not OK, OK?"

"OK, OK."

He grunts out a laugh, says, "We had another fight. Last night."

"Wow. Better phone NBC."

He turns to look at me. "What's up with you?"

"Nothing. You and Coco are always fighting. What's the difference this time?"

He sighs. "The difference is I said some really hurtful stuff. I told her she was a phony, I said I was sick of her game-playing and crap."

I stare at him, at his beautiful face. This news ought to make me frantic with hope and joy but it doesn't. I just feel tired.

"She went ballistic," he goes on. "Then we made up, but this morning . . . she kicked me out. Said she needed time to think."

"And when she's had time to think, you'll go crawling back again?"

"Ro-anne—what the hell is up? Why are you being so mean?"

"Why are *you* telling me about Coco?"

"Well . . . *sorry*. But you asked what was up. And I thought we were friends . . ."

"We've never been friends."

There's a silence. I look around me at all the beauty. The lake, and the great-leaved plants, and the strong bright shadows moving across the surface of the water. Like the essence of the place is all distilling down into this moment, this where-we-are. "You," I go on calmly, "are an idiot. A loser. And probably a masochist too."

"Jesus, anything else?"

"You're pathetic. You're an addict. You know the games she's playing with you, but you still go back for more. You're hooked on dope and you're hooked on her and neither of them is doing you any good and both of them are keeping you away from your life. Your *real* life."

"*Are you done?*" he snarls.

"Yup," I say, and I walk back to my cabin to fall on the sofa and sleep some more.

Several hours later, there's a tap at the half-open door. "Yeah?" I call drowsily. Ben walks in, and comes straight into my bedroom. I'm not surprised, but then I wouldn't be surprised whatever walked in. An alien, say, or an elephant. Right now it feels like someone very, very strange is writing the script.

"Er, Rowan?" he says. "Just thought you should know something."

"What?"

"Coco's gone. Packed her bags and left."

"Oh really."

"Yeah really. Just thought you should know, OK?" Then he turns to go, and as he's leaving he says, "Don't be too hard on him."

I track Landon down on the far side of the lake, sitting propped up against a fallen tree trunk. Iggy's sharing the trunk, basking in the last hot rays of the sun. I can't think of anything to say, so I call out, "Iggy looks enormous, all stretched out like that."

Landon doesn't answer, but Iggy's claws rasp pleasurably against the bark as I walk up, and he nods his head towards me. He's still got his lizard-smile, but he looks tougher, somehow, more determined . . . "His spikes look kind of scary now, don't they?" I say. "They're bigger. And going orange."

"He's growing up," mutters Landon.

I take this as an invitation, and sit down beside him. "I'm sorry," I say again. "About Coco, I mean."

"Don't be."

"D'you wanna . . . talk? About it?"

"No. I know what you think. And you're probably right."

"D'you want me to go?"

There's a silence, and then his hand comes down, covering mine on the ground. My throat kind of seizes with wanting to cry, so I stare hard straight ahead.

And then we just sit there for what feels like hours, side by side, facing ahead, in silence. Iggy shifts on the tree trunk and his claws catch in my hair, but Landon's hand on mine stays steady. The lake's shining in front of us, and crickets are whirring in the grass. Slowly, the sun dips down towards the trees, and just as it's disappearing, a little unseen bird starts up with this wonderfully clear liquid, fluid song, like a jewel in the silence. It's so beautiful I can't breathe for a minute. And

Landon says, "I was in Greece, last Easter."

"Yeah?"

"What they do there—they put these songbirds in tiny little cages. They love the way they sound, so they capture them and put them in these horrible little boxes. And the birds still sing. They shouldn't, but they do. It's—I couldn't figure it out. How those people could love the sound, but not care about the birds, how they could hear that beautiful sound, and not connect it to how *fucking* cruel they were being, sticking these birds in those tiny . . ." He breaks off then, because I've started crying. Not silent tears—great ugly throat-tearing sobs I can't control. "Ro," he says, anguished. "*Ro!*" He puts his arms round me, gathers me up. "Hey, come on! *Hey*—you're scaring Iggy."

I hear Ig scrape his way off the tree trunk behind me, thud down into the grass. "Sorry," I snivel into Landon's shirt. "*Sorry.*"

"What was it? Thinking about the birds?"

I hug him close. "Yes," I breathe. "No. Just—*everything. You.*"

"Me?"

"I love the way you said that, about the birds . . . I love the way you thought about it . . . I . . . I *like* you, I like you *so much*. I was *so hurt* when you went back with Coco . . ."

He's looking down at me, straight at me. I know when I look back at him he's going to kiss me. I sniff hard, and look up. He kisses me softly, on the forehead, on the nose. Then the mouth.

Maybe this is when you decide to sleep with someone. When your emotions are so wrung out you almost don't care one way or the other. Whatever, I stand up, and pull Landon with me, and we walk back to my cabin in absolute silence, and go inside, straight to the bedroom. "You sure about this?" Landon says.

I nod, and we take off our clothes silently, almost solemnly, separately, and get naked on the bed, and make love like it could be our last act on earth.

THE NEXT DAY, WE CAN'T talk about what happened, about Coco, about any of it. I want to, but I can't find the words. And Landon doesn't want to talk. It's like he's scared of something, scared of uncovering something.

By the end of that week he's moved into my cabin. We don't discuss it, he just sleeps in my bed every night and leaves more and more of his stuff round here until finally, the only thing he's doing in his own cabin is cooking, and that's stupid, especially when he's making us breakfast in bed, so together we shift all his gear into my kitchen, and lock his cabin up for good.

The weeks that follow are idyllic and unreal. A couple of times I try to get him to talk about what's happening to us, but he says, "Hey, don't spoil it. We don't need to talk about it." And then he stifles my next words with his mouth. Maybe he's right, maybe we don't need to talk. We're communicating through sex. He learns how to kiss properly. He learns everything, and so do I. I feel kind of drugged with pleasure, with closeness, happiness. Sometimes I look at him and think how beautiful he is and I say to myself, *he's mine* and I can't believe it, I can't believe I'm allowed to touch him whenever I like.

We bribe, bully and cajole to get as much free time as possible off together. After work, I'll meet him at his bar; or he'll come to the babysitting cupboard to meet me. But best of all is being by the lake together. Swimming in the morning, at night. Lying together drying off on the sandy shore in the low autumn sun. Making a fire, cooking over it; watching the deer, the possums and the bats. Even, once, a little brown bear. Not wanting anything else, stupid with freedom and happiness.

But prowling at the edge of it all is the knowledge that it can't last. We're halfway through September, the season's nearly at an end, and winter's coming. I look at Iggy strolling like an emperor round his lake and worry over how I can get him through the winter, where I can take him, how he'll stand being caged again now he's used to all this freedom. It depresses me, thinking about it, but it's easier than thinking about me and Landon and what we'll do when winter comes.

Half the people in the lakeside cabins have already quit and moved on. Ben and Rick are leaving on Tuesday to get ready for the new college term, and we're going to have a party for them, a big barbecue by the lake. Landon and I go into the wood to pick up wood for the fire and I take a big breath and ask him what he's going to do when his employment here comes to an end.

He shakes his head. "No idea."

I wait for him to ask about me, but he doesn't, so I say, "I don't know either. But I really wanna stay on in America."

He doesn't look pleased, he doesn't look anything. I feel like I'm going to start crying. "Landon—"

"C'mon, Ro. I can't carry any more—let's get back, OK?"

When we get back, Ben's already started to build the fire. Iggy's lounging on one of the thick logs nearby, watching him. We tip our logs on the ground nearby, and Iggy, startled, slithers to the ground. "Oh, Ig, sorry," I say—and break off. Iggy's looking and acting in a way I've never seen before. He's puffed himself up; the loose skin round his neck is all inflated. He's nodding, not slow and friendly, but fast, head punching the air, and his head spikes have all come forward like weapons. Then, just as Landon, oblivious, moves towards the fire, Ig makes a sideways run at him, tail lashing. "*Landon—!*" I shout warningly. "Watch out— watch Iggy!"

Landon stops, bemused, and Iggy stops too, and, facing Landon, starts doing these scary push-ups with his front legs. "What the *hell*?" cries Landon. "Is he *challenging* me?"

Something the exotic pet shop assistant said, the day of my escape from Seattle, comes back to me. "He's territorial," I squeak. "It's 'cos he's ready to mate. You're in his space!"

"Challenge him back, man!" urges Ben. "Show him who's boss!"

Half laughing, Landon takes a step towards Iggy, waving his arms in the air. "*Go away!*" he yells.

Iggy freezes, glaring at Landon. Then he does one more push-up, lurches round, and plods off into the undergrowth.

"Well, well," smirks Ben. "You've moved in on his woman, haven't you? He's *jealous*. He sees you all over Rowan, he doesn't like it—"

"Yeah, yeah."

"You better be careful, man. I've heard iguanas

can give a mean bite. Especially if they hold on and *shake*." Ben laughs, and I watch Iggy's tail slithering through the plants, and suddenly, for all kinds of tangled up reasons I can't even begin to understand, I feel so sad I want to cry.

People start arriving for the barbecue when the sun starts going down, and the party lifts off like a rocket. We build the fire up till it's huge and hot, and shooting sparks into the night. Chicken and steak sizzle on the grid and scent the air, and more and more people turn up, and everyone's behaving kind of sad, and kind of wild, because it's almost certainly the last big party we'll have this summer. This ever.

I drink too much and wind up sitting next to Rick and without meaning to I ask, "Was it as good as this last year?"

He looks at me, slyly. "Better," he says.

I'm hurt. I can't help it, I take it personally. "Yeah?" I croak. "Why?"

"Dunno. It was just better, OK?"

I sit there after that, hunched up and deflated, and Landon comes to find me with another couple of beers and I want to tell him what Rick said, I want to ask him all kinds of things about Coco, and me, and what's going on, but I daren't in case he says it too, in case he says, *It was just better, OK?*

That night, when he's asleep beside me, I watch his face by the streak of moonlight that's coming in through the little low window. I wonder yet again about Coco; I wonder what it was that bound him to her, and I wonder if she kept throwing scenes because he'd never talk, he'd never tell her what she wanted to hear. I feel like if it goes on much longer like this between us I'll start throwing scenes. Does that mean I'm like her?

LaToya didn't come to the barbecue. She says she's not into "that whole hippy thing by the lake." We really only see each other at work now, but we're still good mates. She understands that I'm "all swallowed up by love" as she calls it, and doesn't give me any grief. Today, while we clear up the sand and water play, I make her laugh telling her all about the new nasty Iggy. Maria high-heels over and, for once, because we're not talking about men or sex, I don't feel I have to shut up. She eavesdrops on us for a while then raps out, "It's too cold, here, for iguanas. Far too cold."

"I know," I say. "I'm getting so worried about the winter coming . . ."

"He will die. Where I come from, is warmer, and they survive."

"So they just kinda roam around, do they, in Mexico?" asks LaToya.

A mist comes over Maria's eyes, and she says, "Near my home, is ruins of ancient temple. Great steps, and columns . . . places where sacrifices were made. Chichen Itza, it's called. The iguanas are free there—they live in the trees, take shelter in the ruins, just . . . *hang* in the branches of trees, like great fruit. Iguanas—they can reach nearly two metres long there. My aunt—she take food for them."

"There you go, Ro," laughs LaToya. "Y'oughta take Iggy down there."

And Maria actually smiles. "Yes. Take him to Chichen Itza. He'll find nice wife there, raise a family."

Another week goes by, and everyone but Landon and me has moved from the lakeside huts. It should be idyllic, perfect, but it isn't. Things are getting bad between us. Landon still refuses to discuss the future, and I know if I hear him say "live it a day at a time" once more, I'm going to start screaming. A couple of times I do lose it and scream at him, and I remind myself of no one so much as Coco, standing helpless and ridiculous in her open-toed scarlet sandals by the side of the lake.

I can't enjoy the ordinary stuff any more. Being together, swimming, cooking. Even making love is spoilt by the uncertainty, because I can't bear it that something this sweet might have to stop. He accuses me of being tense and uptight, and we row, and one or the other of us storms out, and then we make up again. When we make up I feel as though I've come back to life again. But it's like we're in some kind of a stupid time loop, doing nothing, stagnating, waiting for something to happen.

Then one day, I go as usual after my morning shift to pick up our mail. I only bother to do this a couple of times a week. Mum writes to me, and Mel—just basic keeping-in-touch stuff now. Landon rarely gets any post at all. But this time my pigeonhole's empty, and there's a letter for him.

The writing on the envelope is big and curly. My mind races. Where have I seen it before, that "o" in Landon like a little heart . . . of course. The writing was in red before, red lipstick. Pinned to Landon's door saying, *Guess who's here?*

CHAPTER 51

I WATCH HIS FACE AS I give it to him. He crumples it in his hand and jams it in his pocket, like he wants to pretend it's not there. "Aren't you going to open it?" I demand.

"Later."

"It's from Coco, isn't it."

"Yeah. I think so."

"You *think* so? Come on—you *know* it's from her. Why don't you open it?"

"Look—get off my back, Ro, OK? I said I'll open it later."

And he walks out.

He doesn't come back that day, even though he's not working. I spend the time on my own torturing myself with what's in the letter, all the love messages and pleadings to start over again. Then when I can't bear that any more, I start planning.

I set off for the graveyard shift, and every time I get a break from plugging in and plugging out, I plan some more. Landon doesn't come to meet me; as I walk through the woods I'm preparing myself to be on my own all night. I feel kind of shut down and frozen; the only thing that's keeping me going is the plans I'm making.

When I let myself in the cabin, though, Landon's there. He's fast asleep in bed, just like nothing's happened. I say his name, but he doesn't move. I feel so lonely, looking at him asleep and shut off from me, that I almost wish he wasn't there.

In the morning I pretend to be asleep as I watch him get up and go out. As soon as the cabin door slams I clamber out of bed and go into the front room. He's left me a note, scrawled on a scrap of paper. *Helping Clint.* That's all. No love, no name, no kiss, no nothing.

I go straight up to Kiddie Heaven, even though I'm not on till the afternoon shift, and tell Maria I have to hand in my notice. I tell her what I really want to do—and I know I'll lose wages over this—is leave right now.

Her jet black eyes narrow at me. "That boy, is it?"

"Yes," I say. There's no point in lying. For once,

I find Maria's bluntness quite a relief.

"It's a shame, Rowan. I was going to ask you to stay, after the summer. I can only keep on three girls, but I wanted you for one of them. You're a good worker, the little ones love you."

I shake my head. "I've made up my mind, Maria. I'm sorry."

"So where you going to go? You have other work fixed up?"

"No, but I've got quite a bit of money saved."

She nods. "I'm sure you have. It's cheap, living here. Cheap and good."

"Yes." And suddenly I choke up with regret at leaving it behind, this weird mixture of fantasy castle and Eden, that weird existence between the hotel and the lake.

"Where you going to go?"

"To Chichen Itza. Like you said. I'm going to let Iggy free there, before the winter."

Then Maria does something I've never seen her do before—she laughs. "To *Mexico?* You want to *go* to Mexico? Hah!"

"Is it very dangerous? I mean—there'll be hotels there, won't there, little places I can stay . . ."

"It can be dangerous, of course it can be. A girl on her own . . . but it's beautiful. The beaches—white sand, palm trees—the sea is wonderful . . ."

Suddenly her face shifts, all excitement and resolve. "My sister. I give you her address—in Cancun—you stay there. You take a parcel of clothes for the children, yes? I can't send money—they spend it on things I don't want them to."

"But—but—will she *mind*?"

"No. Why should she? You can help with the children. I phone her. I tell her about the clothes, she'll be glad to have you."

I move fast then, like war's just been announced and I'm fleeing the destruction. While I wait for Maria to pack up the bundle of clothes for her nieces and nephews, I huddle in the side room with LaToya and tell her of my plans. She hugs me and tells me how much she'll miss me; she says she's staying on to work here, and makes me promise to write to her. Then Maria arrives looking almost sheepish with a very sizeable bundle, and her sister's address, and an envelope containing my wages absolutely up to date. I start to thank her and she bats my words aside, like she's embarrassed to be caught out being soft-hearted. "Exceptional circumstances," she says. "No notice required in exceptional circumstances."

At the Travel Information Bureau in the hotel central concourse, I check out the Greyhound route to Cancun; I have to change in San Diego; I can leave early that afternoon. I book a ticket, and a cab to take me to the bus station, then I go back to my cabin and pack. What I'm doing is functioning. My heart's hammering; I feel like I'm permanently holding my breath. I feel like if I exhale, I'll collapse. With Maria's bundle, I can't fit everything in, so I leave some of my heavier stuff behind, just lying on the bed. With one side of my mind I'm waiting for Landon to come back to the cabin, waiting for a showdown, waiting for him to put everything right again. But he doesn't appear.

I crush three herbal tranquillizer tablets in some mashed papaya, and set off to find Iggy, cat-carrier in hand. It takes me nearly thirty minutes to round him up. He slurps the papaya quite eagerly, and follows it into the carrier when I lob it at the back. I seize up with panic when I see how cramped he is. I have to wind his tail in, to get the door closed.

The cab's about to arrive, up at the hotel. No time to write a note for Landon even if I wanted to. No time.

THAT NIGHT—I NEVER AGAIN want to go as low as I go that night. After seven hours on the Greyhound coach, I make a stop in San Diego. The motel is cheap and seedy, with harsh overhead lighting in the room and scary warnings on the door about not opening it to anyone because of all the robberies and assaults in the area. I leave Iggy in the cat-carrier while I scurry out to get a lovely mug of coffee and a nasty mixed salad, and when I finally let him out he's furious. He canters round the room like a dragon on a revenge mission; then he clambers up the Venetian blind with a loud clatter, and dives back off on to the bed. He eats a bit of the salad then spews it back up again on to the side of my backpack. I feel sick with guilt about what I'm putting him through, what I've taken him away from. I can't bear to think about the next day, shutting him up for another seven or eight hours on the Greyhound bus.

I manage to fix up his heater lamp but he's too distressed to use it. All night long as I try to sleep I hear him shuffling about, scrabbling at the door, scratching at the walls, trying to get back to the lakeside.

The morning is bright and light but I feel like I'm in an iron box, lid fastened down against any feeling coming in. I keep chanting to myself: get to Mexico, get to Chichen Itza, free Iggy, get to Maria's sister. I feel overwhelmed by what I've got to do and by the shadowy knowledge that when I've *done* it—that's when the really hard time will start. That's when the iron box will open, when I'll have to start facing what happened with Landon, start letting myself feel it.

Iggy won't go back in the carrier. Of course he won't. He ignores the tranquillizer-spiked apple I hold out to him and runs from me. When I try to corner him he goes on the attack, lashing his tail, jerking his body aggressively up and down. My mind goes thin and focused with desperation. I haul the carrier over near him, chuck the apple in the back of it. Then I pull out the thin damp towel that lines the bottom of it and throw it over his head. While he struggles to free himself I shove him as hard as I can into the carrier, and the claws on one of his back legs catch my hand, and I slam the carrier door and fasten it.

I make it to the Greyhound station with about ten minutes to spare, and stow my case in the storage space beneath the waiting bus. I can feel Iggy still struggling to free himself from the towel but I can't bear to look inside the carrier to see how he is. I sit down on a bench to wait for instructions to board and I feel so heavy with despair I'm not sure I'll be able to get up again. I don't know what's keeping me going, why I'm waiting here for the bus. I'm like an automaton, like someone who's dead.

And then I hear: "I think it's mean, cooping up a big lizard like that."

CHAPTER 53

I FEEL LIKE MY HEART'S stopped beating. I turn, not smiling. Not anything.

Landon's standing there, just standing there, about four metres away. He's panting, like he's been running, and his hands are clenched at his sides.

I want to ask him what the hell he's doing here, how he got here. I want to race at him and fling myself on him and burst into tears. But all I do is mutter, "That's exactly what you said when we first met."

"I know it is. And it's even more true now."

He's trying to look cool, he's trying to sound all suave and slick and in charge, but his voice is coming out like a croak and it could be the early heat making the air shake, but he looks like he's trembling.

There's a silence. He takes a few steps towards

me, but I don't move, I can't, because I'm clogged, heavy, weighted with an incredible sweetness like my blood's turned to honey. "Where are you off to, Ro?" he asks, softly.

"I'm going to Chichen Itza," I croak. "There's ruined temples there, and trees and stuff, and iguanas live there, and I'm going to set Iggy free."

"Setting Iggy free. That the name of your summer, Ro?"

I look at him. I want to say something like—*I can think of better names*. Instead I say, "Why are you here?"

"Why do you think?"

"I don't know. I honestly don't know."

There's a silence. Landon's mouth is working a bit, but he's not saying anything. Our eyes fuse together for a moment then I look down and whisper, "How did you know I'd be here?"

"LaToya. I went looking for you and at first she bawled me out and then she told me where you went. So I checked out the Greyhound schedule and rented a car to get here for your connection."

"Why?"

He doesn't answer.

"*Why*?" I shout.

"*Jesus*, Ro-anne—do I have to spell it out?"

"*Yes!* Yes, you do!"

"OK—let's get this bus loaded!" calls the driver. "Everybody on board—we'll be leaving in two minutes."

I stand up, although I know I'm not going anywhere, and pick up Iggy's carrier from beside the bench. And then Landon speeds over and hangs on to it, just hangs on to it, like we're battling for custody, his face about a centimetre away from mine. "I drove all through the night to get here on time," he says. "Don't you dare just go, Ro-anne."

"Why not? You *just went* after Coco."

"Yeah, well I was wrong. That's over, and I'm with you now, OK?"

I fight to keep a fierce look on my face. "I didn't feel like you were with me. I felt second best, always. You were all distant, you never *told* me anything—"

"You never gave me a chance."

"Yes, I did. I tried to talk about things. But you'd just shut me up."

"I'm sorry. Look—I'm *sorry*. I was scared of talking, I was scared of it going wrong, like it did with *her*—"

"I'm nothing like her."

"I know you're not. I know it. When I found out were you gone—I can't tell you how I felt. Like you ripped my fucking heart out. You just left—

without any *warning*—without *talking* to me—"

"You wouldn't talk to me about Coco's letter. You didn't say a word."

"I tore it up, OK? When I found out you left, I tore it up. You wanna see the pieces?" And he pulls a fistful of mauled paper from out of his pocket. "She was horrible, Ro-anne. She's over."

"Come on," shouts the driver, "hurry it up. I wanna leave on time, OK?"

"*Tell him to take your bag off,*" Landon hisses. "Please, Ro. Tell him."

God, I'm *loving* this. I've no intention of getting on the coach but he doesn't know that and the fine side of me just wants to wind my arms round his neck and kiss him to death but the not-so-fine side is *loving* it.

"I'll drive you to Chichen Itza," he says. "We can let Ig free together. And after that—I'll do what you want. Just gimme a second chance, Ro, OK? *OK*?"

My Dear Rowan,

Flossy was so pleased with your postcard. Mexico—how adventurous! And all for Iggy's sake—he certainly struck it rich when he found you for a protector.

Big drama here—we're moving on too! Sharon was fired (I leave you to imagine the hysterical scenes) and after all kinds of discussion, we've agreed we'll both sell our places and get somewhere large together with a granny apartment for me and a lot more land. Taylor is insisting Sharon gets a job with fewer hours and less stress. At the moment they're going through a second honeymoon period. Long may it last.

I know my chief attraction is as a babysitter, but I don't care. My little grand-daughter means the world to me. She's so excited about moving, although she thinks she'll be able to have a horse where we're going! Well, perhaps she will.

Keep in touch, dear. Flossy still talks about you.

With love,

Stasia Bielicka

HI RO-THANKS FOR THE POST-
CARD! THOUGHT YOU MIGHT NEVER
SPEAK TO ME AGAIN AFTER I PUT
LIZARD-BOY ON YOUR TRAIL. GLAD
IT WORKED OUT! MISS YOU BAD
HERE. MAYBE I WILL COME VISIT. YOU
SAY THE SHERATON HOTEL IS GOOD?
WOULD THEY GIVE ME A JOB?
    STAY ON TOP, GIRL!
    YOUR FRIEND, LATOYA

Dear Rowan

Thank you for delivering the clothes to my family. My sister write to say how much she liked them. Also you and your husband. I hope you lie to her and have not got yourself hitched!

The Sheraton Hotel contacted me for a reference. I gave you an excellent one—ask them for a raise! My aunt told me about the lizard. She says you still visit him, and he knows her too and comes to her for food. She says he has a nice girl friend now!

You must always come back here if things not work out.

Your friend, Maria Reyes

Dear Ro

CANCUN, you cow??!! And I take it the complete stud in the background of the photo of Iggy is HIM? Guess you're right. Even I would have to forgive someone like that who chased me all the way to Mexico . . .

Only (only??!!) another four and a half months behind the till at Tesco and I'm off too. And I plan to save more turtles than you saved lizards, so nyah! God I miss you, babe! Glad you got into Warwick. I'm off to Southampton. We have to get some serious time together when you come back. You are coming back aren't you Rowan??!!

Loadsa luv, Mel

PS YES you have to tell your mum where you are! She'll only find out and go ape!

My darling girl,

Your letter from Mexico has just arrived!! Are you trying to give me a heart attack, Rowan? Never again will I accuse you of being unadventurous! It all sounds wonderful, especially letting the iguana free at Chichen Itza, and watching him plod off in to the sunset. You must have felt such a sense of achievement. Thank you for the photo. He looks so splendid in it, up against those ancient stone ruins. Jack's borrowed it for an art project he's got to do—I hope that's all right.

The hotel you're working at sounds very good too. How lovely to have a room with a sea view. I am a bit worried about this young man you've met, though. Where exactly did you meet him? Don't go getting all serious, will you, dear? Not right before university.

Jack says to tell you anyone who wants to go out with his sister has to be able to knock him down first. You see what I'm living with? When are you coming home? I miss you so much!

Love and kisses, Mum xx

Also by Kate Cann . . .

Pb 0-06-056160-2   Pb 0-06-447302-3

Spanish Holiday

Laura thinks her vacation in Spain can't get worse until she and her traveling companions stumble on a perfect villa—with a perfectly gorgeous guy living right next door.

Grecian Holiday

When Kelly opts out of a summer of roughing it with her intimidating, intense boyfriend, Mike, she doesn't realize she's opted in to a summer that will change everything, especially herself.

AVON BOOKS

www.harperteen.com   An Imprint of HarperCollinsPublishers